Kinfolk Killers

An Olive Reader Mystery

by

L. V. Nield

Copyright 2018 © by L.V. Nield

For information, email Cozy Cat Press, cozycatpress@aol.com or visit our website at: www.cozycatpress.com

COZY CAT
P R E S S

ISBN: 978-1-946063-53-3
Printed in the United States of America

Cover design by Paula Ellenberger
www.paulaellenberger.com

10 9 8 7 6 5 4 3 2 1

To Dave, Daniel, Beth and Lillian

Acknowledgements

My deepest thanks to my husband, Dave Somerfield, for his early reading and constant encouragement of my efforts. My thanks also to Professor Joy Guegler, freelance editor, who read the first draft and provided much helpful advice.

To Patricia Rockwell of Cozy Cat Press , whose timely comments, faith in the story and decision to publish it, I offer my sincere gratitude. My appreciation to Jaimie Patterson, Cozy Cat Press editorial assistant, for her meticulous review of the manuscript. Thanks also to Laura Hunt and Blair Wrean for their help in inputting and formatting the manuscript.

And lastly, my appreciation to our daughter, Beth Somerfield, for her patience in helping me set up online marketing tools.

Chapter 1

"Maybe your move here wasn't such a great idea," Jean remarked. "Christ on a bicycle! Did you bring half of North Dakota with you?"

As usual, Jean was exasperated with her younger twin. She and Olive had been born only twenty minutes apart, but had grown to be completely different women. After sixty-eight years, the dynamic of their relationship still hadn't changed.

Olive just grinned and looked around at the remaining unpacked cartons. "I didn't realize how small this apartment is. I'll probably have to store some stuff in the room in the basement."

Maggie shook her head at the two sisters, both so different in appearance and temperament. She and Jean were more like sisters than the twins were; Jean had been married to Maggie's only brother, Jimmy, and they'd lived next door to each other in Queens for many years. Now they shared an apartment two doors down from Olive's at Flushing Village.

Olive grabbed a lamp and placed it on one of the end tables by the couch. The furniture store had made its delivery yesterday and the delivery men had arranged the pieces as instructed, but the boxes she had shipped to Jean from North Dakota were still lying in the middle of the living room floor, waiting to be unpacked.

"I agree with Jean, Olive," Maggie said. "There's no way all of this stuff can fit. Thank God that when Jean and I decided to move here, she was able to sell her home and buy all the new furniture for our apartment. Chantelle is living in my house now and she's okay with my old furniture, at least for the time being—I can't imagine it fitting in any apartment in this complex."

Olive paused while opening another box. "I still can't believe I got this unit. Senior living facilities are few and far between out West, so you'd think getting into one here would be even more difficult."

Jean nodded. "You were lucky. Some old lady put a deposit on this unit and then apparently drowned in her tub at home. Kind of creepy. You were lower on the waiting list, but the only one who could move in on such short notice."

"I'm glad she didn't die here!" Olive exclaimed, taking a box of cutlery to the kitchen.

It was a small galley kitchen—so different from the one in her old farmhouse in Grafton, North Dakota. Then again, she wouldn't be cooking for harvesting crews anymore. And the appliances here were all so new. She looked into the small freezer in the fridge and chuckled, thinking about the old chest freezer back home. She'd also miss the sun shining into the kitchen like it had in the farmhouse, but the living room and bedroom here both had decent windows with a view of the park across the street, so she couldn't complain.

Heading back into the living room, she noticed Jean unpacking some photos and prints. "Just leave those leaning against the walls," she instructed her sister. "I'll probably take a few days to place them. And leave the boxes of books, too; I may buy another shelving unit for the bedroom. Oh, I feel guilty that I wasn't here to help both of you move."

Maggie shook her head. "No problem. Chantelle and her friends gave us a hand. We had the furniture store deliver right to the unit and one of the boys borrowed his father's truck to help move the rest. Sometimes not having a vehicle can be a pain. It would have helped us move the boxes a little at a time; I'm just getting too old for heavy lifting."

Olive nodded in agreement. "What does Chantelle think about moving back into your home?" she asked.

"Well, growing up, it was her home, too, and now that she and Brad have parted, living back in the neighborhood will probably be good for her," Maggie mused. "I liked Brad, but I guess it just didn't work out. She's almost forty now, so my shot at being a grandmother is likely gone, but oh well. Her monthly payments are helping me out and eventually she'll own the home."

Jean looked at her watch. "The dining room doesn't serve dinner past seven o'clock. Let's say we have a cold beverage around five-thirty before we leave for dinner?"

Olive nodded, and then opened a box of towels to put them in the hall closet. "I wish you hadn't told me about that lady who died. I feel badly that she didn't get to move in." Olive folded the towels carefully and closed the closet door.

Maggie shrugged. "Apparently she was in her mid-eighties," she said. "Yesterday, I heard a couple of women talking in the laundry room; people have nothing better to do than spread rumors. One of them was saying she heard the woman might have committed suicide. And that she was in the nursing home next door for a while, too."

Olive withdrew her mauve comforter and matching bedding from one of the boxes, and took it all into the bedroom in order to ready it for the evening. She'd slept on Jean's sofa for a couple of nights and couldn't wait to get into her own bed.

She was happy that the carpets here were a neutral gray, which accommodated the color of her comforter as well as her blue couch and chair in the living room. The walls were painted eggshell white throughout, and apparently she was free to wallpaper them as she chose. The tile flooring in the kitchen and bathroom complimented the appliances and fixtures, too. All in all, she was pleased with the setting.

After going back into the kitchen, she took out three cold Budweisers from the fridge, knowing that the brand was Maggie and Jean's favorite. Hearing the pop of bottles being opened, the other women yelled "Hallelujah!" and plopped themselves down on the couch.

Jean looked around the room. "I'm glad you brought those photos of the old homestead with you. When I left for New York—lo, those many years ago—I didn't really care if I ever saw the place again, but I guess I'm getting nostalgic in my old age. Are those the ones that Jon took?"

"Yes," Olive answered. "I think he captured the home and yard at sunset just perfectly, and I'm really glad that I have one of him and his father next to the equipment. It brings back a lot of memories."

Jean and Olive reminisced for the next half hour about their home in North Dakota, with Maggie throwing in a comment here and there. After rinsing out their empty bottles, Maggie and Jean headed for their apartment down the hall, telling Olive to stop by after she washed up.

"Do you think Olive's going to like living in the city?" Maggie asked as they walked down the hall.

"I hope so," Jean replied. "Bill's heart attack last year was so sudden. Olive's faith is pretty strong, but she was really tested. Jon and Karen were protective of her at first, but then I think they realized that a change of scene might be good for her. Even though we weren't that close as kids, I'm glad she moved here. I think we'll all have a good time together."

Soon they were rejoined by Olive. Together, they all walked to the elevators. Being on the tenth floor gave them a nice view, but sometimes the elevators were a little annoying; they were always traveling and stopping at very slow speeds to accommodate the older residents. This trip didn't take too long, and soon they were on the first floor.

The lobby could have been part of a Manhattan hotel—another elegant feature the women appreciated. Flushing Village was engraved on one wall, and enlarged photos of early twentieth-century city life adorned the others. On the way into the dining room, they could hear various conversations, some muted and others fairly loud—no doubt involving those with hearing loss.

The women gathered around the menu board. Jean and Maggie were now acclimatized to the dining hall, but so far Olive had only experienced dinner the night before and a quick lunch earlier that day. It appeared that each dinner featured three choices: some kind of meat, a fish or seafood selection, and a dish for vegetarians. Since Jean was an avowed carnivore, her choice was predictable, but tonight the chef had thrown her a curve.

"Liver and onions?" she exclaimed. "I want flesh, not organs! So it's either fish and chips or pasta primavera. The pasta sounds way too healthy, so I'll go with the fish and chips."

"It's Friday, so I should probably have the fish," Maggie chimed in.

Jean just groaned at her. "It's the twenty-first century, for heaven's sake! And when did you last go to church? Jeez."

Olive observed the two bickering women. Growing up, her sister's curly, bright red hair had been so different from her own straight, sandy-blond locks. While Olive's hair was now a decided shade of gray, Jean's was still as vibrant as ever. And coupled with her Italian temperament, Maggie's coal-black Irish mane made her pretty unforgettable. Both women obviously chose to "outsmart Mother Nature," so their hair seemed to get respectively redder and blacker as time passed.

Even after visiting Jean in New York many times over the years, Olive was still trying to cope with Maggie's overbearing personality, but she had learned to ignore the sharp exchanges between Jean and Maggie. They had been through a lot together.

"Well, little sister, what are you having?" Jean tapped Olive on the shoulder, bringing her back into the moment.

"I'll try the pasta," she replied. "Might as well get into a 'New York State of Mind,' as they say."

They found a table in the corner of the room and Maggie ordered a carafe of wine. Olive protested, offering to pay for it, but realized there would be many other nights for her to do so.

Jean spied an older couple across the room and waved. "I met them on the elevator a couple of days ago," she explained. "They got an offer they couldn't refuse on their house in Astoria, Queens, so they decided to move here. Apparently, the old guy was in the nursing home next door for rehab a year or so ago, so they figured this place would be a good fit if one of them needs more care. I know we're all younger than the rest of the residents, but having our own suites and enjoying two meals a day cooked by someone else works for me."

Jean was right; most of the residents of Flushing Village were well into their eighties, but the three women were still under seventy. Olive just enjoyed having the company of women her age.

Soon a young waiter brought their salads and the wine, and they began to eat.

Jean looked over at Olive. "So, are Jon and Karen going to do alright without you in the kitchen?"

Olive laughed. "Karen's a good cook, and I think she feels ready to take on the role of 'farm wife' full-time. Before Bill died, we had talked about moving into town anyway. But it does seem strange to be sitting here in this elegant dining room, being served instead of serving. I feel a little fidgety."

Maggie gazed around the room. The walls had a mutely-patterned design and the tables were covered with linen, sporting fresh cut flowers. Soft jazz played in the background. "I have no problem being waited on," she declared. "If I'd ordered another pizza or served Chantelle one more frozen dinner when she was growing up, she would have phoned me in for child abuse."

Jean shook her head. "She survived just fine. Being Clerk of Court in Queens County wasn't the easiest job, and trying to raise a child on your own at the same time? Don't beat yourself up. Look at me. Jimmy and I didn't get to start a family before some creep shot him, and I ended up eating a lot of pizza rather than cooking for myself. That's one thing about working at the NYPD—there were usually other takers when I suggested pizza for lunch, and nobody minded if I took the leftovers home. That was a great place to work." She paused and found her mouth watering at the mere thought of pizza. "You know, we should plan on going to a movie once or twice a month at the theater down the street. There's a pizzeria only a couple of blocks further on where we can eat too."

The waiter brought their food then, and the women dug in without a lot more conversation. Over dessert, Olive asked if Jean could take her on a little tour of the building. She'd read the brochure Jean had mailed to her back home, and the place was pretty impressive. It seemed so self-contained, which was probably a good feature for folks older than she.

"We'll take you to the roof, for sure," Maggie piped up. "There's a garden and lounge area with a great view of the skyline. Jean and I stopped by a couple of weeks ago for happy hour. There were snacks and everything—even a guy with an acoustic guitar. We can also check out the bulletin board on the way out."

They got up from their table. With Olive and Jean following closely behind, Maggie strolled to the bulletin board out front.

"Oh, look," Olive commented. "They post events by the week. And community groups can put up posters too! This looks interesting: the Flushing Rehabilitation Center—that must be the nursing home next door—is calling for volunteers. I did that kind of thing one afternoon a week back in North Dakota and it felt really good to bring a little cheer to the patients."

Maggie looked skeptical. "I don't know about that. A bunch of old people drooling on me and crying because they have no family? No thanks."

Jean wagged her finger at her roommate. "In the Surrogate's Court you were only dealing with dead people. Maybe it's time you helped out the living."

"Look who's talking," Maggie replied, shooting Jean a glare. "You're hardly 'Miss Volunteer of the Year.' You know very well that we both spend most of our free time either bowling or watching sports on television."

Olive took that opportunity to interject. "It says there's an orientation meeting tomorrow afternoon at three o'clock. I'll be tired of unpacking by then and we'll have plenty of time to get back for dinner. Let's just hear what they have to say and take it from there."

Despite Jean and Maggie's bickering, Olive was looking forward to volunteering again. It would be good for her to have some regular activity here in New York as she was getting settled.

Thinking about it made her shiver with excitement all over again—here she was, living in New York City! She couldn't wait to see how her life changed after this.

Chapter 2

Boxes, boxes—still so many boxes to unpack! Olive had enjoyed breakfast at Jean's and then returned to her unit to try and make sense out of it. A couple of hours after unpacking "half of North Dakota," she heard a knock at the door. She opened it to find Jean and Maggie fresh from their exercise class, ready to help her finish unpacking before going to the orientation session at the nursing home in the afternoon.

"I can't tell you how I appreciate this," Olive sighed, letting them in. "I really wanted to have all my books with me, but space is certainly an issue."

"Sorry we're not able to help you out with that. Our place is already jammed," Maggie replied. "But you know, I do have room at my old home if there isn't space in the storage unit downstairs. Just in case you want to hang onto stuff until you make a decision."

Olive nodded. "Maybe if I buy a floor-to-ceiling shelving unit for my bedroom and one for my closet, that could hold most of it."

Jean looked around. "Let's do this. We'll finish unpacking what we can and Olive can make a list of things she still needs. The local market and pharmacy are good, but we'll have to make a trip to the Queens Center mall within the next few days. I've started a list of things we should get as well, Maggie. And we can spring for a taxi rather than try to haul shelving units by bus. Actually, the ride will give Olive a better feel of the Flushing and Corona neighborhoods."

"Even though I've visited you over the years, I still feel like I don't know this area at all," Olive agreed.

"Anytime anyone visits the area, all they want to do is stroll around Manhattan, so I always took you there to see the sights," Jean said with a shrug. "But Queens has a lot of stuff going for it. I wouldn't have lived here all these years if it didn't."

Grunting, the women put together Olive's entertainment center stand, muttering as they tried to put square pegs in round holes. The cable fellow was scheduled for the next day, and while Olive wasn't much of a television addict, she was happy that computer service would be part of the cable plan.

Around half past two, Maggie straightened up and stretched. "If we're going to make it to that meeting, we'd better stop now," she announced. "It looks like we're just about finished with it anyway, at least until we get the shelving units for the bedroom."

Stopping then gave them ample time to walk next door to the nursing home. Stepping outside onto the sidewalk, Olive was struck by the leafiness of the trees and the quiet of the street. She knew that the main thoroughfares in Queens were noisy, and she'd certainly found Manhattan a cacophony of vehicle traffic and bustling pedestrians, so she'd been apprehensive about adjusting to city life. But in fact, she'd slept very well the past two nights, and looking around now, Olive anticipated truly exploring her new neighborhood as time went on.

"I never really paid attention to the nursing home building until you saw the volunteer notice yesterday, Olive," Jean said, turning onto the sidewalk leading into the next-door building. "It's pretty big. Looks like six stories, but thinking about it, given the lack of land around here, the only thing you can do is build up if you want to put up any kind of facility. Probably good for the patients, too, because they've got a bit of a view."

The women spied the administration offices to the left of the entry and walked over to the window.

"Can I help you?" asked a middle-aged woman in a pale blue nurse's uniform.

"We live next door and saw the notice requesting volunteers, so we thought we'd attend the orientation session today to see what it's all about," Maggie answered.

Smiling broadly, the woman pointed toward a door across the hall. "I believe that Bea Jones is in. She's in charge of volunteer services. She may have a questionnaire for you to complete before the session."

In response, Maggie looked at Jean and raised her eyebrows. "They don't kid around here, do they?"

Olive had already started toward Ms. Jones' office, so the two women followed her. A young black woman sitting behind a desk rose and introduced herself as Bea Jones.

"Hello, my name is Olive Reader," Olive said in response. "This is my sister, Jean Corcoran, and her sister-in-law, Maggie Poplinski. We live next door and wanted to attend the volunteer orientation session."

Ms. Jones moved away from her desk to shake hands with each of them. "Wonderful to meet you!" she exclaimed. "Many of our patients have family who visit them regularly, but some don't, and our staff just doesn't have a lot of extra time to sit with them. I feel bad because I know they're very lonely, but with budget constraints we have to look to volunteers to help in this area. If you could just have a seat in the lounge at the end of the hallway, I'll be with you shortly."

Walking down the hallway to the lounge, the women briefly looked into some of the rooms. They didn't want to pry, but were curious about the layout. None of their parents had lived long enough to require nursing home care, so this was rather new territory for all of them.

"I wonder if we're the only ones attending the session," Jean whispered. "Maybe they'll have someone who's already a volunteer tell us the routine. The administration probably desperately wants bodies, but I'd prefer to hear it from the horse's mouth, so to speak, before I sign up for anything."

Olive scoffed. "Jean, you're not joining the army. Try it, and if you don't like it, you can always quit. You won't end up in the brig, for heaven's sake."

"You've forgotten how competitive your sister is!" Maggie chortled. "If she starts anything, she won't quit. That's why she doesn't ever start many things."

They reached a small lounge with a couple of tables and comfortable-looking chairs.

"This is where many visitors meet patients who are able to walk, because it gets them out of their rooms." The women turned and saw Bea Jones, accompanied by a young nurse. "This is Elfrieda Summers, one of the nurses here."

After Bea completed the introductions, she sat at one of the tables and directed the women to do the same. "I've brought a questionnaire for each of you, which you can complete either while we're talking, or take home with you. Elfrieda, these ladies have moved into Flushing Village next door."

Elfrieda nodded. "It's wonderful you're so close at hand," she said. "The patients here appreciate any time you can give them. Some like to play cards, while others want you to watch television with them, and some just want to reminisce or talk about the news. It's best to take your cue from them and to not impose your own values."

"You also have to remember that many of them are very old, and pretty set in their ways," Bea added. "Some days they'll be glad to see you, and sometimes they'll be downright grumpy. The facility has a lot of patients who are here temporarily for rehabilitation after falls and strokes, that sort of thing—but there are also people who are just too old and frail to be alone, and they'll probably end their days here. They're the ones most prone to depression, it seems, but sometimes patients who are frustrated with rehab can get depressed as well, particularly if they have no one to stop by and discuss their progress with."

Various issues were coming to Olive's mind, and she found herself wishing she'd written out a list of questions. "Are we assigned to a particular patient or do the three of us visit a number of them?" she asked.

"Since you all know each other," Bea answered, "you may get to know, let's say, three patients initially, and take turns brightening their days. Often, though, patients like to think of one person as a personal friend. A lot depends on how gregarious they are to begin with."

Jean raised her hand. "Can we discuss patients with each other, particularly if we know the same people? We might be able to brainstorm, come up with things to make their days more interesting. Also, if they're able to move around or even sit comfortably in a wheelchair, can we take them out of the facility for a walk?"

Elfrieda responded, "All good questions. If a patient tells you something in confidence, it's better to keep it that way, although I've noticed that when people are lonely they'll share a lot of information with whoever will listen. The staff finds it that way, anyway. If a patient wants to be taken out of the facility, you have to clear it with a floor nurse like me first."

Maggie had been silent throughout the discussion until now, when she spoke up: "Our parents all died before needing this type of care, so I haven't dealt much with old people. Someone was telling us that an old lady was discharged from the nursing home and had planned on taking the unit in our building that Olive got, but died in her bathtub at home. If I'd been her volunteer, I would have felt terrible."

"I read about that in the papers," Bea sighed. "Apparently the police investigated because they thought it might be a suicide, but there was no note, and they did find alcohol and barbiturates in her system. As a volunteer, you have to recognize that a lot of the people here are very old and that death is inevitable. You cannot assume responsibility for it. You are certainly free to grieve, and if you ever have any issues with it, feel free to talk to me. Don't let those fears dissuade you from trying this. Your help is sorely needed."

Maggie sat up straight in her chair. "You know, I recently retired from Queens County Surrogate's Court, and it just hit me now why the rumors people have been discussing bother me. The week of my retirement, we had a file come in from a lawyer for the estate of a lady who died, and the death certificate said it was by drowning. I didn't read her will or anything because I wouldn't start a new file just prior to retiring, but in the office we all thought it would be a bad way to die. A coincidence, I suppose, but I wonder if it was the same lady. Ethel something."

Elfrieda just nodded. "I think her name was Ethel. If she had died here, it would be easy enough to look up."

Worried that Maggie was starting to fixate on this woman's death, Olive changed the subject. "What's the best time in the day for volunteers to come here?" she asked. "We have set meal times in our dining room, but if someone wanted me to eat with them, I could, I suppose."

"I believe the best times are in the mid-afternoon or early evening," Bea responded, "when time hangs heavier for them. In the mornings and around mealtimes, they interact with the staff, so it's better to come when they aren't busy."

Falling silent, the women looked at each other and the questionnaires on the table. Maggie stood up and smiled. "We'll take these home and return them tomorrow," she promised. "Bea, do we bring them to you and then discuss pairings with patients? What's the next step?"

"If you can stop by at one o'clock, I'll block out some time to go over specifics. In the meantime, I'll look at our patient list to consider likely pairings. See you ladies then!" Bea shook hands with each of them again.

The women filed out and left the nursing home. Outside, Jean stopped and looked down the street.

"Olive, you've got your pocketbook," she said. "Let's walk down to the little strip mall a couple of blocks from here. I want to buy some wine from the liquor store, and Pignolli's Market next door has enough staples to last you for the time being. It also has a good deli department for sandwiches if you don't feel like dining room food sometimes. Maggie and I've done that already when we're in the middle of Saturday baseball on the tube. There's a pharmacy, too, and a bank branch at the corner. So, there's everything you need on a daily basis, as far as I'm concerned. We'll still have lots of time to get back for dinner, and then we can give you a building tour like we promised."

Olive agreed and the three women went to the strip mall. Olive was pleased with it; it reminded her of the shops back in Grafton, which were nothing too fancy. She and Bill had always gone to Grand Forks for major shopping, but the shops nearby had had enough to get them through the week. Here, she filled a shopping basket with bread, butter, jam, mayonnaise, grapes, sliced ham, cheddar cheese, skim milk, cereal, coffee and filters, orange juice—as well as some paper towels, Kleenex, and toilet tissue.

"Whoa!" Jean laughed. "I know we can be your beasts of burden, but don't clean out the store all at once! Maggie and I are picking up a few things, too, you know, and we still haven't gotten to the liquor store!"

Grinning sheepishly, Olive began to put some items back, but Jean stopped her, saying they would manage somehow. "I'm just so used to buying for the old place that getting just enough for one person will be an adjustment," Olive explained.

"It's okay," Jean said. "You're buying enough to get you started, at least. Let's head for the liquor store."

Maggie had arrived at the liquor store before them and was talking to the clerk, already having put a six pack of beer and a box of red wine on the counter. She called out to Jean, "Do you want me to buy some scotch while we're here?"

Jean shook her head. "We've already got too much stuff. Olive, do you want to buy any wine? Did we drink up your beer yesterday?"

Olive was still looking at Maggie's box of wine with a somewhat skeptical expression. "Are you going to drink all that before it goes bad?" she asked. "What's it taste like, anyway?"

Maggie glanced over her shoulder while paying the clerk, and answered, "You'll find out soon enough. I store it in the fridge."

"You refrigerate red . . . ?" Olive stopped herself before finishing the sentence, stifling a smirk. *That should be interesting.*

She decided to hold off on any more purchases and passed on buying any wine; she could always come back herself another day.

They returned to the complex laden with shopping bags. While they strolled through the lobby, Jean peeked into the dining room. "The early birds are enjoying themselves. I bet if they go to Florida in the winter, they eat dinner at four-thirty too. You know, one dollar off!"

Olive remembered how judgmental Jean could be; she certainly hadn't changed. Sometimes she and Maggie could be really funny, but other times they were pretty cruel. It would be interesting to see how they would interact with the nursing home patients.

After reaching their floor, they separated for the time being. Jean and Maggie invited Olive to join them for a beer before dinner, and then went straight to the kitchen with their parcels. They'd known each other so long, they were like an old married couple and didn't need a lot of conversation to put away their purchases.

Maggie put the box of wine in the fridge. "Let's skip wine with dinner and then introduce Olive to the joys of chilled boxed cabernet after we give her the building tour."

Jean laughed as she turned on the television. She'd been happy to use some of her home sale proceeds on furniture that was suited to this smaller space, like this TV. The flat screen television was huge—Olive was astounded by it whenever she walked into the room—but being a wall unit, it was less intrusive than Jean's old television had been. Jean and Maggie had also chosen a couch, loveseat, and lounge chair combination in striped strawberry and gray, which went well with the gray carpet. Maggie had brought her bed from home, but Jean had given hers to Chantelle so that she could buy a whole new set. Her back had been bothering her for a while and the new mattress was a godsend.

Jean turned to Maggie. "You know, seeing those photos at Olive's makes me think we should bring a couple of Chantelle's photos from your old place," she said. "If she hadn't chosen nursing as a career, she could have made a living at photography."

Maggie flushed with pride. Jean was like a second mother to Chantelle and had been able to intervene in some of Maggie's mother-daughter battles during adolescence. "Great idea," she replied. "Oh, by the way, we've been invited to dinner next Tuesday. Chantelle wants to welcome Olive, and I know that Olive is looking forward to seeing her again. And, unlike mother, daughter is actually a pretty good cook."

Just then, they heard a knock on the door, and they both yelled, "Come in!"

Olive entered; she had brought her questionnaire and set it down on the table. "Shall we look at these now, or wait until tomorrow?" she asked.

Maggie retrieved three bottles of beer from the fridge and distributed them. "Glasses are in the cupboard if you want one. And while I'm thinking about it, let's make a rule. If our door is unlocked, just come in without knocking; it's a lot easier that way. But to answer your question, I'll get out my questionnaire. Jean, where did you put yours?"

Jean retrieved the form from her handbag and they all sat down at the table. The first part of the form was pretty innocuous: name, address, age, occupation. The next portion contained space for a reference and both job and residential history.

Maggie wrinkled her nose. "Are we applying for a mortgage or what? I don't think I should have to give that kind of information."

Olive patted her arm. "You hear all those stories of elder abuse, Maggie," she explained. "Maybe they don't want us to use our status as volunteers to get our grubby hands on old people's money. If we just show a stable work history and give a reference, I don't see how that can hurt. You two have no problem. Jean worked with the NYPD and you worked in Queens County Court. It's me that might look a little suspect. Lady moves here from North Dakota. Farm wife. No New York area references. Not even a local bank account yet!"

"Why don't you put down the name and telephone number of the nursing home administrator back in Grafton?" Jean suggested. "You said you volunteered weekly, so I'm sure you'll get a great recommendation. And besides, I'm sure that Ms. Jones took note of your earnest face and caring smile. Hardly the look of a crook."

"You never know," Maggie said. She inhaled some of her beer, but bubbles came out of her nostrils and she choked just a little at the thought of Olive doing something at all devious, let alone criminal. "Alright, I'm done," she announced. "Let's finish our beer and get down to dinner. It's already almost six o'clock and if we're going to eat and show Olive around before sundown, we'd better get going!"

Dinner that night offered stuffed pork chops, vegetarian lasagna, and poached salmon. "Now they're talking!" Jean exclaimed as she passed the menu board. Olive opted for the salmon, while Maggie joined Jean in choosing the pork chops.

"I would have taken the lasagna, but what's this with leaving out the meat sauce? That's not lasagna, that's something else. Next they'll make it with tofu or something. Marone!" Maggie cried.

Olive began to laugh. She could live in Queens for the rest of her life and still not become accustomed to the "Noo Yawk" accents here, and Maggie's expressions cracked her up. And she was so loud! Olive tried to picture her in the muted confines of a court office.

After finishing up their meal with a mixed fruit cup, the women checked the bulletin board in the lobby once again.

"I really want to go to a movie and have pizza tomorrow night, but it looks like they're having a guitarist at the rooftop lounge," Jean mused. "How about we try the rooftop tomorrow and then do the movie on Saturday?"

"I have no problem with that," Olive responded, while Maggie nodded in agreement.

"Olive, let's start with the roof now for a quick peek while there's still a lot of daylight ,and then we'll show you the amenities on the other floors." Jean led Olive to the elevator, and soon they were exiting onto a partially-covered portion of the roof, where some chairs and tables had been set up.

Two older couples were sitting, sipping wine and looking out on the city. The women strolled over to the railing and Olive gasped at the view. It wasn't the Empire State Building in Manhattan, but the view from the roof was different from anything she had seen in North Dakota. She could make out some of the parks in Queens, as well as many houses and some of the thoroughfares.

"I've lived in Queens all my life and was still blown away by the view," Maggie murmured, understanding Olive's reaction. "When we come for the music tomorrow night we'll have longer to look at it, so let's carry on with the rest of the tour. The Yankees play the Red Sox in about fifteen minutes and I don't want to miss much of the game."

The next stop took them to the corner rooms on the second floor, which housed a beauty salon on one side and a combination internet cafe and lending library on the other. Seeing the salon, Olive commented, "I'll need to find someone to cut my hair occasionally. Have you tried the person here yet?"

"We haven't been here long enough, but I want to see some other heads before I let them touch mine— although it would be more convenient than trying to go back to the old neighborhood for a color and cut," Jean answered. "I think Maggie feels the same way. You can be our guinea pig, Olive."

On another floor, they found an activity room with a pool table in the middle and a couple of small tables with half-completed jigsaw puzzles on them. Twice a week it was used for a morning arts and crafts class, which Jean heard didn't please the men of the building, who thought it was their own personal domain. Next door was an exercise room large enough to hold three stationary bikes and a treadmill along the wall, with plenty of space in the center for free exercises.

"This is where we go for aerobics," Maggie explained. She then pointed across the hall to a small chapel. "And if we overdo it, we can always crawl across the hall to seek divine intervention!"

The tour ended in the basement. Olive looked into the coin-operated laundry room and Jean opened up the storage room so they could see the size of the individual units. Maggie began looking at her watch, which meant the game was about to start, so they all took the elevator to their floor.

Maggie invited Olive in for a glass of wine, who replied, "Thanks, but I'll come back later. I'm going to call Jon and also do some measuring for the shelves I need to buy."

The Yankees-Red Sox rivalry had been a passion for Jean and Maggie over the years. When Jean first arrived in Queens, she had no particular interest in baseball because her parents had tended to just tune in to the World Series. Meeting Jimmy and Maggie had changed all that. With Shea Stadium smack in the middle of Queens, Jean thought that the Corcoran family would have been rabid Mets fans, but the moment Jimmy took her to Yankee Stadium, Jean was hooked on pinstripes.

Maggie turned on the television as soon as they entered their unit. "Jeter's up! Grab me a glass of wine, will you?"

For the next hour or so, Maggie and Jean watched the team change leads, so they were on the edge of the couch when Olive finally came in. As she went to the fridge, she glanced at the screen to learn the score so she wouldn't be completely lost. Gingerly removing the wine, she used the dispenser to pour herself a small glass.

At the end of the inning, she felt free to speak. "I've been thinking about the volunteering," she said. "If we get a choice, what's your preference? Do we tag-team three or four patients? Or each just settle in with one of them, and if so, do you care whether they're male or female?"

Maggie and Jean both thought for a moment before Jean responded. "This is all so new to me, I don't know what to say. What did you do in North Dakota?"

"The nursing home was pretty small, so I looked in on only a couple of patients," Olive answered. "Thankfully, most of them had either friends or family around, so loneliness didn't seem to be an issue like it is here. I think I'd prefer to stay with one patient initially, although I'd certainly like to be introduced to anyone you're visiting, if that works out. I'm kind of excited about tomorrow."

The game resumed and Maggie, not being particularly tactful, immediately turned up the volume. Olive took the hint and watched in silence, although when Maggie and Jean commented on Derek Jeter's backside she couldn't help but groan, "You two could be his grandmothers, for heaven's sake!"

Chapter 3

Bea Jones looked over their completed questionnaires, nodding as she read about their job histories and other information. "Olive, I'm glad to hear you've done this before," she remarked. "If you don't mind, I'll call the nursing home in Grafton, as we have to do due diligence in vetting our volunteers."

"I have no problem with that," Olive replied easily. "Please pass along my regards."

"Since I assume that my calls will prove all of you to be upstanding, I'll let you know the general type of patient we'll be targeting for your help," Bea said. "There are two elderly women and one elderly gentleman right now who are all without family, and our volunteers are spread so thin that they haven't had a lot of regular visits. I suggest that we pair each of you with one of them, although you're free to help each other out if you think it won't be too disorienting for the patient. The patient's emotional and physical comfort is paramount, so you always have to bear that in mind when you're proposing activities.

"One of the ladies worked at Con Ed for years, and took care of her mother, too. Sounds like she had a hard life. The other lady is a retired school nurse; she was diagnosed with diabetes a number of years ago and is recovering from a foot amputation. Neither of them were ever married. The man, a widower, is recovering from a stroke and has some heart problems, but apparently he's working hard at rehab with the hope of returning to his home on Long Island. These are just the thumbnail sketches I got from the staff to give you a bit of background information. The patients may be willing to talk about their lives, but if they aren't, don't take it personally. Sometimes it takes a while to build up trust, but sometimes people never feel comfortable confiding their life histories."

"When can we start?" Jean asked, beginning to fidget. Being uneasy about the whole notion of working with the elderly, she wanted to jump in before she talked herself out of it.

"I have to call your references, so hopefully I can do that this afternoon," Bea answered. "Why don't you come back at one o'clock tomorrow? Lunch will be over and we can visit the wards then. In the meantime, you can discuss the profiles I've given you, in case you want to decide among yourselves who you'll be paired with."

Maggie and Jean still looked a little hesitant, but Olive couldn't wait.

The women returned the next day and Bea greeted them warmly. "Olive, I had a nice conversation with Ellie Nordstrom, the administrator at the nursing home in Grafton," she said, "and she had great things to say about you. How big is Grafton, anyway? Here in Queens we sometimes feel so anonymous, so we envy people in small towns."

"Grafton has about four thousand people, I think," Olive replied. "Just about the right size. You get to know a lot of folks and the kids grow up together in the school system. Except for the cold winters, it's a great place to live. Our farm was about two miles from town, so after-school activities were sometimes a problem, but Jean was pretty active in high school, wouldn't you say, Jean?"

"Yeah, but I still couldn't wait to get out of there," Jean snorted. "Best thing I ever did was take secretarial training and head for the Big Apple."

Maggie grinned, remembering the first time Jimmy had brought Jean home to their parents' for dinner. She and Jean had hit it off immediately and had stayed friends for life.

Bea began the tour of the nursing home, walking ahead and pointing as she went. "There are six floors, with ten rooms on each floor," she explained. "Some rooms have two patients, some are single. It depends upon our availability at the time; people come and go, you know, especially if they're only here for rehab. Our first visit will be Irma Weiss, the lady I talked about who worked at Con Ed. We're just going to meet the three patients today and introduce all of you to each of them, and then you can take it from there."

They turned into room 310, which held two beds, although only one was occupied. The television was blaring, so Bea went over and reduced the volume.

The patient, a clearly elderly woman, whose long indigo hair lay in obvious contrast to her wizened face, cleared her throat. "Thanks," she said. "One of the cleaners turned it on and then cranked up the volume before she left. She must think I'm deaf!"

"I'll speak to her about it," Bea promised. "Irma, I want you to meet some gals who live in the senior living center next door. They just moved in and want to help out around here, and meet some new people."

Irma looked at each woman in turn, growling, "I can't imagine why you'd want to meet an old hag like me."

Jean and Maggie glanced at each other, both wondering whether volunteering was such a great idea.

Luckily Bea just laughed, lightening the moment. "Would you like an occasional visit from one of these ladies, Irma?" she asked. "Perhaps play cards or Scrabble with them a couple of times a week? It's your choice, but it probably beats watching daytime TV. I told them that you worked at Con Ed, so you likely didn't get hooked on soap operas like a lot of women. Am I right?" She didn't wait for an answer. "I'm just introducing these gals to various residents today, but one of them can come back another day, if you like."

Irma appeared to relax and reached into her side table, pulling out a cribbage board. "I used to play cribbage with a co-worker on my lunch hour, but she's long dead and the staff here don't have time to sit around for that long. Do any of you play?"

Jean stepped forward. "Irma, you've met your match," she announced. "I used to play crib with my mom when I was growing up and I showed Maggie's daughter how to play when she was a kid."

Irma obviously warmed to the challenge. "Cocky, huh. I like that," she chuckled. "How about sometime tomorrow? You other two—once I wipe the floor with Jean, you can try your luck with me, too! I've got lots of time on my hands."

Jean nodded. "We're going to do some shopping for Olive tomorrow morning, but I'll be back by two or three o'clock. Does that work for you?"

Looking around, Irma waved her hand. "Does it look like I'm going anywhere?" Still, she managed a rueful laugh, prompting Jean to pat her shoulder.

Olive and Maggie had been standing at the end of the bed, but during this last exchange Olive wandered over to the window and looked outside. There was a courtyard below with potted plants and hanging flower baskets, the whole area shaded by the building at that time of the day. It wasn't visible from the street and was probably fairly quiet, too. It would be a nice refuge for any patient able to walk or be taken in a wheelchair to it. She would keep it in mind as a volunteer.

After they exited the room and were out of earshot, Bea thanked Jean for stepping forward. "I think you'll help Irma a lot," she said, leading the women into the elevator out in the hall. "She's pretty depressed and it seems nobody comes to see her. Her admission documents showed no next of kin, not even a contact person, which is so sad. The staff gets her up and walking sometimes, because otherwise she would just sit there all day. Some fresh air would definitely do her good."

Bea took them to the fifth floor next. They turned right after exiting the elevator, and she led them to room 506. Again, the sound of the television greeted them, although the volume wasn't as high this time. A female patient looked over from the only bed in the room. Unlike Irma, this patient had a rounder, more youthful face, with her white hair pulled back in a bun. She smiled at this unexpected group, a little shy at the attention, and raised her eyebrows at Bea for an explanation.

"Elizabeth, I want you to meet Maggie Poplinski, Jean Corcoran, and Olive Reader, who all moved recently into the building next door," Bea said. "Ladies, this is Elizabeth Billingsley. Elizabeth had her right foot amputated but is recovering nicely. I hope we're not interrupting your show, Elizabeth. I'm just taking these folks around to introduce them to residents in case they want some company once in a while."

Elizabeth replied, "That's fine. I always have the set on either to the Food Network or the Travel Channel. I'm punishing myself because now I can't eat much due to the diabetes, and I sure won't be traveling much in the near future."

Maggie saw that Elizabeth was watching Molto Mario, a show she watched occasionally because of her partial Italian heritage. "I just drool when I watch him cook," she told Elizabeth, gesturing toward the TV. "I don't cook food all that much, although I did learn to make my mother's marinara sauce—but the way he puts things together so effortlessly? I'm jealous."

Elizabeth brightened and looked at Maggie. "His show comes on every afternoon at two o'clock," she said. "If you have the time and want to watch it with me sometime, that would be wonderful. There are other shows, too, which are just as good—there's probably something for all three of you." She nodded at Olive and Jean.

"If it's on tomorrow, I can come back then. We have errands in the morning, but I'll be done by two." Maggie squeezed Elizabeth's hand before following the others out of the room. "If her room is an even number, then shouldn't her window also look out on the courtyard?" she asked Bea in the hallway. "I'm surprised her bed isn't closer to the window."

Bea laughed quietly. "Elizabeth is pretty stubborn. We suggested moving the bed, but she thought it might be too warm with the sun in the afternoon, and she also worried that there would be a glare on the television if she was watching it by the window," she explained. "I think she prefers to look at life through a television screen. Maybe you can help her with that."

Another elevator ride, another floor. Turning into room 608, they could hear no television, no sound at all. Bea put her finger to her lips, indicating that the women should wait at the door while she investigated.

She disappeared into the room, and they heard a man's voice. "Well, Bea, what brings you to the penthouse?"

"Howard, I'm bringing some ladies around to various residents to introduce them. Two of them are sisters and the other is their sister-in-law. They all moved into the building next door rather recently and they want to help out a few hours a week. Ladies, why don't you come in?"

They filed into the room, where they met Howard sitting up in his bed.

Bea introduced them and Howard smiled. "My name is Howard Kenner, and hopefully I'll get out of this joint soon, if my rehab progresses," he said. "You all look so different, so which ones are the Brewster sisters?"

Olive burst out giggling, while the others looked puzzled at his comment. Howard grinned at her, a twinkle in his deep-set blue eyes.

Olive turned to Jean. "You remember the sisters who murdered various gentlemen they thought were lonely in *Arsenic and Old Lace*? The movie with Cary Grant?" She could tell that Jean didn't get the reference. She shrugged and turned back to Howard. "Mr. Kenner, this is my sister, Jean."

"Please call me Howard," he said. "If any of you ladies want to stop by and see me, that would be great. Having some real conversation will be a treat. The staff tries to take a moment or two, but we just get started on the news of the day and then someone needs them in another room." He pointed at the open *New York Times* on his bed. He looked expectantly at them, moving his shock of white hair left and right.

Jean and Maggie subtly turned toward Olive, who found herself blushing a little. "We have errands to run tomorrow morning, but I'll be home a little before two o'clock. Do you have rehab then?" she asked Howard.

"No, it's only scheduled during the week," he answered. "Actually, I have a favor to ask. Could you buy me some black licorice and I'll pay you tomorrow? I meant to ask one of the staff this morning but forgot. There's a tuck shop on the main floor that sells it."

Olive nodded as the other women began to make their exit. Given that Howard was a man, she didn't feel comfortable taking his hand as Jean and Maggie had done with their patients, but she gave him a wave goodbye instead.

Out in the hall, Jean gave her a playful shove. "So, one man on the list and you get him! Just my luck!"

"Oh, stop it," Olive replied, blushing. "He has to be in his early eighties anyway, and we're just going to talk about the news, for heaven's sake!"

"You're right," Bea said. "Howard's eighty-two, I believe. Lost his wife many years ago, according to the staff. No children. He always seems pretty upbeat, though, and works hard at his physical therapy. He does want to 'get out of this joint,' as he puts it, and I can't say I blame him. He apparently kept his home on Long Island. He's a real gentleman, though, Olive, so you needn't worry about anything like that. If we had a male volunteer I'd probably team them up, but it will do Howard good to have someone stop in regularly to discuss the day's news."

They reached the elevator and returned to the main floor. After bidding the women good day, Bea returned to her office.

Jean looked at her watch. "Let's stop by the market again to get any small items Olive might still need. When we get back, it'll be time to go up to the roof for the happy hour entertainment." She paused. "Also, I may regret this, but I suggest that we let Olive pick tomorrow night's movie."

Olive chuckled at her twin's reluctance. They'd always had very different tastes in film.

As they walked toward the market, Maggie looked at Olive. "You may want to buy the licorice today," she suggested. "The tuck shop probably has limited hours."

She turned to include Jean in the conversation. "Tomorrow should be interesting, though. I'm used to watching television with Jean or Chantelle—or alone, for that matter. Sitting there with a stranger will be a new experience. I meant to ask Bea about Elizabeth's age; I'd put her in her seventies. I think Irma's probably a lot older, but she's much skinnier than Elizabeth, so maybe she's just kind of wrinkled. I'm not sure if we're supposed to ask patients questions or just let them talk. I guess we'll find out. Irma seems kind of bitter."

She exchanged a glance with Jean. "Olive," Jean said, "you have to know that we're willing to spend some time with these gals, but we've got other stuff on the go. If you want to pick up the slack, fine, but once a week is probably our limit for volunteering."

Olive supposed she couldn't hope for any more from Maggie or Jean, but it was fine by her. She could already tell she would enjoy volunteering.

Arriving at their units loaded with shopping bags, Jean let out a deep breath. "Olive, are you planning on opening a restaurant with all the stuff you're buying?" she cried. "You do get two meals a day here, you know."

"I like to have some canned goods on hand and something in the freezer in case I don't feel like going down to dinner all the time," Olive replied. "Shall we meet in, say, twenty minutes to go to happy hour? I don't want to be the first one there."

Maggie and Jean agreed, and they parted ways. By the time Olive had put all her groceries away, though, it was time to meet up with Jean and Maggie again, and they went up to the roof.

The late afternoon was sunny, and at that height, a slight breeze cooled the September air. The leaves had not yet begun to turn, but would provide a gorgeous view when they did. A middle-aged bearded man was tuning his guitar and smiled at the women as they passed. He had a tip jar set up by his microphone, and like so many small-time musicians, he'd self-recorded a CD, displaying a number of copies in a box marked "$10 each."

A small bar was set up under the awning and there were more tables available than before; the organizers had obviously prepared for a good turnout. It would be a nice way for residents to get to know one another.

Jean led Maggie and Olive toward the bar. "What will you have?" she asked. "My treat." She proceeded to buy the women drinks.

The tables were filling up, so they took one as close to the railing as possible. On another small table they noticed plates with crackers, pepperoni, and cheese, so Maggie filled up a plate and brought it back. "I don't know about you two, but I'm kind of hungry, and if I'm going to have this scotch, I'd better eat something!" she exclaimed. "We can go to the dining room a little later than usual."

They watched as couples and single people emerged from the building. Some clearly knew each other; the couples were particularly friendly with each other.

Jean chortled quietly. "This certainly matches with the demographics they talk about on television. There are more of us senior women than men, that's for sure.

I'm glad we have each other for company. It would be pretty slim pickin's otherwise, if this is a sample of the population."

Maggie snorted. "Like either of us is in the market for a man at our age," she said. "After I divorced Chantelle's no-good father, I vowed I wouldn't make that mistake again. It was different for you, Jean. You and Jimmy had your life ahead of you. But he was just like Dad. Even though Jimmy'd been shot in the line of duty before, I think they both thought the badge would protect them. Although to be fair to Dad, he made it to retirement with only one gunshot wound."

"It's true," Jean sighed. "I never found anyone who could replace Jimmy, and now I can't be bothered."

Olive was quiet during their conversation. Finally she gulped some of her wine. "I still miss Bill. And if someone came along like him, I might take the plunge again," she admitted. "Married life was good, and I still feel pretty lonely, although coming to New York has certainly been an adventure. But you'll have to put up with me—sometimes I feel pretty glum."

Jean reached over and stroked Olive's cheek. "Don't worry, kiddo," she said. "We're here for you. And once you get settled—especially if you enjoy volunteering—life in the Northeast won't seem so bad."

The guitarist started his set with an old James Taylor tune, so the women turned toward that area of the roof to sit back and enjoy the music.

Maggie wondered what the assisted living center did in wintertime, whether they would organize something in the activities room or the lobby, or perhaps just forget about happy hour until the warmer months. She'd have to ask someone later.

During the musician's break, Jean looked over at Olive. "I wonder what types of things Howard likes to talk about," she said. "He doesn't seem shy, which is good. One thing about Irma and Elizabeth is there will be an activity we can focus on, at least initially. Maybe Howard likes sports, although that wouldn't be such a good fit for you, Olive. But who knows, you might learn something!" Jean and Maggie began laughing and Jean gave Olive a little tap on the shoulder.

They sat through the second set and then adjourned downstairs for dinner. Afterward, Maggie and Jean returned to their unit for the Yankees game, while Olive opted for a walk.

Before Olive left the building, Jean called after her, "Let's meet tomorrow at nine-thirty to get a taxi to Queens Center, so we can be back before two o'clock. If your walk takes you by the theater, take a look at the choices and show times so we can plan for tomorrow night. See you in the morning!"

Chapter 4

The mall trip went splendidly, as did the outing at the movie theater, and soon Olive had the extra shelving units she needed all set up. With her apartment set and nothing else to do, she threw herself into volunteering with gusto. But it soon became clear to Olive that Jean and Maggie weren't all that committed to volunteering, particularly with the baseball playoffs and the beginning of the hockey season coming up. Since Olive liked all three of the patients, she decided to make it a point to check in on each of them regularly, whether Jean and Maggie did or not.

Some nursing home patients like Howard were only in the facility for rehabilitation, with broken hips and the like, but some were living in it to finish out their days. Olive noticed that many had photographs in their rooms showing off better times—shots of themselves and their now-deceased spouses in younger, happier days, and children and grandchildren all smiling— while others, like Irma and Elizabeth, had only bare, lonely shelves. Olive took some extra time with them; they both had stories to tell, but people had probably quit listening years before.

She learned that Elizabeth was seventy-seven and had long retired from her school nursing career in the Bronx. As an army nurse in World War II London, she had met a young Scottish airman—she just "loved his accent"—and they had gotten engaged. When the war ended, he wouldn't leave the UK and she wouldn't stay, both homesick for their own countries and both certain the other would come to love that country as much as they did. They'd agreed to part and think it over, but neither of them ever crossed the Atlantic following their return, so here she was. She had met other men, but none she wanted to marry. Olive listened to Elizabeth's story without comment, knowing she couldn't imagine having lived her life without Bill or Jon.

Elizabeth had used her vacation time to travel around the country. Her keen observations kept Olive in stitches. Elizabeth had a fear of flying that she could never conquer, so all her travel was done by rail or bus. Although she had a driver's license, Elizabeth could never justify the expense of a owning vehicle in the city; she also felt that it was exciting to let someone else drive her places.

On longer trips she'd joined tours. As Elizabeth told Olive, she wasn't particularly afraid of traveling alone as she enjoyed meeting people, and traveling in tour groups was less hassle than traveling unaccompanied. Five years ago, she had joined a "leaf-peeping" tour to the Adirondack mountains in upstate New York. She hadn't returned to the area since her childhood vacations with her parents in Lake George, and she had been curious to observe the changes.

She laughed when telling Olive about the new highway that had been built over the years. "Why, you can zoom up from Albany in upstate New York to Montreal in no time!" she exclaimed. "You don't have to go through Glens Falls or Lake George anymore if you're driving to Canada, but you can still easily get off the highway and go into town, because they put a lot of exits along the way."

Olive had already told Elizabeth of her recent move from North Dakota, and the fact that she hadn't traveled outside the New York metropolitan area. She told

Elizabeth that she'd like to join a tour and might be able to interest her sister in it.

"Well, my dear, don't wait or you'll end up like me, stuck in a bed somewhere with only one foot!" she warned.

Elizabeth then told Olive about a train trip that she and a now-deceased colleague had taken to Montreal one summer, exclaiming, "I absolutely love the train! You can get up and move around, have a cocktail in the bar car, and look at the scenery without any problem. When we got into Montreal, the station was right near our hotel downtown, so after we checked in, we got a little map and did some research. What a time we had! It was like being in France—although I've never been to France. People generally spoke some English, but lots spoke French, and the bread and other food was just delicious. Since there were two of us, we felt all right about going out at night, so we went to Biddle's Jazz Club. I'd go back in a heartbeat if I were healthy!"

Elizabeth's eyes were dancing and she began rocking a little in her excitement, so Olive realized that even with ill health, Elizabeth still had a lot of memories to carry her through the rest of her days. It was a comforting thought.

Irma, on the other hand, was more shy about opening up to Olive. They'd had a nice conversation or two, but it was clear that it would take time for Irma to warm up to her enough to share her life story. Olive didn't mind; she just enjoyed brightening her day every once in a while.

But even from the beginning, Olive enjoyed her visits with Howard the most. At eighty-two years old, he'd been admitted to the facility after suffering a stroke, but with his attitude and daily physiotherapy, his condition was steadily improving. As his left side had been entirely affected, he was frustrated with his lack of dexterity. Luckily he was right-handed, so he could feed himself, and, just as important, he appeared to have suffered no mental impairment.

In their discussions, he spoke of his late wife, Winnie, with unguarded affection. She had been the love of his life and he felt so sorrowful that they hadn't been blessed with children. They'd considered adoption but had ultimately decided against it. They'd shared an active involvement in their church and also enjoyed their mutual love of traveling together.

In his travelogues, Howard was somewhat typical of North Americans. He told Olive about trips to Europe and Asia, and Olive had to stifle chuckles when he frequently referred to the people there as "foreigners," forgetting that he had been the foreigner in their lands.

His description of food in Asia was priceless. Sushi in Tokyo—forget it! Chickens cooked with their heads on in Thailand—I think not! And dog in Vietnam—no way! Fortunately, in Asia, Howard and Winnie had taken organized tours, where the continent's customs and cuisine were presented to them through the filter of a tour operator. The guides had been instructed to include buffet meals that offered both local and North American dishes, and to use air-conditioned buses with handy toilets when traveling through the grittier parts of a country. This had suited Howard just fine. Olive felt like she couldn't sit in judgment because she'd never traveled to those places herself. It did make her a little wistful, though, wishing that Bill had wanted to see the world outside North Dakota.

Howard also recounted his wartime experiences, particularly about taking part in the Allied invasion of Normandy in 1944. Olive got the sense that he left out a lot of the horror, instead talking about how scared everyone was and how seasick he got waiting to land.

She could only imagine the terror those young men—kids essentially—must have felt seeing the shoreline come into view.

Howard felt comfortable telling her about his life, but he didn't exaggerate just to impress her. For years, Howard had been a foreman in a meat packing plant while Winnie had worked in the business office at a school. He laughed when sharing some stories about mishaps at the plant, and about trying to teach the routine to kids just out of high school; he felt that worker attitudes had definitely changed over the years. He did sound like he'd cared about the people under his watch, and maybe his observation was correct, but Olive couldn't help but think it must be hard to be enthusiastic about a job with such mind-numbing repetition—filling up boxes with wieners eight hours a day. She and Bill had worked hard on their farm, but at least each day had offered some variety.

Maggie and Jean occasionally teased Olive about her visits with Howard, but she brushed them off. She just enjoyed spending time with him—that was hardly a crime!

Chapter 5

As she was walking across the lobby one day, Olive spied Jean getting into the elevator. She called to Jean and asked her to hold it for her.

On the way up, Jean started to laugh. "You won't believe what Maggie is doing right now!" she chuckled. When Olive just looked at her, waiting for an explanation, Jean continued, "She's been on redial for the last half hour trying to win four tickets to the Ranger's game against the Islanders! A Manhattan radio station does this once a month and Maggie has sat on the phone for years, cursing when she doesn't win."

Maggie's antics never ceased to amaze Olive. "I assume she's not the only fan wanting tickets?" Olive asked.

Jean just chortled. "You got that right. The lines must just light up when the DJ hits the noisemaker. You can't just phone in and wait; you have to keep dialing when you get a busy signal! I couldn't take it anymore, so I went down to check the mail. Let's go commiserate with her."

Since Olive couldn't care less about a hockey game, she felt "commiserate" was too strong a word, but kept that thought to herself. When they came in, Maggie was on her cell phone, jumping up and down. She held up a finger, signaling them to wait, and whispered, "I think I got in!"

Jean and Olive took a seat at the kitchen table. They watched Maggie and listened to the radio. The DJ said,

"We have lucky caller number ten on the line. What's your name?"

Maggie shrieked and yelled out her name.

The DJ responded, "Okay, sweetheart, just settle down! So you're a big Rangers fan?"

Trying to sound less maniacal, Maggie told him that yes, she'd been a fan for many years. The DJ told her to stay on the line to give him her address and other information, and then began playing another tune. Maggie got herself under control, gave him the information he wanted, and then hung up. Dancing around the room, she grabbed both Jean and Olive and began shouting, "We're going to a Rangers game, we're going to a Rangers game!"

Both Jean and Olive had to laugh. Jean was secretly pleased, because the only live hockey she'd seen was years ago when Jimmy had taken her to an Islanders game. Maggie had never felt free to spend money on tickets during the regular season, so she'd contented herself with a couple of preseason games. This experience promised to be a real treat, since the Islanders and Rangers didn't like each other, and both teams had just begun the new season fairly strong.

Olive thanked Maggie for including her, but asked if there was someone else she might prefer in the party. Maggie answered quickly. "Nope! I want you to see a game live so you'll understand why Jean and I like it so much. It's not all about fighting, you know; that stuff just gets a lot of attention on the sports news. The pace is fast and these seats will be pretty good."

Olive then asked, "If there are four tickets, may I make a suggestion? Howard's improved enough in his therapy that I think he could probably handle going to the game, as long as we take it slow when we walk along. I know he's getting cabin fever being cooped up in his room most of the time."

Maggie looked skeptical. "Well, Madison Square Garden holds a lot of people and the subway will probably be jammed. Does he use a wheelchair?"

"I've seen him walk with a cane a few times. He uses the wheelchair to go to physio, probably just because the nurses want him to."

"Let's try this," Jean interjected. "Mention the game to him and ask him to be honest about whether he can handle the trip. Has he been to a game before?"

"He told me about the times he and his late wife watched the Islanders play, and I assume that most arenas are pretty similar, wouldn't you say?" Olive answered.

Maggie nodded slowly and said she'd go along with the plan. Olive agreed to speak to Howard that night, as the game was only a few days away.

Since the Rangers were playing that night in Tampa and the game was televised, Maggie insisted that Olive join them to watch at least one period so that they could explain the game to her. Jean thought that was a good idea, not wanting to spend half of the live game answering Olive's silly questions. Better to get them over with in front of the tube.

Olive crinkled her nose; she could smell the microwave popcorn already. They agreed to meet at the dining hall at six o'clock, which would give them plenty of time to get back to Maggie's apartment for the seven o'clock start.

After dinner, Olive stopped by Howard's place to ask him about the game. Arriving at his room, Olive heard sound from his television and realized that the pre-game show must have already started. She called in through the door to ask if he had a couple of moments to spare for her.

"You bet!" Howard answered. "Come on in."

Olive took a seat in his room and told him about Maggie's good fortune.

He was enthusiastic. "Lucky stiff!" he exclaimed. "Tickets are like gold these days, what with regular fans and all the tourists coming to Manhattan."

"Well, here's the thing. Maggie won four tickets and she insists that my sister and I join her, but I know so little about hockey that I may be a pest with questions during play," Olive explained. "Would you be interested in using the fourth ticket and explaining the game to me while we're watching? I'm a pretty fast learner, but knowing my sister all these years, she'll be upset if I interrupt her train of thought."

Howard's face lit up. "I'd love to accompany you fine ladies! And since my ticket is free, I'll pay for a taxi. That way we can be dropped off at the door and I won't slow you down. The Rangers are playing tonight, so if you want to pull up a chair, I can give you some pointers."

Olive thought this was a great idea, and since she still had her cell phone in her pocket, she gave Jean and Maggie a call to let them know that Howard would be explaining the game to her instead. She grinned at Howard and said, "I'll watch the first part of the game with you, and then during the last part I'll go back and impress them with my knowledge!"

As the game carried on, Olive found she required fewer and fewer explanations. She wasn't particularly interested in the intermission chatter because it was more information than she cared for, but she sat quietly, as Howard appeared to be interested. After the end of the second period, the game was tied 1-1, so she thanked Howard and said she'd try out her newfound knowledge on her cohorts.

As she was getting up, Howard spoke: "I want to thank you for the invitation to the game. It means a lot to me. I'll get a cab to pick us up at a quarter after five, because it will take a while to get into Manhattan, and I'll probably slow you all down reaching our seats."

"That's no problem," Olive replied. "I'll pass it on to Maggie and Jean."

When Olive reached the apartment, Jean's television was blaring and the usual microwave popcorn smell bowled Olive over. She'd mentioned it once to Jean, but her sister didn't seem to notice it, possibly because she and Maggie always lived on the stuff during football season. As far as Olive was concerned, the popcorn smelled neither "original" nor "buttery good," or whatever other descriptions the manufacturers used.

Olive opened the sliding door of the balcony just enough to let in a little air without cooling off their lair. Maggie always struck Olive as a hot-blooded Irish-Italian—almost a caricature of the fast-talking, loud, emotional "mamma-mia" types in the movies—but when it came to the apartment, Maggie kept it as hot as a thin-blooded old lady with poor circulation would. Olive was used to keeping her home in North Dakota rather cool, even in winter, and did so here as well, so walking into their apartment was like walking into a kiln. And there was Maggie, wrapped in an afghan!

The second intermission had just ended so Olive pulled up a chair. "Do you have any wine to accompany that popcorn? Chateau Vin Sherry, perhaps?" Her attempt at sarcasm was lost on Maggie, sitting there in her Rangers jersey and engrossed in the tube, but Jean grinned and pointed to the fridge.

In it, Olive found the box of red and poured herself a glass. She took a suspicious sip, and found herself mildly surprised—not bad!

That Friday—or "game day," as Maggie insisted upon calling it—they had the dining room prepare take-out chef's salads for dinner and ate in Olive's apartment at four-thirty. A little while later, Maggie stepped out of her bedroom, resplendent in her Ranger jersey.

Together, the three women walked down to the nursing home entrance to find Howard already seated out front, ready for their arrival. He stood as they approached, thanking Maggie for her generosity. Jean in turn thanked him for his patience in explaining the game to Olive. Howard raised his eyebrows, replying that Olive was an apt pupil indeed. Olive looked smugly at her sister in response.

Getting from Queens to Manhattan was no mean feat, and the cabbie decided to do it as quickly as possible. Howard, sitting in the front, braced his cane on the floor and, in jest, began to pray. When the cabbie looked at him strangely and asked in broken English if he was okay, Howard explained that he just wanted to see a hockey game before he died. The cabbie heard this and launched into an excited monologue about hockey in general and the Rangers in particular, all the while weaving in and out of traffic. Maggie, for once, was perfectly silent.

The taxi dropped them off near Madison Square Garden, and once Howard got himself righted after stepping onto the sidewalk, he was able to walk slowly but steadily with his cane. They all instinctively turned to look north at the lights on Broadway, which were impressive even in the dusk. They would have an even better view when leaving the game in darkness.

After entering the building, they suggested that Howard rest for a moment while Maggie looked for the elevators. Howard noticed a bathroom close by, so he decided to visit it before they got settled in their seats.

People were filing into their seats and even though it was very early in the season, there was a lot of energy in the crowd. Obviously some Islanders fans had gotten tickets and were determined to make up in volume what they lacked in numbers. Already there were horns blowing and the organist was warming up the crowd.

"And now, your New York Rangers!" The announcer's voice brought the crowd to its feet as the players skated onto the ice, spotlighted in the darkness of the arena.

Everyone then stood for the national anthem. Olive found herself singing along and feeling somewhat overwhelmed. She couldn't help it. When the anthem was sung on television during the Olympics it was very stirring, but this was different. She felt so proud to be an American, sharing in the bounty she was lucky to have.

The spell was broken quickly, however; after the referee dropped the puck, fans around her started shouting epithets at opposing players. "Oh, my," she murmured to Howard. "People take this really seriously!"

Howard patted her arm. "Don't worry about it. They're just letting off steam."

The play began at a fast pace, and it occurred to Olive that she really had to pay attention, because there were no play-by-play announcers or slow-motion replay. With the crowd chanting and hearing all the "oohs" and "ahs," it was more exciting than she had imagined it would be. Maggie was shouting at the top of her lungs, and Olive was startled to hear Howard tell the referee he should get glasses.

When there was a break in the action, either the organist played or the sound system blared some song or other. A favorite appeared to be "We are the Champions." At one point Howard leaned over to the three women and said, "I never much cared for Queen." Maggie and the sisters swiveled in their seats to look at him, stunned that he would know of the band, but he just sat back quietly with his eyes on the game.

The game wound down and Olive noticed that Howard looked to be a little tired. She nudged Maggie and since the score was 5-1 with only five minutes left in the third period, they all stood up and began to leave.

Down at street level they caught a cab and headed home. At the entrance to the nursing home, they paused to laugh again at the antics of the cab driver on the way into the city, vowing to attend church that Sunday in case they ever had another cabbie like him.

Chapter 6

Olive had been volunteering for a few weeks when she entered Elizabeth's room to find her very excited. A man in a suit had introduced himself to her earlier; he'd said he was a lawyer and had been contacted by a possible relative of hers, which was news to Elizabeth. She hadn't realized she'd had any. Elizabeth showed Olive his business card bearing the name Edgar Barnes, the company name *Kinfolk*, and the phrase "Bringing Families Together."

Olive was puzzled. "What did the fellow tell you?"

"He said he understood that I have no close relatives, but he could connect me with a relation on my father's side," Elizabeth said, her eyes bright.

"And why would he do that?" Olive asked.

"I never asked him! He seemed so sweet and he told me it's comforting to us older folk to know there's family out there."

Now Olive was really puzzled. "But how does this family member know about you? And why haven't they contacted you sooner?"

Still excited, Elizabeth replied, "I don't know. Mr. Barnes says he'll visit me again in a few days, and he even asked if I enjoyed chocolates. He seemed like such a nice man!"

Olive was beginning to feel distressed. "Did he ask you anything about your will, that sort of thing?" she pressed.

Elizabeth was quiet for a moment. "He did say that my, what did he call it?—my estate plan—was my business and I shouldn't discuss these things with the nurses or other patients. You're so good to me, Olive, but maybe we shouldn't talk about this anymore."

She closed up after that, and they spent a few more minutes making polite conversation. Despite her concern, Olive told Elizabeth not to worry and bade her goodbye.

Apparently, Elizabeth hadn't been Barnes' only stop that afternoon. Howard couldn't wait to tell Olive about the man. As with Elizabeth, the man had left him his *Kinfolk* business card too and had given Howard the same warning he gave Elizabeth, so Olive didn't press for additional information. Barnes had told Howard that he would return in a week or so for a longer talk. After learning of this, Olive made her excuses and left for her apartment.

Back in her unit, Olive thought about what she had—and hadn't—been told that day. Senior magazines always featured warnings about con artists, and heaven knew the news on television ran all kinds of stories, but back in North Dakota that had all seemed so far away. Maybe this Barnes fellow was on the level, but it was all pretty strange. His secretiveness certainly raised Olive's suspicions, but then again, lawyers were like that.

Maybe Jean and Maggie could give her some perspective. Her knock on their door brought a joint "Come in."

They were glued to the tube, as usual. What the two of them saw in college football, and Rutgers University football in particular, was a mystery to Olive. She guessed it might have something to do with the young Italian coach, but who knew? Halftime was coming up, so she opened a bottle of iced tea and waited.

"I'm a little upset," she said when the game reached halftime. "There's something going on over at the nursing home and I'm not sure what to do."

Maggie leaned forward. "How so?"

Olive began to explain. "A man has talked to Elizabeth and Howard and he might be persuading them to change their wills. I don't want to play Miss Marple and interfere in their affairs, but they may be vulnerable." She told them the rest of what she knew about this Mr. Barnes.

"Christ on a bicycle!" Jean exclaimed. "This guy just waltzed right in there?"

Olive thought about this. "I guess so. Visitors must sign in and out, but unless a patient complains, anyone can visit."

"You said Elizabeth and Howard," Jean said. "Do you think that's it?"

"Well. I only spoke to those two. There may be more."

Maggie shot them both a look. "Listen, Sherlock and Watson!" she admonished. "The best way to follow up is to check patient records, see if other residents have no living relatives listed. When I worked in the Surrogate's Court, I was surprised at the number of people with no immediate family. But if you ask me, it doesn't sound like anything to worry about yet."

Olive pondered this for a moment. "I have access to patient records if I want to check a telephone number or address. Sometimes a patient asks to send flowers or a card to a family member. Next of kin are always shown."

"Then check out anyone who fits the bill and check the visitor's log while you're at it," Maggie said with a shrug.

"Look who's Sherlock now!" exclaimed Jean. "I gotta check out this guy online. Maybe that's how he 'brings families together,' or whatever it says on his card."

"Good idea!" answered Maggie. Olive agreed, knowing that the business office closed at noon on Saturdays, so she wouldn't be able to look at patient records until Monday without attracting attention.

A moment later, the second half of the game came on and Olive knew it was time to depart. They'd agreed to do a movie and pizza that night rather than eat in the dining room so that the three of them could talk about this plan without any eavesdropping from other diners.

Sure enough, Jean and Maggie bounced into Olive's room at four-thirty. They always took turns choosing movies after learning that Olive preferred more family fare—"tear jerkers" to Jean and Maggie—while they enjoyed grittier films, usually involving some violence. Having been around cops for so long, both of them loved *Gangs of New York* and *Goodfellas*, either of which would have driven Olive out of the theater. Tonight was Olive's choice and she was excited to see *The Blind Side*. They decided to catch the five o'clock feature and get pizza afterward.

Gianetti's Pizza was a block from the Cineplex. They were able to find a table in the corner that looked out onto the street. There was still a little daylight left and Olive enjoyed watching people get off the bus and stride home, usually weighed down with various parcels. The women ordered a large pizza to share— pepperoni and mushroom—with a carafe of the house red to wash it down. As usual, Jean launched into her "pizza monologue."

"I'm glad we live in a place with decent pizza," intoned Jean. Both Maggie and Olive rolled their eyes, knowing that there was no point trying to stop her. "I mean, the Swedes can make meatballs, but North Dakota doesn't know real Italian meatballs, let alone a good pizza crust. And don't get me started on the sauce! Whoever heard of sauce without oregano?"

Olive had tried to tell Jean of the improvements in North Dakota since her departure, but she did agree with Jean that pizza in the New York area was delicious.

Now Maggie got onto another gripe: Olive's choice of movie. "Olive, with all the choices out there—*Crazy Heart, The Hurt Locker, Sherlock Holmes,* three of the best movies this year—you pick *The Blind Side*," she complained. "I gotta tell you, watching Jeff Bridges or Robert Downey Jr. beats the hell out of listening to people around us weep through Sandra Bullock's righteous bleatings!"

Olive had enjoyed the movie and wasn't going to let Maggie browbeat her. "You just can't make up your mind, can you?" she retorted. "You're crazy about sports and you liked Sandra Bullock in *Miss Congeniality*, so I figured this choice would shut you up!"

Maggie shot back, "Yeah, but there was precious little real sports in this flick and Sandra Bullock kicked butt in *Miss Congeniality*. And her partner in that movie was easy on the eyes too!"

Jean decided she'd better weigh in to stop any further argument. "Well, next week is my turn and I'm going with *Invictus*, so that should keep both of you happy," she declared.

The pizza and wine came, ending the discussion for the time being, although Maggie tried to continue their earlier conversation about Elizabeth and Howard. Her mouth still full, she mumbled something about the website.

"What are you talking about?" asked Olive.

Jean leaned in and said that she and Maggie had looked up the *Kinfolk* website on the internet.

Maggie finished chewing. "First off, *Kinfolk* isn't a very original name, but it is catchy."

Olive couldn't contain her curiosity. "But what did the website say?"

"Well, the title is at the top of the screen with the 'Bringing Families Together' tagline typed out in fancy print underneath. There are a couple of short videos embedded in it with younger to middle-aged white people, I'm guessing actors, saying how grateful they were that *Kinfolk* found their second cousin Tillie in her later years, and that they were able to learn so much about their family history, blah, blah, blah."

Jean chimed in, "And there was also a video of an old, frail-looking lady in a nursing home bed who said she knew she didn't have long to live, but finding her late cousin's family was making her last days so much more peaceful." She rolled her eyes.

Maggie added, "I think the message is that the old girl is loaded and hasn't long to live, so the late cousin's family will help themselves to a windfall when God calls her home. My guess is that Edgar Barnes, being a lawyer, gets the old lady to update her will while she's still able, and probably also names himself Executor too, so everyone gets a piece of the pie."

"It sounds like something out a movie!" Olive exclaimed. "Did the website say what it costs?"

Jean answered, "No, it didn't really get into specifics. It gave a toll-free number and invited viewers to call for further information."

"I'm wondering if it isn't a two-way street," Maggie said. "Perhaps this guy gets calls from people, but maybe he also gets to know someone in the business office of a nursing home, and then tries to find patients who appear to have no immediate family."

Olive nodded. "Yes. When I think about Elizabeth and Howard, if there are long lost relations, they would have contacted the nursing home themselves. Although I suppose that people could also contact this Mr. Barnes with names they believe are elderly relatives, and he'll do a search to locate them—for a fee."

Jean interjected, "But you did find it pretty creepy that he just happened in on both Elizabeth and Howard and didn't really lay out his business during the first visit. And I, for one, am not too sure about a guy who seems so secretive."

Olive mulled this over. "I wonder if he knows that Howard is leaving his estate to his church?" The thought made her uneasy.

When dinner was done, the trio walked back to the complex and parted for the night.

Knowing Maggie and Jean would be incommunicado during all of the televised NFL games, Olive decided to try some online research herself after church the following day. Maggie and Jean were so much better and faster at using computers, as with everything else technological. Olive preferred to putter and ponder, not even attempting computer searches with either Maggie or Jean in the room.

She found the *Kinfolk* website and watched the videos Maggie had described. Things are so different now, she thought as she watched the old lady in the nursing home bed. Everyone was so spread out and families lost touch. But drumming up some distant relatives who had nothing in common with an elderly nursing home patient didn't seem like the answer either, particularly if they were more interested in getting an inheritance than bringing the patient any real joy. Olive then berated herself for being so cynical. What had the morning's sermon just said about reaching out and sharing joy with others? Still, she couldn't help feeling uneasy, picturing either Elizabeth or Howard in that website's video.

Chapter 7

On Monday morning, Olive went to the nursing home office as usual. Her presence caused no comment other than the usual greetings and small talk about the weekend weather. The accountant and her assistant were busy reviewing bills that had been prepared for the previous month, so Olive was free to look through the vertical files relating to the fifty or so patients currently in the facility.

She first looked at Elizabeth and Howard's records to confirm who, if anyone, was listed as their next of kin. As expected, none were shown. Olive began flipping through the other files alphabetically, only looking for next of kin, not wanting to spend a lot of time there or draw attention to herself. She found no next of kin for Irma, either, and made a note of it. Olive knew that Irma had entered the nursing home from her apartment in Queens about three months before and was confined to bed with a variety of complications, not the least of which her age: eighty-seven. Although Olive had been in her room during the initial tour, Jean was supposed to play cribbage with her. But when Olive thought about it, she realized Jean hadn't said much about Irma of late. If she wasn't visiting Irma regularly, Olive would stop by. It had been a while since she'd seen Irma, anyway.

Olive had almost completed her file review when the accountant called her name. "Can I help you with anything?" she asked.

Olive was somewhat startled, but recovered quickly. "Elizabeth Billingsley had a visitor on Saturday morning who thought he might know some distant relatives, so I'm checking her file before I see her today to confirm if anyone was listed as next of kin when she was admitted," she hastily explained. "I don't see anything here, so I'm going to talk to Elizabeth since she's expecting him to return sometime this week." The accountant was satisfied with her answer and Olive quickly wrapped up her search in the office.

She moved on to the lobby. On a table by the entrance, she found the guest book and proceeded to review the entries for the past few weeks. Sure enough, an Edgar Barnes had signed in and then signed out a couple of hours later. His notation indicated a meeting with Elizabeth, but there was no mention of his visit to Howard.

Olive decided to try Irma's room. It was past breakfast and unless Irma had regular physiotherapy or other treatments, she should be in bed. Olive grabbed a few flowers from a vase in the hall and knocked gently on Irma's door. A faint greeting called her in.

Seeing Irma, Olive wondered what she herself would look like in twenty years. Maybe Irma had always been small, but she seemed so shriveled and frail that Olive could not imagine her as a young woman. Unfortunately, there were no photos in Irma's room, so Olive was left to speculate.

The television blared a morning show with two women giggling at each other. Perhaps one of them was that Regis woman, Olive thought, but she couldn't be sure because she wasn't much of a viewer. It appeared that Irma wasn't really interested either, so an aide had probably left the TV on again, thinking she was doing Irma a favor.

Olive came up to the bed with the flowers and said good morning. Irma had been staring blankly into space, but brightened at the sound of Olive's voice and the sight of the small bouquet. Irma asked her to turn the television off, muttering, "The people on that show speak such drivel!"

Olive grinned, realizing that Irma had more vinegar in her than she'd imagined. She replied, "I agree. There's so much time spent staring at the box. I love to listen to music and get my news from public radio in the evening." She turned the TV off as per Irma's request.

Irma looked wistful. "I used to do that at home, but here there isn't much privacy. I think I'm getting a roommate soon."

"Why don't you have a radio or a CD player by your bed?" asked Olive.

"I don't have anyone to get one for me."

This irritated Olive, because either Jean had stopped visits altogether, or hadn't bothered to listen to Irma. "Do you still have those things at home or in storage?" she asked. "If you do, I can pick them up and bring them to you."

Irma shook her head. "Thanks anyway. They were part of a home entertainment unit in my bedroom, but they were sold along with the furniture in my place. I couldn't stay by myself any longer, so it was easier to just get rid of the stuff."

Olive responded, "I'm sure some family member could lend you a player, or buy you one of the new smaller radio-CD player combinations. They aren't expensive."

"It isn't the money. I have a lot of it." Irma looked at Olive bleakly. "It's terrible to be eighty-seven years old and not know any living family, let alone anyone near enough to visit or help out."

Olive patted her shoulder. "Well, I can run an errand for you; I'd be delighted to buy you one."

"Please don't make a special trip on my account," Irma said, "but I can give you some money before you go. If you can also buy earphones, they'll be my salvation if I do get a roommate, particularly if she likes the TV." She smiled ruefully.

"I'll just pick them up and bring you the receipt. You don't have to give me money ahead of time," Olive said. She paused, and then asked, "What type of music do you like? The office has a video and CD library that's quite varied."

"Big Band and classical CDs are my favorites," Irma responded. "During the war I remember dancing to Glen Miller at the USO with the young GIs being shipped out. I was still relatively young myself. You'd never know it to look at me now."

"I bet you were a beautiful young woman!" Olive said with a grin. "I have to go out later today for some weekly shopping, so I'll see what I can find. I'll try to stop by after dinner." On her way out, Olive paused. "Are you still playing cards with my sister, Jean?" she asked.

Irma grunted. "She hasn't been around for a while. I'm just a boring old woman to her, probably."

"Well, I also like to play cards, so we'll have a game tonight." Cribbage was a leisurely game and allowed for conversation. Perhaps she could find out a little more background on Irma in the event that Barnes decided to add her to his list.

Olive returned that evening with a combination clock radio and CD player, and enjoyed watching Irma clap her hands with delight. Olive set the clock and then brought out a couple of CDs she'd borrowed from the nursing home's collection, together with a Benny Goodman CD she'd found while shopping.

"This one is a gift from me," she told Irma, "but I'm going to enjoy listening to it while I beat you at crib."

Irma teared up, saying, "I haven't received a gift in so long. Thanks so much . . . but I still intend to win!"

As Olive had hoped, Irma became more talkative as the game progressed. Olive wondered if Irma had just forgotten the art of conversation during her lonely years following retirement. Irma shared her story about working most of her adult life in the billing department at Con Ed, bored with the job but afraid to leave because she had no husband to support her and was caring for her mother as well. When she retired at sixty-five, her mother was still alive, so she didn't do the things people often do in retirement; her days were a dreary routine of making meals for herself and her mother, putting her mother in front of the television in the living room, and either retiring to her own bedroom or the porch in good weather, desperate to escape the noise of the set and her mother's carping at the screen. As Irma explained, it was one of the reasons she hated the television here in the nursing home. In her bedroom she could at least enjoy public radio programs and music whenever she chose.

Her mother had come from the UK and had raised Irma on a fairly bland diet—and her mother's tastes had become even more parochial as she aged. Olive thought that this was such a shame, for Irma had missed out on the great ethnic restaurants springing up in the area over the years. At least Irma had been spared the adjustment to nursing home cuisine.

While counting both Olive's cards and her own, Irma related the rest of her history. When her mother finally did pass away at the age of one hundred and one, Irma herself was then old, and her own health—

particularly her lack of mobility—interfered with any travel. She'd gone into Manhattan a few times on bus trips from the local senior center, and had been thrilled to attend a matinee concert of Beethoven's Sixth at Lincoln Center, but museum trips proved too difficult, so she had to choose her outings carefully. The local senior center also hosted bridge and blackjack tournaments, but she had always been reluctant to leave the apartment for too long.

"I haven't even been to Atlantic City, and I love to play cards!" Irma moaned. "And look at me now! A frail, bitter old woman who'll spend her last days in this bed."

She began to weep and all Olive could do was pat her shoulder.

After a few moments, Irma gathered herself and said, "I'm better now. Thank you for listening. I think I just want a shoulder to cry on after all of these years!"

Olive responded, "Well, if you don't let me win a game or two, you'll have to find someone else's shoulder!" This broke the tension and Irma burst out laughing.

They resumed playing and Olive inquired whether Irma had any more distant family she would like to contact to advise of her change of address.

Irma snorted. "One thing about a long life is that you outlive everyone. Years ago, I knew a couple of cousins in the Midwest, but we only met once or twice when I was young. They may have children, but I've never heard from anyone—not even a card at Christmas."

Olive could see that Irma was beginning to tire, and Olive herself felt ready for some respite. She excused herself and promised to play another game with Irma soon.

Walking across the compound in the early evening, Olive considered Irma's situation. If Barnes visited Irma, she would be so susceptible, given her loneliness and bitterness about a life wasted. On the other hand, was it any of Olive's business? With those conflicting emotions, she reached the residence and caught the elevator to her floor.

She didn't feel ready for sleep quite yet, so she stopped off at Maggie and Jean's apartment. Jean was on her cellphone and waved her in; Olive went to the fridge for some water.

When Jean was finished with her call, she exclaimed, "Where have you been? You were going to look in the files at the business office today, right?"

"I tried to find both you and Maggie this afternoon but you weren't home!" Olive responded.

"You know we do our laundry together on Mondays!" Jean took on her usual exasperated tone whenever she and Olive disagreed on anything. "You could have just come down to the basement to check on us."

"Alright, I forgot about your laundry day." Olive was also a little jealous on this account as well. It wouldn't kill Jean and Maggie to ask if she wanted to throw some articles in the wash with theirs, but it clearly never occurred to them. Olive tried to hide her irritation when she asked, "Irma says you haven't been around to see her lately?"

A little defensive, Jean blurted, "All that boo-hoo was getting to me, so I'm taking a break."

At that moment, Maggie emerged from the bathroom. "Whatcha up to? We've been looking for you!" Olive related her day's experiences, concluding with her concerns about Irma. "Hmm," Maggie responded. "Irma didn't mention any visit from our Mr. Barnes?"

"No." Olive shook her head. "But we talked enough about her boring life and loneliness, I think she'd have shared that sort of excitement." She stood to leave. "I plan to make brief visits tomorrow to Elizabeth and Howard, so I'll let you know if anything changes. I feel awkward sneaking around like this, but who's going to look out for these folks otherwise?"

Chapter 8

Olive felt somewhat listless on Tuesday morning. She hadn't slept well, and thought about staying in bed for part of the day to catch up on her newsmagazines. Usually she made herself some toast or instant hot cereal, but looking out at the fall sunshine, she decided to go out for a walk and to have breakfast out. She thought about calling Jean to accompany her, but instead chose to just get up and go out alone. She was still a little disappointed in her twin for her negligence regarding Irma.

It had rained a little during the night and the leaves were floating in puddles on the sidewalk. At this time of year, Olive truly loved living in the East. While spring and summer were her favorite months— especially when the corn and wheat began sprouting— North Dakota was flat and dry, and its early winter offered few mornings like this.

At eight o'clock, people were still hustling by on their way to work, heads down, dodging puddles. Olive chuckled, knowing that her walk could be leisurely, its only purpose to find a place for breakfast. She decided to stop at Neighborhood Bagels, a cozy little place that was fairly quiet at that time of day.

She sat down at a small table where someone had left the *New York Post*, so she glanced at the headlines before turning her attention to breakfast. "What to order?" she asked herself, looking at the chalkboard menu. In the movies, actors were always eating plain bagels spread with cream cheese, but here there were so many choices. She decided on cinnamon raisin with butter only, and a medium coffee. She was glad this place offered understandable sizes. Medium was medium, not that "tall," "grande" nonsense!

Turning back to the *Post*, she was amazed at some of the stories. So lurid! Maggie and Jean both commented on the *Post*'s descriptions of players for the sports teams in the area, and how difficult the media and fans could be—while at the same time making their own judgments on these same players.

No wonder *The Times* was called "The Gray Lady" compared to these Technicolor descriptions in the *Post*. "All the News That's Fit to Print," thought Olive, but for the *Post* it's "All the News That Fits, We Print!"

She finished her bagel and carried her coffee with her over to a nearby bulletin board. She liked to check out local events, especially free ones. In early October there had been a Friday evening concert in the park. The band hadn't been professional, she remembered, probably only a community group, but she'd talked Maggie and Jean into coming, and even they had enjoyed it. Olive vowed to do more of these outings, now that she was getting settled in "the city."

She was proud of her ability to adapt, something which Jean appeared not to notice. It had been a big change—first losing her husband and coming to grips with life as a widow, and then agreeing to join Jean on the East Coast—and all within the past year or so.

Life on the farm had possessed a certain cadence; it had been much slower and more predictable, although not without its worries. Weather and grain and beef prices couldn't be predicted, much less controlled, and as any parent would, she'd worried about her son, Jon, as he grew up and away from the farm. It had been a welcome call when he'd told them of his plan to move back and farm with his father—especially when he'd mentioned that he was bringing along a young woman who he'd chosen as his wife. While Olive had had some early misgivings about her daughter-in-law's commitment to the farm, Karen and Jon seemed to enjoy their life, and Olive had hoped that a grandchild might join the family. As the years passed, she'd begun to doubt there would ever be a grandchild, but she kept that thought to herself. She was finding it was nice enough to call them every Saturday evening just to say hello.

Olive was also trying to carve a niche for herself in her new home. Aside from her hours volunteering in the nursing home, she wanted to get to know the residents in her complex. In speaking with the activities director in the assisted living wing, she discovered that various craft courses were available at a local senior center. She'd done some knitting over the years, but preferred reading to needlework and that sort of thing, so the craft courses didn't hold much appeal for her.

When Olive was a child, her father had tried to interest both Jean and her in musical instruments, but unfortunately his choice had been the accordion—probably because he played it and already had one in the house. Jean had made it clear she wouldn't be caught dead with it, and when Olive had tried to learn, Jean always cackled that it sounded like a couple of cats fighting in a bag. Olive had had trouble with the size and weight of the thing, and trying to coordinate the buttons and keys had proved too much for her, so she'd put it aside and concentrated on singing in the church choir.

Now, with all this time on her hands, she imagined herself learning an instrument. Her hands were too stiff to consider playing the guitar or piano, and besides, she didn't want to practice on the piano in the activity room downstairs because it was too public. One of the "oldies" stations had featured a Bob Dylan tribute a month or so before, and it struck her that maybe the blues harmonica might be something she could work on.

Recently she'd gone to a music store and found a new "harp" for around eight dollars, so she figured there would be nothing lost if she had no talent; she also found a small instruction booklet for around ten dollars. Olive decided to keep these purchases to herself because she could only imagine the ridicule she'd have to endure from Jean and Maggie. She'd gone through the booklet and done some of the exhale-inhale exercises, concluding that she sounded less awful exhaling on a note than inhaling, but other than that, she hadn't done too much.

Walking back to the residence from the bagel shop, Olive resolved to look in on Elizabeth and Howard, and then spend an hour exhaling and inhaling. If nothing else, it would expand her lungs. Apparently the senior center had a little music group that met on Friday afternoons, so Olive figured that she could go over for one of the sessions, listen, and perhaps sing along, and then decide if it was the type of group which would accept rank amateurs learning a new instrument.

Getting out of the elevator, she spied Maggie and Jean knocking on her door. "What are you two selling, besides aggravation?" she called out as she walked down the hall.

"There you are!" yelled Maggie. "We're going to have to put a bell on you!"

Olive unlocked her door and invited them in. "So, what's up?" she asked once they'd settled down.

"We decided to do a little sleuthing ourselves!" Jean replied.

"And?"

"Maggie and I went to the lobby of the nursing home, and guess who signed the visitors log this morning!"

"I gather Mr. Barnes has reappeared?"

"We didn't see him, and even if we did, we don't know what he looks like," Maggie answered.

"But did the log indicate the room he intended to visit?" Olive inquired.

"He's got himself listed as a visitor to Elizabeth, or whatever a person puts in the log," Jean said.

Olive looked at both of them and realized that the ball was in her court. "Alright, I planned to see both Elizabeth and Howard today, so I'll stroll by and get a look at him," she decided aloud. "I don't want to go into their rooms if he's there, though, because it's supposed to be none of my business. Where are you two spending the rest of the day? I can report back if you want me to."

The two women agreed, nodding their heads. It was good to see them so concerned about the nursing home patients' well-being—Olive just wished it wasn't under such suspicious circumstances.

When Olive arrived at the nursing home, there was the usual late-morning lull in activity. The patients had eaten and bathed; some were off to physiotherapy and others were either resting or enjoying the company of visitors.

Olive greeted the floor nurse, Nurse Elfrieda. She was the same nurse who had first spoken to Olive, Jean, and Maggie at the volunteering information session, and Olive had since developed a rapport with her.

Olive told Elfrieda that she was going to stop in on Elizabeth Billingsley, but Elfrieda held up her hand and whispered, "There's a visitor in with her and she says she doesn't want to be disturbed, not even by staff. She's never done that before."

Olive shrugged and went back to the elevator to travel to Howard's floor. Sometimes he asked her to purchase licorice for him at the tuck shop, something he'd eaten for years to stave off the need for nicotine. He'd quit smoking decades before and had eaten tons of licorice since, but he said it never truly replaced the satisfaction he'd felt in lighting up. Neither Olive nor Bill had ever smoked, so she couldn't truly empathize, but if it worked for Howard, that was just fine.

"Hi, Olive!" Howard shouted when she entered his room. Like a lot of older folk, he'd lost some of his hearing, so assumed that everyone else was nearly deaf too.

"Just thought I'd stop by to see if you want anything from downstairs," Olive replied, looking around his room to see if anyone else was with him. He had his television on SportsCenter, although it was on mute. Olive guessed that he'd watched it earlier at a higher volume and now just kept it on to enjoy the video replays.

"I'm fine, thanks, but guess what? I had another visit this morning from that Mr. Barnes. He just dropped in and said he wants to come back later to talk some more. I can't figure out why he wants to see me, unless he came across a long-lost rich uncle!" Howard snorted out a half laugh.

"Maybe you have distant younger relatives who want to meet you?" asked Olive.

"I'm sure he'll tell me, but I can't for the life of me think who that would be. Still, I am a little curious."

"I'll get out of your way then, but I have to come back to the ward tomorrow, so I can stop by to see if you want anything."

"Thanks, Olive. If you don't mind, can you pick up some more licorice for me? Just put it on my tab at the tuck shop."

Olive grinned and agreed. After leaving Howard's room, she realized that she still had time to check on Irma, so she headed down to her room. The television was blaring. Olive turned it down and went to Irma's bed. Irma looked up and Olive saw her headphones.

"Thank goodness you bought these for me!" Irma exclaimed. "The cleaner cranked up the television just as she was leaving and I couldn't get her attention to turn it down." Taking off her headphones, she asked Olive, "Do you have time for a game of crib?"

"No time like the present!" Olive replied.

As they settled into the game, Olive asked Irma if she'd heard anything about a roommate. Irma said there was no word yet, and that she hoped it wouldn't happen; although she enjoyed Olive's company, she valued her privacy. She went on to say that she did have a gentleman stop in for a few moments that morning and it had been a nice surprise.

Olive asked, "Is he with the nursing home?"

"No. His name is Edgar Barnes and he gave me his business card," she said, passing it over to Olive. "When I asked him what *Kinfolk* was, he said he didn't have long because he was meeting with another resident, but would stop by later to explain it to me."

Olive glanced at her watch, noting that it was almost eleven-thirty. "What time did he visit? It'll be lunchtime soon."

Irma looked at her clock radio. "I think it was around nine o'clock or so, because I'd finished breakfast and put my teeth back in, and the aide had brushed my hair, thank God! The sight of me first thing in the morning would scare the horses, I swear!"

Olive had just finished pegging fourteen points to bring herself even with Irma on the board when Irma groaned. "Let's stop flapping our gums and finish this game. Lunch will be along soon."

Olive smiled at Irma, but on the inside, she was worried. Just what was this Barnes fellow up to?

Chapter 9

Olive hurried toward her apartment and spied Maggie and Jean coming to the elevator; when they saw her, they both gave her expectant looks.

"Are you two on your way to lunch?" Olive asked.

"Yes," Maggie answered. "I didn't have breakfast this morning, so I'm famished. Are you coming?"

"No. I had a bagel earlier and there's some fruit in the fridge, so I'll pass. I've got some things to do around the apartment, so stop by when you're finished and I'll fill you in."

This worked out well for Olive because she wanted to spend a little time on her harmonica lesson, but also wanted to be done by the time Maggie and Jean returned. When she brought out the harp and instruction booklet, she chuckled to herself, wondering why she bothered. But she'd made a promise to herself to try as many new things as she could, and to not let her late start hold her back. So Olive began the tedious exercises, exhaling and inhaling into the instrument, glad that the apartments were pretty soundproof and that any neighbors were probably at lunch.

After forty-five minutes she put it away, knowing that Jean and Maggie would be along shortly. She made some coffee and got out a box of Pepperidge Farms biscuits. Olive had a sweet tooth and knew that neither Maggie nor Jean would decline the offer, so she set a tray on the table by the couch. Out of habit, she turned on the radio and listened to the rest of the noontime news. It was usually followed by a jazz program, which she also enjoyed.

About twenty minutes later, Jean and Maggie walked through the door.

"Service a little slow today?" Olive asked.

"Christ on a bicycle!" Jean exclaimed. "Not only slow, but the food wasn't great either! Lunches around here are so hit-or-miss. Sometimes the soup is delicious and other times the food tastes like the cook just took all the leftovers, put them in a pot with some ketchup, and called it goulash! I guess we should have ordered sandwiches, but I can make those in my apartment, for God's sake."

"Enough of the culinary criticism," Maggie admonished. "Let's get Olive's report."

Olive updated Maggie and Jean, and then told them that she could do nothing more that day without arousing suspicion. She really wanted to speak to Elizabeth, but knowing that Barnes was in the building, she preferred not to run into him in the event he returned to Elizabeth's room after seeing Howard and Irma.

"Is there any other research we can do before tomorrow?" she asked.

Maggie and Jean both shook their heads, but then Maggie said, "Why don't you get out your laptop for a moment so we can take another look at the website?"

Rather than fuss with it herself, Olive just handed her laptop to Maggie and told her the password. Jean laughed and shook her finger at Maggie, saying, "Now, don't try to get into Olive's online accounts!" knowing full well that Olive wouldn't even consider online banking.

"Her secrets are safe with me," Maggie said with a grin, her fingers flying over the keys. "Okay, here it is."

She put the laptop on the table so they all could view the screen.

They ran through the videos again and sat back silently.

After a couple of minutes Jean suggested, "Maggie, why don't you call the number from your cell phone and see who answers?"

"That's an idea," Maggie said, "but the address on the website gives me another thought. If Barnes is a lawyer, he must be on the rolls in New York State. I'm going to call an old colleague still working in the Queens County Surrogate's Court to find out if she has any open probate files listing Barnes as attorney of record or named executor in a will." She started toward the door to retrieve her phone from the apartment, pointing to Jean. "Why don't you go online and search for attorney names in active practice? The Court Administration department must have a list, or maybe the New York State Bar Association will have names on its website. They may be shown by location or alphabetically. If there's any biographical information, just bookmark it on the computer so that I can look at it, too."

When they were alone, Olive just looked at Jean and said, "This is making my head spin. You and Maggie know so much about these things."

For once Jean didn't respond with sarcasm. "Truth be told, Olive, you're doing the hard part. I'm not sure we should be involved in other people's business, but I agree that we should at least check out this Mr. Barnes and then take it from there."

Giving Jean a brief hug, Olive quickly brushed her eye with her sleeve; she was glad to have such a supportive sister. She poured herself another cup of coffee and watched in silence as Jean began her online searches.

Maggie burst back into the room a few minutes later. "Jean, don't bother with your search. My friend Agnes told me that Barnes has three active files in their court right now, both as attorney and named executor. She said she didn't have time to review them over the phone, but we can do it ourselves if we want to. I asked her if there was time this afternoon and she told me to come in at three o'clock."

Olive clapped her hands in surprise. "We can do that? I thought all that stuff was confidential."

Maggie grinned. "Heavens, no. We can't take the files out, obviously, but we can look at them in the clerk's office. Haven't you ever seen the ads by estate planning attorneys telling us to hire them to prepare trust agreements rather than wills, so no one will know how we give away our estates? Property owned by trusts usually isn't subject to administration by the Surrogate's Court."

Olive shrugged. "I guess I never paid attention to that. I'm hardly the person those attorneys care about anyway, I suppose."

"Me neither! *National Enquirer* won't care about my estate," Maggie chortled. "So, how about it? Should we do some hands-on research at the Surrogate's Court?"

The women were all on board, so they began to get ready to depart. As they were getting into their coats, Olive asked Maggie for more information about Surrogate's Court. Maggie explained that when someone dies and leaves property to their family or friends in a last will and testament, it has to be processed through the County Surrogate's Court to make sure the will is legal and so that the executor named in the will has the legal authority to pay the debts of the dead person before distributing any property to the beneficiaries named in the will.

"But why is this necessary?" Olive wondered aloud. "Bill and I signed a will after Jon was born, but when Bill died, I didn't have to go to court."

"Were you and Bill both named on the deed to your farm and your bank accounts?"

"Yes."

"Okay, since a will only covers stuff in just one person's name, and you and Bill owned your property together—or 'jointly,' in legal terms—even though you had wills, there was no need to bring Bill's will to Surrogate's Court after he died," Maggie explained. "Now, if you and Bill had been killed together in a car accident, Jon would have required a lawyer to prepare a petition and present your will to the Surrogate's Court so that he could get title to the farm and your other assets as a beneficiary of your estate. The other thing the Court does is ensure there's no hanky-panky regarding the will itself."

Olive nodded. "But if the will is signed and all, how could there be?"

"You'd be surprised at the greed in some families," Maggie responded. "Let's say one kid wants to cut other children out of the estate and that child lives a lot closer to a widowed parent. The kid can bring a new will and a couple of witnesses to the parent, and essentially browbeat Mom or Dad into signing. Then Mom or Dad dies, but because the will must be 'proved' in court, it allows the other children to contest the legality of the new will based on what is called 'undue influence' by the greedy child, and if the judge agrees, he can declare the new will invalid. It's what probate is all about."

"That's just terrible!" Olive exclaimed.

Jean joined in: "And that's what Barnes may be up to in visiting all these people who have no family members to contest what's being done."

Maggie cautioned them to not jump the gun until they actually had proof of some wrongdoing, hoping that their trip to Surrogate's Court might provide some answers.

Jean had already been to the clerk's office when Maggie worked there, but Olive had never been inside a courthouse before, so while Olive was enthusiastic, Jean was just curious about the files. They set off by bus, taking a notebook and some coins for the photocopier.

On the way, Maggie mused about Barnes' website, wondering if he had open files in courts in the other four boroughs of New York. She didn't share this concern with Jean or Olive because she didn't want to alarm them. It might be that Barnes was totally legitimate and just happened to have a busy law practice. Maggie couldn't help but speculate, though, given the language on the website—but time would tell.

They arrived at the courthouse fifteen minutes prior to their appointment in order to allow enough time to show their driver's licenses and pass through the metal detectors. Olive was intimidated by the process, never having passed through security checks except at airports.

"It's such a sad comment on our society," she murmured to Maggie and Jean after they were cleared to proceed.

Maggie exclaimed, "It's a sad comment on the world! When the World Trade Center went down, you were safe and snug in North Dakota. Your sister and I were in the midst of it! It changes your perception on a lot of things. I'd sooner take a few moments at a checkpoint than have some nutball blow me to kingdom come!"

"Alright, I'm sorry. I'm not being critical. It just makes me sad," Olive sighed.

When they reached the office, Maggie went in first, greeting people she still remembered from her days on the job. Some of them were now approaching retirement, too, so they kidded Maggie about having too much time on her hands and asked if she'd found a rich old boyfriend.

Maggie laughed. "No, I just hang out with these old hags."

After introducing Jean and Olive to her friend Agnes, Maggie asked her if she could look at the files they'd spoken about on the telephone.

Agnes was obviously curious. "What's your interest in Attorney Barnes?" she asked.

Maggie explained that Olive volunteered in the nursing home where Barnes was meeting with various patients who had no known next of kin, and that they were trying to find out a little more about him after having looked at his website.

Maggie asked Agnes if she'd ever met Barnes. "Nope," Agnes replied. "You know how it is with probate. Unless there's a problem, you never see the attorneys. Their staff usually brings in any documents, or they send them through the mail. If there's no objection to the petition, the judge signs the order appointing the executor without a court appearance. These three files don't seem unusual, but feel free to look."

Jean and Olive followed Maggie to a side table and watched as she opened the first file. It was clear that she'd done this before and that she knew what she was looking for; she grunted occasionally and made some notes on her legal pad. After her review, Maggie pushed the file over so that Jean and Olive could look, and then she took them through the petition and the original will in the file.

The estate in question concerned an elderly lady named Beatrice Summer—who had died in the nursing home that was part of their own complex! The death had occurred about seven months earlier, and the death certificate listed heart failure as the cause. The will had been signed by the deceased only one week before her death and it named Edgar Barnes as Executor. It left a cash gift to the lady's church and the rest of her property to a person named as her friend.

Maggie murmured, "I'd love to have seen the will she had before this one. I'll bet my pension that her previous will left everything to her church! But we'll never know because no one contested it, nor probably had any reason to, unless the church actually knew the contents of her previous will—and that's unlikely. Barnes was smart, too. He had her sign an affidavit of heirship."

Jean was busy flipping through the file, so Olive asked, "What's an affidavit of heirship?"

"When someone has immediate family—you know, a spouse, children or grandchildren, or even brothers, sisters, nieces, or nephews—the lawyer lists them on a family tree signed by the executor, which names people who would be eligible to inherit the person's property if there was no will," Maggie explained. "Even if the will only names some of them as beneficiaries, each and every person on the family tree who could share in the estate had there not been a will—it's called 'intestacy'—must be notified that the will has been submitted, and given a chance to contest it. Normally those people just sign what's called a 'waiver' unless they suspect foul play.

"Now, when someone dies with only very remote relatives, many of whom are already dead, the lawyer tries to get all the information relating to family connections on both the person's maternal and paternal sides, and then he prepares the affidavit of heirship, showing the connections and who is now dead, usually attaching copies of death certificates. The purpose is to give the judge a lot of information so that he won't order the executor to publish a notice in a bunch of newspapers saying that the will of John Doe is in probate and any possible heirs should contact the court. Having to publish notices is a really expensive and time-consuming step, so lawyers try to avoid it if possible. Because the person signing the will has also signed the affidavit, the Judge is usually satisfied that no unknown heirs require notice, and allows the will to be probated. It appears that Barnes got through this without having to publish anything in a newspaper."

Olive and Jean sat quietly, shaking their heads while Maggie looked through the other file. She gave them a quick summary.

"This other file follows a similar pattern. A male patient at another nursing home signed a will a short time prior to his death. The will contains a couple of charitable cash gifts, with the rest going to a friend, and the file has an affidavit of heirship. Barnes made sure there were cash gifts, but he didn't divide up the estate into percentages among the charities and the other beneficiaries. If he'd used percentages, he'd have to notify the State Attorney General, who makes sure that any charity receives the stated percentage, and obviously he didn't want the Attorney General anywhere near these files! With a cash gift, all the court requires is a receipt signed by the charity showing it received its gift.

"And sure enough, it looks like Ethel what's-her-name also signed a will and affidavit of heirship before she drowned in her tub at home. Olive, that's the lady who was going to get your apartment!"

Olive was shocked—and now she was sure that this Mr. Barnes was doing something suspicious with Elizabeth, Irma, and Howard.

Chapter 10

Maggie had flipped on the television on the way in, so while Jean poured them glasses of wine, Olive surreptitiously reduced the volume to manageable decibels.

Maggie smirked on her way into the living room. "Olive wants to get the crop report, Jean, but all I get here is sports news. Damn!"

Olive shot back, "Very funny, Maggie. I think I'll buy you a hearing aid soon, before the noise level in here gets the whole complex in trouble."

"All right, you two," Jean interjected. "Let's review where we stand with this Barnes thing before we go down to dinner. What's our next step?"

Olive had thought about this on the way home. "I promised Irma a game of cribbage after dinner, so I'll try to find out if Barnes visited her today. Where will you be if I want to report after we're finished?"

Maggie hooted. "Rangers vs. Philadelphia at 7:05. Be there or be square!"

Rolling her eyes, Olive said that the game gave her a good idea. If she finished with Irma in time, the hockey game would give Olive a reason to stop by Howard's room to watch a little of it with him.

Maggie squinted and whispered, "If I didn't know any better I'd say that our Olive is getting a little sweet on old Howard!"

Blushing, Olive took a gulp of wine and told Maggie to stop her foolishness. Jean just looked at Olive, shrugged, and then asked about Elizabeth Billingsley.

Olive reminded them that Elizabeth appeared to heed Barnes' instructions for secrecy regarding her estate plan, so they agreed she must be handled carefully.

"Yes, but before Barnes' arrival, Elizabeth had been pretty open with Olive about her life, so Olive should decide how to play it," Jean concluded, standing to put her glass in the sink.

In the dining room, Maggie had forgotten her glasses, so Olive read out the menu items to her from the table. Since it was a little past six o'clock, the early birders had departed and the waiter came promptly to their table. Jean settled on the shepherd's pie while both Maggie and Olive opted for turkey à la king. The dessert that night was an old favorite, chocolate chip mint ice cream with a small brownie.

Even though there was repetition in the menu and some days were significantly better than others, the whole format was still new enough to the three women to hold some luster. The idea of sitting in a well-appointed dining room, with preparation, service, and clean-up done by others, was such a pleasure. Knowing that they could vary their diet by making small meals in their apartments or just meeting for pizza helped, too. The dining room seated approximately forty people, but with some early eaters and others preferring to dine late, the room never appeared crowded. The residence management company had spared no expense in furnishing the room or in its choice of dishes, glassware, cutlery, and linens, so the atmosphere was more like a restaurant than an institutional eatery.

Dinner arrived and they each surveyed their plates. Jean's pie had a garnish of peas and a side salad, while the other meals featured the turkey meat and vegetables spilling out of a puffed pastry cup, with a pile of coleslaw on the side.

Maggie sat in silence for a moment and then spoke: "I wonder how they get the pastry container to puff up like that." Maggie was always coming out with statements like this, attesting to her complete lack of culinary knowledge, and this continued to confound Olive. How could Maggie know so much about so many things and be so ignorant of others?

Olive tried to explain the construction of puffed pastry and how fussy it was to make, but looking across at the blank faces of the other two, she stopped in mid-sentence. "Oh, never mind!"

After finishing their dinner, they left the dining room, Maggie and Jean talking about the game that night and Olive thinking about Irma.

Olive arrived at Irma's room a short while later to find her with her cribbage board and cards all ready for battle. Shortly after they began the game, Irma burst out, "Guess what happened today!"

Olive shrugged, saying she couldn't imagine.

"I had a nice talk with Edgar Barnes."

Apparently, he had returned to her room just as Irma was finishing lunch and they'd talked for a while. Irma had been surprised at his knowledge of her background. He'd also told her that a young man had contacted him through the *Kinfolk* website, wondering if perhaps she was a distant relative. Barnes had told Irma about the searches the young man had conducted through the free Mormon genealogy online website—Irma thought he may have called it the "Family Search Site"—and had asked Barnes to follow up.

"What is the young man's name? Weiss, like yours?" Olive asked.

Irma shook her head. "The man's name is Matthew West."

Barnes had explained that this was the interesting part, telling her of the family tree that traced her own immediate family back to her great grandfather, Albert Weiss, who'd lived and married in the Midwest, siring four children. During World War I, one of his sons had supposedly changed his surname to West in order to cope with the anti-German sentiment prevalent in some parts of the country, and it was that branch of the family to which Matthew West belonged.

This was all news to Irma, but she found it interesting. Irma's father had died when she was young and her mother had never really spoken about his family, but Irma was able to confirm to Barnes the name of her grandfather, who had lived in Ohio—and whom her mother had detested. According to Barnes, the online search had revealed that West was her only living next of kin.

"What a coincidence!" Olive muttered.

Barnes had then informed Irma that West was an attorney in Maryland, and that sometimes his business brought him to Manhattan. He was scheduled to travel to the area in a few days and wanted to meet Irma. Olive obviously looked a little skeptical, because Irma quickly added, "I told him to come here. I mean, what's the harm in just talking with him?"

Olive couldn't disagree with that, telling Irma it would be fun to meet him if Olive happened to be in the ward when he paid his visit. Olive didn't share that Barnes had actually connected with two other residents because she could see that Irma felt special, maybe for the first time in a long time.

Finishing up their cribbage game, Olive congratulated Irma on her victory but declined a second match, explaining that Jean was expecting her to stop by for coffee.

In the hallway near Howard's room, Olive was a bit startled to see Elfrieda again, who had been on duty that morning, as well. "No rest for the wicked?" she said with a smile as she walked up to Elfrieda.

"Connie called in sick at the last minute, so I agreed to cover her shift. Been a busy day, lots of people coming and going for some reason!" Elfrieda remarked.

It occurred to Olive that this would be a great opportunity to get a little information. She told Elfrieda about Edgar Barnes' visit to Irma, and Elfrieda confirmed that he'd also met with Elizabeth Billingsley and Howard Kenner.

"Have you spoken to Barnes?" Olive asked. She was hoping to get a professional caregiver's impression of the man.

"I gave him directions to Irma's room. Apparently he already knew the way to Elizabeth's and Howard's. He seemed pleasant. Tall, rather good-looking, middle-aged fellow. Well-dressed and nice shoes. Had one of those expensive soft leather briefcases slung over his shoulder. Looks like he's used to making the rounds at facilities like ours."

Olive had an idea. "A friend of mine retired from the clerk's office at the Queens County Surrogate's Court, and she heard from a colleague that Barnes is an attorney and has a file at the court for the estate of Beatrice Summer, who used to live here," she said, gauging Elfrieda's reaction as she spoke.

Elfrieda nodded in recognition. "I didn't know that patient all that well because I was assigned mostly to another floor at the time, but she was pretty old, so no one was that surprised when she died. As for Barnes, he may have been coming around, but I personally didn't see him until these recent visits."

"Well, thanks, Elfrieda. Howard Kenner and I sometimes watch hockey on TV, so I'll stop in there now."

Howard was yelling at the television when Olive entered his room.

"Careful, Howard, or you'll have another stroke!" she admonished, pointing at him and chuckling.

Howard was undeterred. "Either the referees are blind or they've been reached!" he croaked, beside himself at some call either made or not made—Olive couldn't be sure. He went on, "I bet the refs have some money on the game!" He looked a little sour when Olive asked if that was legal. "Oh, never mind," he said. "I'm sorry, sometimes I get too worked up about silly stuff. Have a seat."

He gave Olive a quick summary of the game to that point. The first period was just ending. When the intermission began, he reduced the volume on the set and turned to Olive. He was more agitated than usual and Olive wondered if it was more than just the game that had him on edge.

She asked about his day and the course of his physiotherapy. He told her that he was progressing, but he was getting restless lying there day after day.

Howard finally got around to recounting his meeting with Edgar Barnes. Barnes had stayed with Howard for almost an hour, telling him he'd been contacted by a young man in England who thought he might be a relative, and using the rest of the time to ask Howard questions about his family history. It was becoming obvious that Barnes used this type of information to concoct a "long list of relatives."

Barnes had told him he was following up on some research and believed that Howard might, in fact, have a relative previously unknown to him. Howard told Barnes that this was unlikely in light of the information he'd already given him about his family.

Olive listened with interest as Howard described his early life. His father had apparently returned from World War I a changed man. He and his older brother had fought in the same unit, but his brother died in September of 1918, during the Allied assault on the Hindenburg line in Belgium. Even though Howard's father was a decorated veteran, he'd carried the guilt that often burdens survivors of war. Knowing that his brother had been his parents' favorite, Howard's father had almost been afraid to return home to rural Pennsylvania. He'd tried to ease his pain through alcohol, but his growing dependence on the stuff had only made it more difficult to keep his temper, and any job he was lucky enough to get. He did manage to marry a local girl—truly a girl, much younger than he—and Howard had been born a year later, in 1921. The difficult birth had taken the young bride's life, though, for which Howard's father never forgave him.

Howard had been given over to his grandmother and maiden aunt, and rarely met his father, who'd drifted until the early years of the Great Depression, looking for odd jobs to pay for cheap rooms and some booze. One day the family learned that he had lain down on some tracks in sight of an oncoming train, dying destitute and alone.

Olive gasped. "That must have been terrible for you!"

Howard shrugged and told her that he hadn't really known his father. While his grandmother and aunt could be gruff and demanding, they'd taken care of him and had given him the only home he knew. Olive again reflected on Howard's positive attitude and was amazed.

"So now this Barnes guy is telling me he thinks I have family somewhere, but unless my Uncle Johnny fathered a child we didn't know about before going into the army, I don't see how it's possible," Howard said. "My grandmother did tell me a bit about Uncle Johnny, and I remember her mentioning that my father looked through his uniform after Johnny died and found a young woman's photograph. Apparently my uncle told my father that he'd met her in England, but my grandmother didn't know anything about her."

Olive didn't want to share her knowledge about Barnes' visits to Elizabeth and Irma with Howard, because she was careful to keep one patient's confidences from others. But she felt alright about sharing the information with Maggie and Jean, knowing that she needed their assistance. She asked Howard why Barnes was interested in his family history.

"Good question!" Howard responded. "I asked him if he charged a fee for the search and he said I wouldn't pay a dime, but the person who contacted him would pay him at an hourly rate. He said that the person didn't want to actually meet me until Barnes was sure there was a match. The whole thing is a little confusing, for sure, but I figured there would be no harm in this fellow looking into my family tree and seeing what's there. At least it makes life around here a little more interesting."

At that moment, Howard glanced at the television, and, seeing the start of the second period, turned toward it. Olive patted his arm and told him she'd stop by with his licorice the next day, feeling foolish that she'd actually purchased it for him and had then forgotten it in her apartment. Glancing over at her, he smiled and thanked her before turning up the volume on the set.

Olive didn't want to sit through the second period, and, concluding that Howard had told her all he knew at that point, she left the building and took a short stroll on the way to her apartment.

The evening was chilly but clear, and the moon was full. She chuckled to herself, recalling the full moon in the movie *Moonstruck*. Maggie had liked the movie so much she'd bought the DVD, and had recently played it for Olive. Maggie and Jean could quote some of the lines using the same accents as Cher and Nicolas Cage before their characters even came on screen, so Olive wasn't sure if she was enjoying the film or their antics when she watched it with them. Olive actually enjoyed her second viewing more, because she was then somewhat used to the dialogue, and she'd convinced Maggie and Jean to just watch the movie rather than participate in it.

There was a slow rustle in the trees, just enough breeze to lend some atmosphere to the evening. Olive looked up at the buildings—particularly at the huge church near the apartment complex. The developers of her building had clearly been sensitive to neighborhood concerns, because the facade on the complex looked more European, complimenting—rather than obliterating—the facade of the church. Obviously it would have been easier and cheaper to throw up a cement monstrosity, but even with the size of all of the components of the complex, it still had a neighborhood feel to it. In the daytime it was even more apparent, given the shrubbery and seasonal flowers surrounding the buildings. She had already enjoyed the inner courtyard with its fountain and landscaping, and she looked forward to spring and summer when it could offer some outdoor privacy.

By the time she reached her apartment, she assumed that the second period had ended. She stuck her head in the women's doorway and asked if they wanted a report. Jean waved her in, offering her a glass of wine.

"What's the score?" Olive asked, knowing that Maggie would give her an in-depth analysis whether she wanted it or not. Apparently, Maggie fully agreed with Howard's assessment of the referees, adding pointed questions about their parentage. Olive still found all of this somewhat puzzling, but she knew enough not to ask "Who cares?".

Taking the glass of wine from Jean, Olive launched into a summary of her visits with both Irma and Howard.

Maggie cocked her head. "You can see how Barnes gets people hooked," she said. "They're bored, a little curious, and happy for the attention. If it doesn't cost them anything, they say 'What do I have to lose?' and encourage him by disclosing a lot of information about themselves. I bet he just gives a few clues to get them started talking about their family history, and then he takes that information to learn more and gain their trust. I don't know. It just sounds fishy to me."

Olive then recalled Elfrieda's comments. "The ward nurse remembered the lady whose estate was at the courthouse, although she'd only worked a couple of shifts on that floor, so she couldn't give much detail. She hadn't met Barnes at that point, either. She said that Beatrice had been pretty old, so no one was surprised about her death. She talked briefly to Barnes today on his way to Irma's room, and on another day she watched him go in to see Elizabeth."

Jean sighed. "I don't know where this leaves us. No one's been threatened or hurt, so we can't go to the nursing home administrator, and we certainly can't go to the police—Barnes would sue us eight ways from Sunday!"

Olive agreed. "I plan to talk with Elizabeth tomorrow anyway and see if she's willing to tell me more about Barnes. All this activity today has tired me out, so I'll leave you to your hockey game and call it a night."

Olive thought about Howard as she returned to her apartment and got ready for bed. Maybe he was the reason why she was so upset about this Edgar Barnes thing—she would hate for someone she liked that much to get hurt. At that thought she blushed, and set about turning her mind to something else so that she could fall asleep.

Chapter 11

While Olive boiled water for her coffee and oatmeal the next morning, she tried to put "the Barnes thing," as Maggie was now calling it, into perspective. Knowing that she'd visit Elizabeth later that morning, Olive wanted to clarify, at least for herself, the situation she found herself in. Yes, she felt concern about Barnes' visits to the patients, and his apparent routine in dealing with each of them was justified, but what did it all really mean? As Maggie and Jean mentioned the night before, nobody had been threatened, and if anything, Howard and Irma appeared revitalized by the attention.

Because Elizabeth had appeared reticent to discuss Barnes' first visit, Olive wondered whether she should try to open up the topic at all, or just mind her own business. Even if Barnes eventually persuaded Elizabeth to change whatever will she might have, and even if he got her to name him executor of her estate, would anyone really suffer as a result? It wasn't as though Elizabeth had young children to protect.

She considered her conversation with Elfrieda and decided to ask her to watch Barnes more closely. If he appeared one day with a couple of witnesses in tow, it would be proof that he was trying to convince patients to change their wills. Perhaps Elfrieda could ask the staff if anyone remembered his visits to the lady who had died months before. Shaking her head and rising from the kitchen table, Olive told herself she mustn't fixate on Barnes.

The day was dry, so Olive just pulled on a cardigan before walking to Elizabeth's room. She could have traveled through the tunnel connecting the various parts of the complex, but if the weather permitted, she always enjoyed the outdoor stroll. It made her feel part of a new day, and she enjoyed breathing in the fresh air. It also made her sympathize with the patients in the nursing home. Some patients could be wheeled outside on nice days, but when it was cold, the nurses were reluctant to expose them to the elements, so many were forced to merely look through their windows and breathe recirculated air.

Olive passed the business office and waved to the accountant before riding the elevator up to Elizabeth's room.

She called out as she passed over the threshold and Elizabeth, recognizing Olive's voice, responded with a greeting. Olive pulled out a travel magazine she'd bought a couple of weeks previously, interested by the cover story on travel in the Adirondack Mountains.

Elizabeth clapped her hands and cried, "Thank you!" She eagerly began to look over the magazine.

Olive was pleased because she knew that Elizabeth gladly watched any Travel Channel show, enjoying every vicarious experience available. This magazine contained stories on foreign travel, too, but since Elizabeth had never left the United States, Olive assumed that she would enjoy remembering her childhood summer vacations in upstate New York.

Olive looked up at the television near the bed and saw that Elizabeth had been watching a show featuring that Southern cook who sometimes had her family members on as guests. Olive had watched it with Elizabeth once before, both of them commenting on the woman's sense of humor and obvious love for her husband and sons. Elizabeth had said, though, "That girl better watch out with all those sweet and fried foods she makes. That's just a prescription for diabetes!"

Elizabeth had told Olive that she'd been stunned to receive the diabetes diagnosis herself in her late sixties. She had known she was overweight and hadn't done much consistent exercise; in cooking for herself, she'd focused on easy-to-cook, easy-to-eat foods which weren't that healthy. She hadn't been fond of fruits or vegetables, either. She'd tried to lose weight and correct her diet, but it was too late, and so she began daily insulin injections.

Olive now asked Elizabeth if her foot was healing.

Elizabeth nodded, saying that the antibiotics were working well, but she had to be careful. She went on to say, "You know, it's funny. The foot isn't there, but it still feels like it is. The doctor says it isn't unusual. I can't imagine what it must be like for those young people coming back from Iraq with blown-off limbs and hands. At least I've lived most of my life, but their lives are all ahead of them."

While listening to Elizabeth, Olive tried to think of ways to broach the subject of Edgar Barnes. Finally, during a commercial break, she commented, "Boy, it's been busy around here lately! A lot of people coming and going. It seems even busier than the Christmas season. Have you noticed it?"

Elizabeth nodded. "I was just thinking about it this morning because it finally was a little quieter in the hallway. I know that I had a couple of quick visits from Mr. Barnes. He is so nice. He wanted to bring me a box of chocolates, but I told him about my diabetes, so he brought me those flowers instead." She pointed to a bouquet by the window.

Olive grinned. "Well, wasn't that nice of him. I wish someone would bring me flowers! It's nice to have visitors from outside this place, too, I bet."

"Don't get me wrong," Elizabeth exclaimed, taking Olive's hand, "I'm so thankful that you stop by to talk and to share some time with me, but it was such a nice surprise to find a gentleman willing to take time out of his busy schedule to discuss my life and family."

Olive realized that this was her opportunity. "I didn't realize you had any family left. That's just wonderful!"

Elizabeth was obviously excited. "I'd told Mr. Barnes about growing up an only child in the Bronx, the same history I talked about with you, and lo and behold, he came back a day or so later with some information for me. He said a woman upstate had seen his website and had asked him to follow up, but he told me he'd hesitated to mention anything to me until he could verify her information. He still isn't sure, and I'm not sure I want him to be sure, but I may have a younger half-sister in the Adirondacks!"

Olive didn't know how to respond. Elizabeth's eyes were shining brightly and she was smiling, which startled Olive. Had she been told that her father had sired a younger sister out of wedlock, Olive would have been flabbergasted. But then she quickly reconsidered. Olive already had a family of her own. Perhaps if she was all alone in the world, she'd have been surprised but pleased to learn that there was a close relative out there, unknown to her until Barnes shared that information. She broke out of her reverie to hear Elizabeth's whisper that the information was confidential, and Olive quickly assured her that the secret was safe with her.

"Will Mr. Barnes bring your sister here to meet you?" Olive asked.

Elizabeth shook her head. "Apparently, my half-sister—and he hasn't confirmed it yet, mind—is a paraplegic, doesn't have much money, and is currently somewhat ill, so travel is out of the question, but Mr. Barnes told me he may make a video of her speaking so that he and I can look at it together. I told him that if she truly is my sister and if I'm given clearance by the doctor, I would want to go upstate to talk to her. I'd love to hear her life story. All Mr. Barnes said was that apparently my father and her mother met a few times in the afternoon during our vacations near Lake George—or at least that's what the woman had been told before her mother died—so this was news to her, too. Mr. Barnes told me he could make arrangements for us to meet."

Olive didn't want to press the issue, but couldn't help herself. "If her mother and your father are both deceased, how will you know if she really is related to you?" she asked.

"Mr. Barnes said that we can get a sample of my blood or tissue—I believe that's what he said—and check it against hers. I am just so excited to think that all of this may be true!" Elizabeth beamed at Olive.

With that, Olive squeezed Elizabeth's arm, wishing her luck. She thought she'd better leave the room before asking any more questions. She didn't want to spoil Elizabeth's moment, and as with Irma and Howard, Barnes had done nothing which could be construed as harmful.

Olive decided to stop by the dining room for a late lunch after visiting Elizabeth. Spotting Jean and Maggie laughing at a table in the corner of the room, she walked over.

"Hi, Sis!" Jean said cheerily. "We stopped by your place and you weren't there, but I didn't want to phone you in case you were in the middle of a gab with one of your patients. We just ordered the meatball sandwiches. We're assuming the chef can't screw those up because his sauce is usually pretty good."

Olive sat down and looked over the menu. She decided upon a chef's salad with a cup of cream of chicken soup, just the thing for a cool day.

While waiting for their food, Maggie and Jean began to quiz Olive about her meeting with Elizabeth. Olive wasted no time in filling them in.

After she finished, Jean started to laugh. "Imagine if we just found out we had a bastard little brother who wanted to meet us oh-so-much!"

Maggie started to giggle, but Olive didn't find it funny.

"Elizabeth is really excited about the possibility of meeting her," Olive said, "and that's what worries me. She's willing to travel two hundred miles or so to Lake George, and in her condition, that probably isn't very smart."

Jean shook her head. "I can't imagine her doctor recommending any travel in the near future, what with her foot and all. So don't worry about it. We've all been focusing on this guy Barnes for a while now, and frankly, Olive, I'm beginning to worry about you. When you began volunteering, you thought it would take a day or so a week, but now this appears to be a full-time job, and I don't think it's all that healthy for you. You should take a break."

Olive nodded because the same thought had occurred to her that morning. "I agree. There isn't much we can do in any case, so I'll still drop in on those three patients regularly, and I'll continue to play cribbage with Irma, but I'll leave my sleuthing hat at home for a while."

Chapter 12

The next day, Olive planned to only talk about current events with Howard, but decided to pop in on Irma on the way up. She entered Irma's room, hearing her excitedly telling the nurse that "Matthew" was coming sometime that day to take her to lunch.

Olive knew she wasn't supposed to be snooping anymore, but she couldn't help herself, and stood by the door to listen in. Apparently, Mr. Barnes had called with the news that morning; he and this Matthew person would pick her up in a couple of hours. Olive was curious, but didn't want to intrude.

As she started to back out into the hallway, Irma saw her and motioned for her to come forward. The nurse was telling Irma that she was concerned about her leaving the facility, but Irma told her that Mr. Barnes said there was ample room in his trunk for a wheelchair.

"Well, I guess it's your decision, Ms. Weiss," the nurse said doubtfully. "You don't have a fever and your other vitals are good. I just worry about you getting too tired trying to do this."

"I know my body," Irma told the nurse. "If I start to tire, I'll have them bring me back right away. A little fresh air and some different food will do me a world of good!"

The nurse left and Olive asked Irma if she wanted any help in getting dressed. Irma told her that she only had a few clothes with her, so she'd have to settle for the Tan Jay pantsuit, one of her mainstays. Olive took it out of the closet, pleased to see it had been laundered. She knew that Irma wanted to look her best and although the pantsuit—more of a jogging suit really—had the usual embroidered flowers and leaves on it that Olive detested, its light mauve color complemented Irma's dyed black hair and hazel eyes. Following Irma's instructions, Olive also located some pearl earrings and a nice-looking watch in a box on the top shelf of the closet. Olive admired the watch aloud.

"Forty years at Con Ed will get you a handsome watch!" Irma responded to Olive's compliment. "Just help me get out of bed and I'll get changed. Also, I haven't used the watch in a while. Is it keeping correct time?"

Olive checked the watch against her own, and, after finding it correct, she took Irma's arms, helping her to stand upright on the floor. She was surprised at Irma's height, but then she remembered that only Irma's torso was usually visible, so she hadn't realized that her legs were fairly long. Irma straightened and moved toward the bathroom.

"If you want to change next to your bed, I can leave the room to give you privacy," Olive offered.

"It's not that. I just want to wash up again before I change," Irma replied. "Can you look in the bedside drawer and hand me my lipstick and powder? I'll put it on when I'm in the bathroom. You might as well hand me my clothes, too."

When Irma emerged from the bathroom after changing, Olive was startled. With her hair brushed back, her teeth in, some makeup on, and wearing a pantsuit rather than a nightgown, Irma radiated much more vitality than Olive had ever observed since meeting her. She told Irma she looked great and Irma patted her cheek, clearly pleased with the attention.

"Do you know where Matthew is taking you for lunch?" Olive asked.

"No, but I don't care where we eat. I just want to get out of here for a couple of hours, and I'm really curious about him."

"So Matthew is convinced that you're related?"

"Well, Mr. Barnes completed the genealogy search and said it confirmed what Matthew had suspected, so that's good enough for me."

As Irma was speaking, Olive saw her glance past her, and she turned to see two men striding into the room. She stepped aside when Irma called out, "Mr. Barnes!" and the younger man was introduced to her as Matthew West.

Olive quietly left the room, not wanting to intrude, because the three of them began to exchange pleasantries almost immediately. She knew that Irma would give her a full report when she returned. Moving on to Howard's room, she found it vacant. The nurse confirmed that his therapy was running late, so she decided to return to the complex.

She found Maggie and Jean in the laundry room, just finishing up before lunch. She was glad there were no other residents there, as it gave her the opportunity to share her information without worrying about "big ears," as her mother used to say. She told them about Irma's lunch invitation and the arrival of Barnes and West.

"What happened to no more sleuthing?" Jean teased Olive. "Just kidding; this sounds like it's more important."

"What do they look like?" Maggie asked as she loaded her folded linens into a basket.

"Barnes looks just like the ward nurse described him," Olive said. "Very confident, tall, silver-haired, and fairly good-looking. West was almost like a choir boy. Young, with nice, medium-length blond hair, blue eyes, a nice suit, a nice smile—but just thinking about it, if he's a relation of Irma's, there's no resemblance that I could see, because she has dark hair and a darker complexion. But then again, he's supposed to be a distant relative."

"What was Irma's reaction?" Jean picked up her basket and was headed toward the door. "Olive, I thought we'd see you before lunch, so I made up a pot of tuna noodle junk for us to share instead of going to the dining hall."

Although she wasn't sure if she was in the mood for Jean's signature dish, Olive responded as they walked together. "Irma looked radiant, to tell you the truth," she said. "She dressed the best she could with the clothes she has here, put on makeup, the whole shebang. I'm beginning to feel guilty about doubting Barnes and his motives. If he and West brighten her day, then fine by me."

Standing in Jean's kitchen, Olive knew immediately that lunch was ready. Jean had always acknowledged her lack of cooking skills, but she was proud of her noodle concoction. She'd explained its preparation to Olive during a visit a number of years ago. The best thing, Jean said, was that it was cheap, fast, and filling, and you could make as much or as little of it as you wanted. Olive learned that Jean liked to make a lot of it, and then eat it again and again on ensuing days. But to Olive's surprise, it had actually tasted pretty good, a mixture of cooked macaroni noodles, canned tuna—or "tuna fish," as Jean called it—chopped green onion and celery, and grated cheddar cheese, into which she blended mayonnaise and seasoned with salt and pepper.

Jean usually served the first meal warm and ate it cold after that.

They served themselves helpings of the tuna noodle junk and sat around the kitchen table in Jean and Maggie's apartment. They discussed Irma's situation in between bites.

"So, what time do you think Irma will be back?" Maggie asked.

Olive thought for a moment. "Let's assume she'll be gone most of the afternoon, unless she starts to tire quickly. She actually looked pretty spry this morning."

"Are you going over there later today?" Jean asked.

"I don't want Irma to think I'm spying on her. But you or I were supposed to play cribbage with her later today."

Jean looked at Olive. "Well, why don't we go over right after dinner and tell her you told me about the lunch date. I mean, let's face it. She'll be dying, pardon the pun, to tell us about her day!"

Olive shuddered at the pun, but agreed they should see Irma that night. She remembered that Jean and Maggie planned to watch hockey again that evening, so Olive thought she might also stop in on Howard; she hadn't seen him in a few days. This time she would remember his licorice!

Olive offered to help with dishes, but when Jean shooed her away, she went back to her apartment to pick up her checkbook before leaving for the bank.

Jean and Maggie always teased Olive about her banking. They were able to pay their bills and transfer money between accounts online, and Olive's son, Jon, had encouraged her to do the same, but she didn't feel ready. Besides, she enjoyed chatting with the tellers and appreciated the ability to keep her cancelled checks as proof of payment. Olive did use her ATM card occasionally, but she didn't tend to keep a lot of cash on hand. Old habits usually die hard, she acknowledged, but she rationalized that her banking quirks were just another good excuse for a walk.

Maggie, Jean, and Olive had agreed to meet at six o'clock for dinner, and Olive returned just in time to find them exiting their apartments. Entering the dining room, Jean grabbed Maggie and pulled her over to the menu board. Olive giggled and followed behind.

"Alright, Missy. From now on, if you don't bring your glasses, we're going to stop at the menu board so you can read it yourself. My little sister is not here to serve as your social secretary!" Jean announced.

With other diners looking on and Maggie in full blush, Olive and Jean waited until she made her choices. "There. Are you satisfied?" she growled as they all moved toward a table in the corner.

The menu that night offered Swiss steak and mashed potatoes, which Jean immediately chose. Since Maggie and Olive had already enjoyed the tuna noodle junk at lunch, they declined the poached salmon and opted for the third choice, manicotti. Maggie had tried it before and although it didn't match her mother's cooking, as she told Olive, the chef cooked a reasonable facsimile "for a Latino." The dish also came with garlic toast— and Olive already knew that hers would somehow find its way onto Jean's plate.

With dinner over, Olive and Jean went directly to the nursing home. Irma was humming when they entered her room.

"Well, don't you sound chipper tonight!" Olive grinned at Irma as Jean patted her hand.

"Thank goodness you came. I've got so much to tell you!" Irma exclaimed.

Forgetting about any notion of cribbage, Irma launched into a narrative about her day on the town.

Apparently Matthew had hired a limousine and driver for the afternoon, and Irma had felt like a queen. She'd been delighted when they suggested a ride into Manhattan for a late lunch at Bar Americain, off Times Square; Irma had read about Bobby Flay's restaurant in the Lifestyle section of *The New York Times*. Traffic was a little slow getting onto the island, but she hadn't cared, because she was able to gawk at the sights and chat with Matthew and Mr. Barnes. The limousine had driven around Central Park before dropping them off for lunch. Irma hadn't been in Manhattan for years, so she could only gaze at all of the new signs in midtown, imagining what it must look like at night.

Matthew had been so gracious, helping her out of the car while the driver removed the wheelchair from the trunk. Lunch had been divine, beginning with shrimp cocktails—huge shrimp arranged around a crystal bowl holding shredded lettuce and cocktail sauce, atop a bed of crushed ice "just like in the movies!" Matthew had insisted on ordering a bottle of champagne, and Irma admitted to feeling a little tipsy by the time lunch ended. Apparently Matthew had spared no expense, as lunch not only included a delicious blistered Vermont cheddar soup, but also a lobster club sandwich which she shared with him—all quite a wonderful shock to Irma's palette. Pistachio crème brûlée being the finale, Irma regretted not having a camera. The restaurant had actually offered to take a photo of the trio as a souvenir for Irma, but Matthew had declined to have his picture taken, telling Irma he wanted his privacy, so she had nothing to show Olive and Jean.

Irma hadn't wanted to return to the drab routine of the nursing home, but Matthew had to attend a business meeting in Manhattan, so Barnes brought Irma to her room around five o'clock and left for his office.

From Olive's perspective, the afternoon appeared to have gone well, although she found herself curious about Matthew's reluctance to have his photo taken. She asked Irma if Matthew and Barnes brought along any documentary evidence of the family relationship.

"Mr. Barnes said it was being mailed from Salt Lake City, but he and Matthew were given verbal confirmation," she said. "Matthew seemed to know a lot about the family connections, so I'm sure we're related somehow. His own parents were killed in a car accident, and he says he has no family of his own, so he was thrilled to find me. He's quite successful and busy in his consulting business."

This puzzled Jean. "I thought Mr. Barnes told you that Matthew is an attorney."

"I must have misunderstood," Irma replied. "Matthew told me that he attended a law school in the South but found it boring—which made Mr. Barnes laugh—and that he liked working in finance and investing people's money. He explained that he always gets good results for his clients and that he has a lot of different portfolios, as he called them, for people to choose from. He said that some people are more cautious and some like taking risks, so he tailors the investments to their temperaments. I believe that's what he said."

Olive picked up on this. "Did he ask you to invest through his company? I might be interested in seeking his advice."

"He did mention the possibility of looking at my finances for me, but told me he wanted to get to know me as possible family, not as a client. But here's the best part!" She looked incredibly excited. "As we were finishing lunch, Matthew and Mr. Barnes asked if I'd ever been to Atlantic City, and I just about jumped out of my seat. Matthew said he's booked into a conference at one of the big hotels next week, I think maybe one of the Trump ones, and would love to entertain me for a couple of days. He has meetings during the day, so I can rest or sightsee, and then at night we can do some gambling and see a show."

Jean slowly shook her head. "But how will you get there, and how will you get around?" she asked.

"Well, Mr. Barnes has courses he must take every year to keep his law license, so he's also planning to be in Atlantic City on those days," Irma said happily. "He laughed that New York attorneys love to go all over the place to take the courses as a 'perk,' he called it, rather than stay at home. He told me he planned to hire a car and driver anyway, so we might as well travel together. It's almost too good to be true!"

No kidding, thought Olive. Not wanting to dampen Irma's mood, Olive just squeezed her hand, telling her the whole trip sounded wonderful. Irma pulled out a deck of cards, but left the cribbage board on the side table. Seeing Jean's puzzled look, she grinned, saying that for the next few days she wanted to practice blackjack, a game unfamiliar to the women. Irma looked disappointed, but told them she'd played it over the years and believed it would come back to her. She'd already found a nurse who could remind her of the subtleties.

The women bade Irma good evening and peeked into Howard's room. The television set was on but Howard was obviously dozing, so Olive wrote him a quick note, left it with the licorice on his bed table, and quietly headed home with Jean.

Chapter 13

The next day, Olive entered Elizabeth's room to find her almost bouncing in bed. She was looking at a video on television, so engrossed that she failed to notice Olive until she touched her on the shoulder. Elizabeth cried out in surprise and Olive apologized for startling her, explaining that she'd called her name but hadn't gotten her attention.

Elizabeth responded that she was happy Olive had stopped by because she wanted to show her the video that Edgar Barnes had made. Olive drew up a chair while Elizabeth rewound the video tape.

"Elizabeth, before you show me the tape, can you give me a little background?" Olive asked.

"Well, Mr. Barnes told me he had some legal matter in the Warren County Surrogate's Court, which is only a few miles from Lake George, so he stopped off at my sister's house—although we still don't know for sure whether we're related," Elizabeth said. "Anyway, her name is Beverly Williams, and from this video, she seems to be really sweet. Beverly told Mr. Barnes that she had a car accident a number of years ago. Apparently she'd been drinking before she went off the road and hit a tree, so she couldn't make an insurance claim. Beverly was able to obtain social security disability benefits, but they aren't much. Mr. Barnes said he only told me that so I'd understand why her home is so modest in the video. I told him that I didn't care about her home, I only wanted to know about my sister."

Olive nodded, but asked, "If you learn that you aren't related, will you be upset? Maybe Mr. Barnes should have waited to show you the video until he confirms that she is your sister."

"I thought about that," Elizabeth said, "but Mr. Barnes says that he's pretty convinced based on what she's told him. We'll know for sure after the blood test. He had a doctor friend of his come by and take a sample of my blood."

Olive blurted out, "The nurses here could have done that and sent it to a lab, along with your sister's sample!" Realizing that she may have startled Elizabeth, Olive backtracked, saying that Mr. Barnes, as an attorney, probably knew the best way to handle it.

Elizabeth had hardly heard Olive anyway, because she'd begun to play the video for her. The two of them watched the twenty minutes or so of tape, first seeing Barnes on the screen stating the date and place of the recording and introducing Beverly, followed by Beverly's greeting to Elizabeth and her monologue explaining the family connection.

Although Elizabeth's father had made no public or legal recognition of his paternity, Beverly said he'd continued to visit her mother after her birth. Olive realized that somehow Barnes had convinced Elizabeth to give him a photo of her father and mother when they were younger when he appeared onscreen and showed it to Beverly. Beverly, not surprisingly, immediately recognized the man who had visited her mother during the summers as she was growing up. Beverly said she remembered that the visits stopped when she was about six years old, so Olive concluded that Barnes had probably planted a fertile seed of memory to which Beverly was clinging.

Olive broke the silence after the tape had finished. "So Beverly is convinced that your father is the man who visited? She would have been awfully young, even at the point when the visits ceased."

Elizabeth's lips started to quiver and Olive immediately wished that she could take back her comment. Elizabeth whispered, "I know it sounds crazy, and Mr. Barnes won't receive the DNA results for some time, but when I watch the video, it just feels like Beverly is my sister!"

Olive nodded and squeezed Elizabeth's hand, all the while thinking about her vulnerability and the emotional webs which people like Barnes could create to trap people like Elizabeth. Olive asked her if she'd checked with her doctor about the feasibility of a trip to the Adirondacks, given the distance involved and her diabetes—not to mention her fairly recent amputation.

Elizabeth crossed her arms in front of her, and, looking somewhat defiant, declared, "Well, it won't be for at least a month or two from now anyway, so I'll have more time to heal, and Mr. Barnes will be with me most of the time. There are hotels all over the place up there because it's a real vacation area, and there's a big hospital too. I remember that from the leaf-peeping bus tour I took a while back. Apparently the hospital is really modern, too. Services the whole region. So I'm going to go, whether the doctor likes it or not. I'm not a child."

Olive quickly saw that her questions had agitated Elizabeth and she didn't want to alienate her. "I'm sure you're not going to do anything to jeopardize your health; I'm just concerned, that's all," Olive said in an attempt to placate her.

Elizabeth relaxed her posture and lay back. "I know. I shouldn't have snapped at you, but I get tired of people telling me what's good for me. It's hard for you to understand how I feel. You've been married and have a son, as well as a sister. Until Mr. Barnes came to see me, I had nobody, and I don't want to let that slip away."

Olive decided to ask one last question. "I'm not sure how it works with diabetes. If you're going somewhere overnight, do you just take vials of insulin with you, maybe a couple extra in case you're delayed in returning to the city?"

"I used to keep them in the fridge at home, and the time I took the trip to the Adirondacks, I just packed extra insulin because the trip was over two days," Elizabeth answered. "I'm not worried about that."

Olive stood to leave. "Well, it seems that you're all set, then. I do want to wish you bon voyage before you go, so I'll stop by every few days to get a progress report," she promised. "By the way, I was reading in the magazine I gave you that the Adirondack area is very close to Vermont. If you can pick up some of that maple sugar candy for me—if it's sold in the Adirondacks, that is—I'd just love it."

Elizabeth brightened immediately and almost shouted, "You bet! I'll just have to watch you eat it and remember how good it tasted when I was a child."

On the way out of the room, Olive spied Elfrieda. She caught up with her in the hallway.

Elfrieda turned to Olive and raised her eyebrows. "Looks like Elizabeth is excited about doing some traveling," she remarked. Olive was happy that Elfrieda had broached the topic because she didn't want to relate any of her conversation with Elizabeth, but it sounded like Elizabeth wanted to tell anyone who would listen.

Elfrieda continued, "First, Irma on the third floor goes out for a high-end lunch with our Mr. Barnes, and now he's promising to take Elizabeth upstate to see some long-lost sister! What's next, a trip to Paris?"

Olive nodded. "I guess Irma's relative is well-off, so he paid for the afternoon in Manhattan, but Elizabeth's supposed sister is on disability benefits, so maybe Elizabeth herself is picking up the tab. She didn't say."

She asked Elfrieda if anyone on staff remembered Barnes from his visits to the lady who had died eight months before. Elfrieda had asked around and apparently one other nurse remembered his arrival one day with some documents, but beyond that, nothing had seemed unusual.

"Did your colleague know whether the lady had left the premises before she died?" Olive asked.

"The nurse was on vacation when Beatrice died, so she didn't know. But Olive," Elfrieda said, "you have to understand that the patients come here voluntarily, and if they want to leave for the afternoon or for a couple of days, so long as they're mentally competent and have their medications with them, they are free to do what they choose."

Olive thanked her and strode out of the nursing home to see if she could locate Maggie and Jean. As it happened, they were getting off the elevator when Olive reached the door of the dining room.

Waiting for them, she couldn't help but chuckle. Because they'd been neighbors for so long and Jean was part of Maggie's family through her marriage to Jimmy, the two women had developed very similar mannerisms—or maybe Jean had turned into a second Maggie. They both gestured a great deal when they spoke, and spoke loudly. From the beginning, this fact alone had prompted Olive to restrict any discussion of Edgar Barnes to the privacy of one of their apartments.

Today, the two other women were even dressed the same: light denim jackets and jeans, with white blouses open at the neck. Olive couldn't resist. "Yee-haw! Are you two joining a country band?"

Maggie and Jean looked puzzled and then looked down at their attire.

"Good one!" Maggie cackled. "Actually, we're joining the rodeo. Let's eat. Maybe there's steer on the menu today."

Jean squinted at Olive. "You look like the cat that swallowed the canary. What's up?"

"I'll tell you after lunch. We've got a lot to talk about."

Maggie stepped up to the menu board immediately, not wanting to be embarrassed again. Chicken noodle soup and a crusty roll with custard for dessert made the decision easy for Olive, but Maggie and Jean were waffling between the waffles with ice cream or something more savory. Both admitted that guilt prevented them from eating ice cream and waffles for lunch, and instead they chose the hot turkey sandwich.

Sitting down to the strains of "Moon River" playing in the background, they settled into silence. It occurred to Olive that while Jean and Maggie were always talking to each other, the three of them together had few topics of conversation, save for the saga of Edgar Barnes. She hoped this might change over time.

Maggie finally looked directly at Olive. "You're killing me here, Olive! At least give us a couple of clues about the Barnes thing. I don't want to wait till I'm finished lunch."

Olive shook her head slowly and told Maggie that there was a lot to discuss, so they had to be patient. Fortunately, at that moment, the waiter appeared and served lunch, which kept all of them occupied for the next half hour.

Later, sitting in Olive's living room, Jean and Maggie listened intently while she brought them up-to-date. Jean had already told Maggie about Irma's planned trip to Atlantic City, but Elizabeth's updates were news to her.

Maggie whistled when Olive told her about the possible trip to the Adirondacks. "You gotta be kidding me."

They all agreed, though, that nothing dangerous had happened, so no further inquiry would be justified. Olive began pacing, knowing that Maggie and Jean were right, but also knowing how terrible she would feel if Barnes' plans led to any harm to either Elizabeth or Irma. She realized that Jean was staring at her.

"Olive, it's time you got a grip," her sister said.

That night they ordered in Chinese food. As they waited for the delivery and poured their drinks, Maggie surfed the television channels. She mentioned to Jean that baseball spring training was on the horizon.

Olive groaned. "Why don't you try to find a movie we'd all like?" she suggested.

In response, Maggie just handed the remote to Olive while she went into the kitchen to retrieve plates and utensils. As luck would have it, *My Cousin Vinny* was set to begin in about ten minutes. It was a movie they all enjoyed, and having seen it before, they didn't need to concentrate on every point of dialogue. As with *Moonstruck,* Maggie and Jean could recite dialogue along with the actors, but they were learning, albeit slowly, that Olive found this very irritating.

Still, despite Maggie and Jean's strange quirks, Olive enjoyed spending time with them. The move to New York had certainly been a good idea!

Chapter 14

Following church that Sunday, Olive decided to stop by Howard's room. Normally she didn't visit the patients on the weekend, thinking that they might have visitors, but since she knew Howard had no family and that most of his contemporaries had passed away, she felt comfortable dropping in.

Even from their first meeting, she'd enjoyed Howard's dry wit and courtly manner, and could see how he had wooed his late wife. He didn't say a lot, but what he said was meaningful, much like her own husband, Bill. She loved to ask Howard questions about life in the Northeast over the years, and, unlike Jean, he always answered her patiently.

After stopping by the tuck shop to pick up some licorice, Olive entered Howard's room to find him reading *The Sunday Times*. He looked up, grinned, and motioned her into the room.

"I don't want to interrupt your reading," she protested.

"Oh, heavens, no. I'm glad you stopped by," he said. "I just finished the sports section and haven't decided what section I want to read next. Do you like crossword puzzles? Winnie and I always tackled the Sunday crossword together."

"I love crossword puzzles, although I understand that the Sunday puzzle is pretty difficult," Olive responded.

Howard chuckled. "That's why Winnie and I always did them together! Pull up a chair."

Two hours and a couple of oaths from Howard later, the puzzle was complete, or at least complete as far as they were concerned. They'd have to wait a week to see whether it was correct or not. Howard put the paper away and took out a piece of licorice, offering one to Olive.

"Well, you won't believe my news!" he said. "Edgar Barnes appears to have found my unknown relative, or at least maybe my unknown relative has found Edgar Barnes. He came by on Friday and told me the tale."

"That was pretty fast, wasn't it?" Olive commented.

"He told me that this fellow, John Case, had done a lot of research before he ever contacted Barnes. Apparently my uncle Johnny met a woman in England before he shipped out to Belgium and got killed. That much I knew from my father. The woman apparently only realized she was pregnant after my uncle's departure. Uncle Johnny promised to come back to her after the war, and when he didn't, she traced his name through the War Department and found out that he'd been killed. She married another man in 1919, just before the baby was born, and her husband raised my cousin as his own, even giving him the name Case. It wasn't until the son was much older that his mother, knowing she was dying, told him the truth about his real father.

"You know, I never can figure why people do that," Howard said. "If they've kept it a secret over many years, it doesn't make sense to disrupt someone's life with that kind of information late in life.

"Anyway, apparently my cousin didn't follow up on the story his mother told him, but when his son became an adult, he shared the same story with him before he died, and now this fellow, John Case, thinks I'm a long-lost second cousin. He told Barnes that his father always regretted never following up, so he decided to pursue the question in his honor, so to speak. He lives in England but has no children of his own, and he and his wife apparently divorced a few years ago."

Olive nodded. "I can understand people wanting to find their roots, since it's easier now with the internet and free genealogy search sites like the Mormons have."

"You know, Barnes mentioned something about that. I never took much interest in that sort of thing, having—or so I thought—a pretty good knowledge of my family tree."

"Is he asking to meet with you?" Olive asked.

"According to Barnes, John is very interested in World War II history. I didn't know this, but apparently there's a museum outside of Boston dedicated to the War, and since Barnes told Case that I fought for the U.S., he thinks it would be a great idea to meet in Boston, visit this museum, and attend a Red Sox game," Howard said. "I'd pay my way to Boston, but he wants to treat me to the hotel and the baseball game. I don't really care. I can afford it, but I guess he's insisting. Then Barnes said that he may have to go to Boston himself, apparently to take some course or other that New York makes lawyers take, and that I can drive there with him. He said it would be easier on me, because we can stop occasionally on the way. I haven't been to Boston in years; Winnie and I went to a ball game a long time ago when the Sox were a bunch of losers, so I'd like to see them actually win, for once."

Howard's mention of Barnes' legal course in Boston was too reminiscent of Barnes' course in Atlantic City for Olive's comfort, but she opted to stay silent for the time being. Instead she asked, "When do you think this John Case will travel to the States?"

"He hasn't scheduled anything yet. Barnes suggested that we plan it for earlier in the baseball season, because tickets are probably easier to buy in April than in the summer. That makes sense."

"And Case is pretty sure you're related?"

"He knew about my father, and he knew that my uncle had been killed in Belgium, and my father did tell us about my uncle knowing a woman in England, so it may well be true. In any event, it would be good to meet him and hear what he has to say."

Olive remembered that Howard had told her all of the things that Case was using to explain their relationship, so Barnes likely had gotten the same information from Howard during their first meeting. She found herself being drawn into the Barnes saga again, even though she'd agreed with Maggie and Jean that she should mind her own business. Unlike Elizabeth and Irma, Howard was not particularly frail or vulnerable, but still, she liked him and didn't want to see him hurt.

"Is Case going to write you a letter or telephone you before coming to America?" she asked.

"I haven't asked him to, although Barnes said that he'll tell him to email a photo of himself so that we'll know what he looks like. I haven't really decided anything yet," Howard admitted.

Olive looked at her watch, telling Howard that she had to go and join her sister for lunch. As she left the room, she spotted the delivery wagon; it was lunchtime for Howard, too.

On Monday afternoon, Olive paid Irma a visit. She knew that Irma had said she wanted to concentrate on blackjack, but Olive figured she might want company all the same. Walking into Irma's room, Olive found her huddled over a tray on her lap, picking up and discarding a number of cards.

Olive called out, "So, are you going to be the one who breaks the bank at Monte Carlo?"

Irma looked up and laughed. "Maybe not Monte Carlo, but I'd love to bring back a piece of Atlantic City!"

Olive asked Irma whether she intended to try the slot machines or just play cards.

"I'll spend a little time with the slots, but I've always enjoyed cards, and when they had blackjack fundraiser nights at our senior center, I did pretty well," Irma responded. "I've been playing a few hands with one of the nurses after her shift, and that's helped bring back a lot of the rules. She pretends to be the dealer, and has actually gone on bus tours to Atlantic City a bunch of times. She described them to me and the tours sound like fun. You should try one sometime!"

Olive asked Irma about the game, telling her that she and Bill had sometimes played games of whist with friends, and she enjoyed playing cribbage with Irma, but that was the extent of her repertoire. Irma told her to push over the bed table, and Olive removed the water jug and glass to give them room.

Olive tried a few hands of blackjack with Irma, but found herself bored with the game. She asked Irma if the travel plans were set. Irma told her that Mr. Barnes had stopped by on Friday, which reminded Olive that Howard had received his visit on the same day.

"Mr. Barnes is going to pick me up on Friday morning around eight o'clock," Irma told Olive, "so we should arrive before noon, which will give me time to have lunch with Matthew and to rest before dinner at six. Then we're going to see Paul Anka. I can't wait!"

"So, you feel well enough for all of this activity?" Olive asked.

"Mr. Barnes has arranged for a nurse to come with us. She's married to the man who works as his chauffeur, so Mr. Barnes is having her come along as a precaution," Irma said. "He said that she can sleep in my room, too, to check on me at night. I like my privacy, but I understand his concern, and I want to go on this trip so badly.

"Since the drive takes almost three hours, he told me to bring my financial statements and my current last will and testament with me so that he and I can look at them together while we're traveling. He said that since there isn't much to look at on the way to Atlantic City, we might as well use the time to answer any questions I might have. I haven't looked at my will since Mother died, and Mr. Barnes says it's important to review these things every few years. He said he won't charge me any legal fees; he just wants to be sure that everything is in order."

Olive couldn't help herself and asked, "You don't have your own lawyer?"

"Not anymore. My mother's lawyer died a few years after she did and I haven't found a new one, so it's handy that Mr. Barnes came along, isn't it?"

Olive felt her blood pressure rising, so she decided it was time to leave. "I have to meet my sister, but if you need any errands run before you go, here is my cell phone number." She gave her number to Irma and took her leave.

Walking out of the nursing home, Olive looked at her watch and realized it was five o'clock. She could just go back to her apartment and cool off a little bit, but she wanted to vent about "the Barnes thing," and knew she could rely on Jean for a cold glass of white wine while she did so.

Jean answered the door almost immediately. "Maggie is down in the storage room. I figured you'd have something to tell us. Can I get you some wine?"

Olive smiled in appreciation, waiting to begin her report until Maggie joined them.

"I know the two of you think I'm fixated on Barnes and what he's doing, but every time I meet with these folks it seems he's done something else to alarm me," Olive said, taking a sip from her wine glass. She told Maggie and Jean about Howard's mysterious second cousin and Barnes' coincidental legal meeting in Boston, as well as his offer of a nurse for Irma—the nurse who just happened to be married to his chauffeur.

Jean and Maggie both nodded in agreement.

"We agree with you," Maggie said, "but we're still at first base here. Barnes has yet to do anything to any of these people, other than bring them long-lost relatives. And he is a lawyer. If Irma wants to show him her financial statements and her will, and whatever else he'll look at with her, that's her business."

"But I feel like I should warn them," Olive protested.

"And get them mad as hell for sticking your nose in their business?" Maggie replied. "I hate to be the wet blanket here, but Olive, it's time you took a break from all of this. Stay away from the nursing home for a few days, and then maybe visit Elizabeth later to check her status."

Olive managed to stay away from the nursing home for the next few days, but on Thursday morning, her cell phone rang. Picking it up, she heard Irma's somewhat breathless voice.

"Can I impose on you for an errand?" her elderly friend asked.

Olive immediately assured her that she could. Apparently Irma's lipstick was very low, and she wanted to take a full tube to Atlantic City.

"I'll be right over so I can take your old tube with me to the drugstore," Olive promised her.

When Olive arrived at Irma's room, she saw her standing by the bed, folding a new pantsuit. She also appeared to have a new travel bag and nightgown. Irma caught Olive's startled look, telling her that the nurse who helped her with blackjack also purchased those items on Irma's behalf so she'd have a decent outfit for her trip.

"I could have run those errands, you know. That's why I gave you my cell phone number," Olive said.

"I'm sorry. It was kind of a last-minute thing and Gloria told me that the department store was right at her bus stop," Irma responded. "But if you can get me some lipstick, that would be wonderful. Mr. Barnes is picking me up at eight o'clock tomorrow morning, so I'm trying to pack my things today."

Olive returned from the pharmacy a half hour later and put the new tube of lipstick on Irma's table. Irma emerged from the bathroom and slowly made her way to the bed. Once she got back under the covers, Olive asked her if she still felt well enough for the trip.

"I feel as good as I ever will," Irma responded. "Mr. Barnes is bringing the wheelchair so I won't have to walk if I don't want to. I'll take sleeping pills with me in case the new surroundings make things difficult, so I should be alright."

Olive saw a small pile of documents at the end of Irma's bed, and asked if she wanted them added to her travel bag or pocketbook. Irma told Olive that Mr. Barnes had taken her investment account statements with him when he brought her back to the nursing home after their lunch in Manhattan, but she'd received a new monthly statement just the day before, so she thought to bring it along that weekend. Apparently Barnes had faxed the earlier statements to Matthew West, because he planned to review them before meeting Irma in Atlantic City.

Olive started to add the documents to Irma's pocketbook, noticing her will beside the bank statements. "Irma, does anyone hold your power of attorney?" she asked. "I signed a document naming my son, Jon, and my sister, Jean, authorizing them to make financial decisions for me if I become unable to make them myself. You know, for banking and that sort of thing."

"When I was younger I used to have my mother, as well as our lawyer since I didn't have any other family," Irma explained. "But now that I have no one, Mr. Barnes is suggesting that he and Matthew do that for me. I told him I'd think about it, although I may decide to name Elaine Grant instead; she's the accountant here at the nursing home."

Seeing that Irma was tiring, Olive wished her luck at the gaming tables. As she was leaving, Irma told Olive that she hoped to have a visit from her on Monday, so that Irma could tell her all about the trip.

Chapter 15

Irma had asked Olive to stop by on Monday morning so she could tell her all about the trip, but by Sunday evening, Olive decided to go to the nursing home to check on Irma's arrival and to satisfy herself that Irma had returned in good spirits. Walking down the hall, she spotted Elfrieda at the nursing station, and waved to her as she passed. It was then that Olive noticed Elfrieda's stricken look. She motioned Olive to stop. Elfrieda took her by the arm, directing her to a room behind the station and closing the door behind them.

"I guess you haven't heard?" she asked.

Olive shook her head.

Elfrieda motioned Olive to sit down. "Irma died during the night yesterday," she said softly. "Apparently the night nurse stopped in her room around four o'clock this morning and couldn't hear her breathing. Irma's a heavy snorer, so it got the nurse's attention. She took her vitals, and it appears that Irma must have passed a few hours earlier."

At first, Olive was too stunned to speak, but then through her tears, she haltingly told Elfrieda that Irma wasn't expected back in the nursing home until Sunday evening, and that Olive had intended on surprising her with a welcome home.

Elfrieda squeezed Olive's shoulder as she handed her a couple of tissues. "The evening people told me that Barnes and his nurse brought Irma home early because she'd gotten pretty tired. Overdid it at the gaming tables is what they told Gloria, so when Gloria poked her head in after they left and saw Irma sleeping peacefully, she didn't think anything was wrong. I'm so sorry, Olive. I know you two were very close."

Olive stood up quickly. She told Elfrieda about Irma's suspicious call, wondering if Irma had been calling for help. "Can the nursing home request an autopsy?" she demanded. "Irma said something about orange juice in her phone call."

Elfrieda shook her head. "Apparently the nursing home's physician stopped by at eight o'clock this morning and signed the death certificate indicating a heart attack as the cause of death. He told Gloria it wasn't surprising, if Irma had engaged in that much activity at her age. She owned a prepaid cremation plan, so her body had already been taken away before I arrived this afternoon."

"Do you have the name of the funeral company?" Olive asked, feeling desperate. "Perhaps we can call to see if the cremation has been done? If not, maybe we can ask for an autopsy?"

"I suppose it's worth a try, but, Olive, you have to understand that old people die," Elfrieda said gently. "That's one of the hardest parts of working in a nursing home, whether you're paid like me, or a volunteer like yourself. You get attached to people and they become part of your family, so when they pass away, you hurt for a while. But you have to accept it or you can't keep doing it."

This made Olive sniffle all over again. "I know. If Irma had just passed away peacefully after her usual day's activities I could accept it, but after being taken away by this man who had a lot of questions about her will and her finances, and then being returned early just a few hours before her death? I can't accept that!"

"Okay. Let me find the number for the funeral home and we'll give it a call." She gave Olive a little hug and went to find the phone number.

Half an hour later, Olive sat grimly staring into space. The funeral home was nothing if not efficient, because Irma had been cremated before noon that day. The funeral director even assumed that Olive was her next of kin and asked whether she wanted an urn for the ashes. Olive handed the telephone to Elfrieda because she couldn't speak.

Elfrieda finished the call and briefly hugged Olive. "Why don't you go back to your apartment, pour yourself a stiff drink, and then take a hot bath?" she suggested. "There's nothing you can do now. But don't forget that you gave Irma some very good days while she was here. I noticed the difference in her outlook, and a lot of it was your doing. If you ever want to talk some more, you know where to find me."

Olive left the building, her tears drying in the cold night air. Her thoughts turned to Elizabeth and Howard. Were they also in danger? She realized that without an autopsy, her suspicions could never be confirmed, but she'd ask Maggie to check with her friend at the Surrogate's Court in a week or so anyway. Should Barnes submit a new will, it would be proof of foul play, at least in Olive's mind.

If that was the case, she'd certainly share her concerns with Elizabeth and Howard. She decided to defer any visits to them for a few days, because she feared that her grief over Irma would affect her demeanor, and she didn't want to alarm them. Realizing that she didn't want to be alone at that moment, she decided to find Jean and Maggie.

When Jean opened the door, she knew immediately that something was terribly wrong. Seeing Olive's tearstained face, she gasped, thinking that perhaps Jon had been injured on the farm. She took Olive's hand to bring her toward the couch, and breathed a sigh of relief when Olive finally murmured, "Irma's dead." Then she gave Olive a hug, knowing that Olive had become attached to Irma, so that to her this was like a death in the family.

"Do you want to talk about it?" Jean asked while pouring each of them a small glass of scotch. Maggie looked on, nodding.

Olive took a sip of her drink. "I think Barnes killed her," she said, her voice shaking. She began recounting the weekend's events, beginning with Irma's call on Saturday and ending with the cremation at the funeral home. "What are your thoughts?"

Maggie whistled, saying it sounded fishy to her. Jean just nodded, patting Olive's hand.

"On Monday I'll call Agnes at the courthouse and ask her to be on the lookout for a new file from Barnes," Maggie said. "If there's a file, we can go over and look through it. Until then, there isn't much we can do. Do you think that Elizabeth and Howard are in any danger?"

"I'm not sure. Barnes probably won't come to the nursing home immediately, because he's already laid the groundwork with Elizabeth and Howard, and he'll want to lie low," Olive replied, "although Elizabeth did say that she wanted to go to the Adirondacks soon, and that was about a week ago. I'm going to wait for a few days before I resume my visits with them; I'm just too blue right now to do them any good."

Jean finally spoke up. "I don't want you brooding about this, waiting for a file to appear at Surrogate's Court. And clearly walking around and learning the harmonica aren't enough activities to fill your day."

"How do you know about my harmonica?" Olive asked, brushing a tear from her cheek.

"Let's just say that your apartment isn't as soundproof as you think. I heard some braying one day, so I stood at your door until I realized what it was. I almost went out and bought you an accordion, for God's sake," Jean exclaimed.

Olive couldn't help herself. She started laughing and found it released a lot of the tension she'd been holding in. Jean gave her another hug and winked at Maggie.

Chapter 16

It was a week before Olive felt like venturing into the nursing home again. When she entered Elizabeth's room, she was greeted with a pout, realizing that she was in trouble.

Elizabeth wagged her finger. "I thought I must have offended you, or you were ill. I've missed you!"

Olive took Elizabeth's cue, explaining that she'd been a little under the weather. She said she hadn't wanted to bring any germs into her room, given that Elizabeth was still recovering from surgery.

Mollified, Elizabeth began chattering about the letter she'd received from Barnes: "Mr. Barnes wrote to apologize for not visiting me earlier in the week, but apparently he's been busy in court matters. How nice of him. He was asking about my health, because my sister really wants to see me. He wants me to call him today after I meet with my doctor.

"The doctor took a look at my stump and told me that it's still healing. The nurses have been changing the dressings regularly, and someday I'll be fitted with a special cushioned boot to prevent me from hitting my stump and getting any cuts. The plan, apparently, is to teach me how to walk with a crutch, but I told the doctor that at my age I'd be satisfied with a wheelchair, especially if I stay in the nursing home for a while, or maybe move to an assisted living unit next door and pay an aide to spend some hours a day with me. We haven't settled on anything yet."

"So your physician probably won't allow you to travel until you get this sorted out?" Olive asked.

"No. But I told him I'm determined to make the trip as soon as my foot is healed. I can sit in a wheelchair as well as I can sit in this bed. The doctor's coming back after Christmas and if I'm healed, he'll give his approval, so long as I have an aide with me. I told him that I can find one easily enough, but I'll check with Mr. Barnes to see if that's a problem."

Olive asked Elizabeth if she had a cell phone, and in response, she reached into her bedside table drawer and pulled one out. Olive told Elizabeth that if they exchanged cell phone numbers, she should feel free to call Olive should any errands be necessary in advance of her trip.

With their numbers exchanged, Elizabeth began looking up at her television set, asking Olive if she'd ever seen the series *No Reservations*. Olive shook her head.

"It's kind of a hoot because this curly headed chef, a tall lanky guy—kind of cute actually—goes to different countries and eats their food and meets the people," Elizabeth explained. "He's bit of a potty mouth, too, so the producers bleep out his swear words, although you still know exactly what he's saying. It's coming on now, so do you want to stay and watch it with me?"

Olive could see that it was more of a direction than a question, so she agreed to stay. She had to laugh along with Elizabeth at some of the chef's observations, and the show was pretty informative, so she made a note of the day and time for the future. She and Elizabeth both agreed that television had certainly changed; Mary Tyler Moore had certainly never used that kind of language, but then again, maybe television content was just more real than it had been before.

Leaving Elizabeth, Olive considered checking up on Howard too, but remembered that she'd agreed to visit him after church on Sunday to work on the crossword puzzle again. She'd only eaten a slice of toast early that morning, so she decided on a quick lunch in the dining room. That evening was movie night with Maggie and Jean and they'd be dining out, which made lunch in the dining room the most reasonable choice.

When she saw Maggie and Jean approach from the elevator, Olive was convinced that she and the other two actually operated with one brain. Sometimes it was uncanny, although she guessed it probably wasn't that unusual to meet people at a dining room at lunchtime.

"My God, you're actually wearing glasses!" Olive blurted out as Maggie drew closer.

"Thanks, Sherlock! I wore them last night too. Maybe you should check your own prescription," Maggie exclaimed as she strode by Olive.

Jean followed along behind, stage whispering to Olive that someone had gotten up on the wrong side of the broom that morning. They found their usual table was taken, further irritating Maggie, and Olive was beginning to wonder whether joining them that night for a movie and pizza was such a good idea.

"Hey, guys. I'm sorry I'm grumpy, but my back is killing me," Maggie said. "Every once in a while, it does this and then I can't sleep. I must have twisted it at bowling or something. I'll have to pass on the movie tonight."

Olive thought for a moment and nodded to Jean. "Why don't you lie down after lunch and we'll take care of you?" she suggested to Maggie. "Tonight we can order in Chinese, and you can lie on the couch like a queen and just eat and watch a movie. In fact, we'll rent a DVD."

"That's sweet of you. I think I'll take you up on it," Maggie said.

An hour later, Jean and Olive were standing at the local video store, looking at DVDs. Since they knew that Maggie wasn't much of a reader, they decided to rent two DVDs, one for her to watch that afternoon, and one for the evening with them. While there were a lot of new releases on shelves against the wall, they were looking for old standbys which would cheer her up. She hadn't asked for specific titles, telling Jean that she trusted her to choose, while raising her eyebrows in Olive's direction.

Jean grabbed *Goodfellas*, saying she knew Maggie would be pleased, having rented it enough times that Jean couldn't understand why she hadn't actually bought it. Then they moved down the aisle to pick out a second movie.

"Jean, you know I hate violent movies," Olive said. "I heard about *Goodfellas* and I can't imagine sitting through the whole thing. You and Maggie like sports, though; do you think she'd be happy with *Bull Durham*? I was surfing the movie channel a few weeks ago and I caught enough of it to make me want to see it. Maggie can even have her popcorn while we watch it!"

"Brilliant idea!" Jean said. "It's a great film with a few laughs, so it'll be good for all of us."

Still stunned at Jean's immediate agreement after they checked out, Olive held the door for her as they left the rental store. Not wanting to go home yet, Olive left Jean at the entrance to the complex and walked to the grocery store. She had nothing particular in mind to buy, but thought she might purchase some ice cream for dessert that night. She also remembered that she'd been planning to buy some wine anyway, so she could contribute a bottle of Chardonnay with the ice cream. Having brought her cloth grocery bag, she didn't want to overfill it and end up in Maggie's condition with a bad back.

Olive enjoyed trips to the liquor store in her new neighborhood. Her hometown in North Dakota had only one store, which carried mostly hard liquor and beer, with little variety in wines. When in town, she and Bill occasionally picked up a bottle of spirits and a case of beer, but he wasn't really partial to wine, so it was a rare purchase.

She also remembered that life in a small community was somewhat claustrophobic, with everyone knowing or wanting to know everyone else's business, and that trips to the liquor store with any regularity were bound to feed the rumor mill. By her nature and being busy with farm life, Olive never participated in the gossip circles, and she hadn't realized they existed until she moved to town after Bill's death. But Bill must have known. She chuckled to herself, remembering him "stocking up," as he put it, when he went on trips to Grand Forks.

She entered the store, the tinkle of the bell alerting the owner to her presence. She'd talked to him before and discovered that his hours of work weren't much different than a farmer's. She asked him whether he had anyone to give him a break, and he told her that either his son or daughter, both in college, tended to work from six until eight o'clock every other day or so, giving him a chance to have dinner with his wife. In his thick city accent, he explained that his wife worked at a bank during the day, so their dinners together were special. He said that on Saturdays he paid a clerk, allowing him time with his family, and he wasn't open on Sundays, so it wasn't a bad life. "At least I'm my own boss!" he exclaimed.

Olive couldn't disagree with that, moving off as another customer entered the store. She looked at the varieties of wine, and resolved to try something new each time she made a purchase. Maggie and Jean had their favorites, but maybe she could convince them to experiment as well. Today, however, she would purchase the old Chardonnay standby in honor of Maggie's convalescence.

That evening, Olive noticed that Maggie's mood had improved. Advil, alcohol, and a violent movie appeared to have worked their magic, because she was back to her usual talkative self during dinner. Before beginning the movie, Olive gave them a brief report on Elizabeth's current situation. Maggie told them that Agnes at the courthouse hadn't called yet, but that hadn't surprised her, because it took a while for a law office to prepare the necessary paperwork.

"What if there's nothing at court by the time Elizabeth travels to the Adirondacks?" Olive asked, feeling apprehensive.

"There's nothing you can do until we get some actual proof," Maggie responded. "To alarm her and make accusations about Barnes will only bring you lots of trouble, so you'll just have to be patient." With that, Maggie took hold of the remote and started the movie.

Olive supposed she was right, and sat back to enjoy the movie as best she could.

The following weeks passed fairly quickly. Olive enjoyed her Sundays with Howard, and the two of them completed each week's crossword in record time, feeling confident about their answers. Reviewing the previous week's puzzle, they could see where they'd made errors. When the weather was nice during the brief Indian summer, they even did the crossword outdoors in the beautiful little courtyard Olive had admired earlier in the year.

Howard hadn't received a photo of his second cousin yet, so there was nothing further to discuss in connection with Edgar Barnes. Elizabeth had recently called, though, and asked Olive to pick up some underwear and a new nightgown, "just in case" she was cleared to travel. Olive reluctantly complied, truly wanting to hear something from Surrogate's Court regarding Irma's estate before Elizabeth set off on her trip. Taking Maggie's advice, though, she kept her concerns to herself, not wanting to alarm her.

Olive was pleased by the distractions offered by shopping and preparing for her upcoming trip to North Dakota to share Christmas with Jon and Karen. She would leave gifts for Maggie and Jean, and for Chantelle, who was going to host them on the big day. Olive bought sugarless candy for Elizabeth and a *New York Times* crossword puzzle book for Howard to enjoy in her absence. Staying in North Dakota for ten days would give her the chance to reconnect with her friends and tell them all about her new life in New York.

Chapter 17

A couple of weeks following her return from North Dakota, Olive stopped by Elizabeth's room to find her directing an aide to bring her suitcase out of the closet. Seeing Olive's quizzical frown, Elizabeth waved her over by the closet and asked her to take out a grey pantsuit. Glancing at it, Olive couldn't help thinking of Irma; it appeared that she and Elizabeth shopped at the same store, the pantsuits being almost identical except for the color.

"I gather you've already talked to your doctor this morning?" Olive asked, trying not to let her dejection creep into her voice. She still couldn't help but feel that Barnes had had something to do with Irma's death, and she was loath to see Elizabeth fall prey to him, as well.

Elizabeth giggled. "You betcha! And he says I can go so long as I take along extra insulin, in case we get delayed. I told him about the big hospital in Glens Falls, and Mr. Barnes has assured me that his chauffeur's wife will be there to help me out with bathing and such. My foot is all healed and the boot will protect the stump from any contact. I'll be in a wheelchair most of the time anyway, but we're taking a crutch along just in case. I used one when I broke my ankle about twenty years ago, so I sort of remember how that works. I'm just so excited to see my sister!"

Olive saw the aide put an envelope into Elizabeth's suitcase. Noticing a corner of the label, she went over and started to put the pantsuit into the case, giving her a chance to see that it was from a law firm, and it appeared to be fairly thick. Elizabeth saw Olive fold the pantsuit and called out, "No, no, dear, I plan to wear the pantsuit, but you can pack the blue one hanging at the end of the closet."

Seeing that Olive was doing the packing, the aide begged off, leaving them alone in the room. Olive asked Elizabeth how many pairs of underwear and socks she would need, and Elizabeth told her to pack three days' worth.

This gave Olive the opportunity to pick up the envelope. "Will you want this packed too?" she asked.

"Oh, yes! Mr. Barnes asked me to bring along my financial statements and my current will so that he can review them with me on the ride to the Adirondacks," Elizabeth explained. "He told me that he doesn't charge for the service because he feels it's important for people to be up-to-date with their documents. I haven't looked at my will in years—and for that matter, I haven't been to church in years, so Mr. Barnes told me I may want to reconsider giving all my money to the church. But he said not to worry; we can talk about it on the way."

"When do you leave for the Adirondacks?" Olive asked.

"Mr. Barnes will pick me up after breakfast tomorrow, because I have to check my blood sugar after I eat, and then we'll get on the road," Elizabeth answered. "It's about a three-hour trip, so we should get there in time for me to have a light lunch and check into the hotel before we visit Beverly. I'd planned to take my camera, but Mr. Barnes says that he has a newer one, and can even shoot a video of me with Beverly if I want. He's such a sweet man!"

"So the doctor finds no problem with the trip?" Olive asked again, still a little incredulous.

"I suppose if I was a recent insulin user he might have some misgivings, but I'm an old hand at giving myself injections and I even do it myself here in the nursing home, so there shouldn't be any problem. And for heaven's sake, I'm not going to the moon. I'm only going to the Adirondacks!"

Olive still felt very conflicted, but not wanting to ruin Elizabeth's day, she didn't mention Irma or her concerns about Edgar Barnes. Maggie had confirmed that since no papers were filed with the court, there was no evidence of fraud—only Olive's gut feeling that something was very, very wrong.

Elizabeth gave her further directions about the suitcase, having Olive set it aside so that she could pack her toiletries before leaving. Elizabeth happily began packing, humming to herself.

Realizing that she was no longer needed, Olive excused herself, wishing Elizabeth a great trip.

"Stop by on Tuesday morning," Elizabeth told her, "because Mr. Barnes intends to finish his business in the Warren County court on Monday morning, and will bring me back later that day."

Olive promised to do so, praying that her gut was wrong and Elizabeth would be returned to the nursing home safely by Monday night.

Olive had been fretting all weekend. On Saturday, Maggie and Jean showed their concern by insisting on a long afternoon walk in the neighborhood, followed by Chinese food and a movie rental of Olive's choice. She appreciated it, knowing if she sat alone in her apartment that evening, her glum mood would only deepen.

The walk was lovely; she listened to Jean and Maggie josh each other and noticed the spring smells that had begun to drift up from the soil. Spring came much earlier in the Northeast, and Olive was happy about it. In North Dakota, she could remember having snow drifts all the way into May. The local cemetery would even dig graves in the fall, before the ground hardened with frost.

As they walked, Olive laughed at Maggie's jokes and could see why she'd been so important in Jean's life following Jimmy's death. Listening to the two of them, Olive upbraided herself for her jealousy, knowing that she couldn't have offered the solace which Jean must have needed after losing Jimmy, and which Maggie, in her own crude clumsy way, had been able to provide.

Even with the much-needed distraction, her mind still strayed to thoughts of Elizabeth. She wondered how her meeting with Beverly was going. Trying to stay optimistic, she imagined the two women embracing and sharing memories together.

After Olive, Jean, and Maggie finished their walk, they stopped at the video store on the way back to the complex. Olive was torn as she walked down the aisles, because frankly, with the way she felt that day, she'd have preferred the comfort of *Sleepless in Seattle* to anything Maggie wanted. A few weeks before, she'd mentioned how much she liked the movie, only to suffer much scorn from the other two. She'd endured much eye-rolling and enough "You're too old for such a chick flick"s to last her a lifetime. She didn't understand their fascination with sports and violence. Then she spotted what she hoped would be an acceptable compromise.

"You two like horse racing and this is supposed to be really good," Olive said, gesturing at the movie. "I'd planned to read the book and still haven't gotten around to it, but the movie is supposed to be pretty true to the novel."

Jean picked up the video and nodded at Maggie. "*Seabiscuit*. Okay, I'm alright with that. Let's do it!"

Back at their apartment, Maggie poured them all glasses of wine, and Olive agreed to watch the last period of an afternoon game at Madison Square Garden. She had to admit that she was actually developing an interest in hockey. The season was moving toward the playoffs so the games were more important, at least according to Howard. She watched parts of games with him sometimes, getting a kick out of his passion; his tutoring had made her a better viewer, so now even Maggie was impressed.

Now it was time to order dinner. As with pizza, Maggie and Jean had a definite view of acceptable Chinese take-out. Since Olive's only experience with Chinese food in North Dakota was the lone Asian restaurant in town, she didn't feel worldly enough to doubt their choices. Left to her own devices, she might have been tempted to try something new, and had once even suggested it. Maggie's philosophical response? "If it ain't broke don't fix it!"

It wasn't that Olive didn't enjoy their choices. Who could complain about pork lo mein, chicken fried rice, and garlic prawns? But the menu was quite extensive and Olive was curious, for instance, about hot and sour soup. Oh well, another time.

The food arrived and the women set the cartons on the coffee table. They spooned their dinners onto plates. Jean had taken some beer out of the fridge, and they were now debating whether to start the movie or wait until after dinner. Olive asked that they wait, since she hadn't seen the movie before and didn't want to miss any dialogue. Maggie grabbed the remote, telling Olive to be careful what she wished for, turning to a sports channel to look at scores around the league. Since spring training in major league baseball had begun and the basketball season was winding down, there was plenty for Jean and Maggie to talk about.

Olive ate her food and lapsed into thought about Elizabeth. Elizabeth was supposed to return on Monday evening, and Olive hoped that she was having a wonderful time in the Adirondacks meeting her sister. Try as she might, however, she couldn't get the image of Irma out of her mind—of her excitement at leaving the nursing home for a weekend, only to die unexpectedly just after her early return from the trip. She prayed that Elizabeth would have a better fate.

Jean interrupted her reverie by announcing that she was done with dinner and ready for the film. At that moment, Olive couldn't agree more; she sat back, ready for any diversion from her thoughts of Edgar Barnes.

Chapter 18

The next morning, Olive readied herself for church. Seeing the sleet outside, she took her umbrella from beside the door. In North Dakota, she'd taught Sunday school when Jon was young, and she and Bill had sung in the choir. Bill hadn't always been available for church, particularly during the busy season, but he'd told her that he knew lots of men who chose golf over church on Sundays, and at least he was trying to feed his family, so Olive never made a fuss over his occasional absences.

When Bill died, she'd felt angry with God for a while, finding it unfair that Bill should be taken while others lived. Her friends had told her it was God's will, and they'd encouraged her to seek comfort in the church, but she couldn't do it. Oddly enough, her move to Queens and occasionally attending the local Methodist Church had reawakened her interest in religion, and she found the minister and the congregation welcoming.

Olive asked Jean to accompany her some weeks, but her sister wasn't interested, and although Maggie was as lapsed as they come, she pleaded her Catholic roots in declining Olive's invitation. Olive also realized very quickly that her vocal skills were no match for those in the choir, so she contented herself with listening to the sermon and hearing the music.

Recently, Howard had asked about her Sunday mornings, knowing that she came directly from church to join him for the crossword puzzle. He nodded when she told him it was a Methodist church, saying that he and Winnie were Methodists, and that his will left his estate to the church now that Winnie was dead. He told Olive that he liked to sing along with the choir, not having a good enough voice to be part of it. Olive took comfort from this, realizing that others felt as she did.

After church that next morning, Olive went to the nursing home to help Howard with the crossword puzzle, as usual. She was also curious about whether Elizabeth might have called in. On her way up to Howard's floor, she stopped by the nursing station. Recognizing none of the staff, she told them that she was a volunteer and asked about Elizabeth. The nurse on duty checked for any incoming calls, telling Olive that if Elizabeth called, they would buzz her in Howard's room.

She found Howard with the puzzle already unfolded, ready to go, and she dropped a bag of licorice on his table.

"Ah, you are a sweetheart, my dear," he said. "I finished the last of it yesterday but didn't want to bother you. I've already checked last week's puzzle, but here, you can look at the few mistakes we made."

Olive chuckled when she read off the mistakes he'd circled, vowing to do better this week. The next hour and a half passed pleasantly—just what Olive needed after worrying about Elizabeth for most of the weekend.

"Do you miss your home?" Olive asked Howard as they were finishing up the puzzle.

"Yes, I miss it," he replied, "but not the work involved in keeping it up."

He'd been lucky to find a young college professor as a tenant, and he was even considering selling the home to him on a rent-to-own basis, but until he absolutely knew that he couldn't manage by himself, he didn't want to sell for sure. Olive wasn't surprised, given that Howard's stroke had been relatively recent, and him being such a proud, independent man. He reminded her a little of Bill, quiet and strong, although not so quiet when he was engrossed in televised sports. It was easy to see that he'd been a good husband, and he probably would have made a fine father.

"Any photo yet from your second cousin?" Olive asked. She had debated whether to broach the subject of John Case, still unsure about Elizabeth's status.

"Apparently he really wants to arrange a meeting in Boston," Howard said, "and I must admit, I'm bored to death with the people here—present company excluded, of course—so it would be a treat to see a ballgame and go to the museum he mentioned. Barnes called to say that John's computer has gone down, so he wasn't sure if he'd be able to email a photo, but that he planned to phone me soon. I gave Barnes my cell phone number to pass along. I don't have a computer, anyway, so emailing me would have been difficult."

Olive thought about asking Howard for his cell phone number, wondering whether it would be appropriate. Instead she said, "I have a laptop computer which I'm not very good with, but I can bring it next Sunday, and we can Google that World War II museum near Boston if you want to check it out. It must have a website."

"Sure. Sounds great." Howard sighed. "Sometimes I just feel so old. Well, I guess I am old, but you know what I mean. There have been so many new things in the past ten years that I feel like the world has passed me by. You know, Google, for heaven's sake! I used to be proud of the stuff I mastered, but now all I can do is sit here and feel sorry for myself."

Olive knew there wasn't much to say in response, so she just sat quietly. Howard looked at her and reached out to take her hand.

"You remind me so much of Winnie. She didn't say much, but when she spoke, she had something to say. I always appreciated that about her."

Olive felt herself tear up but just looked over at Howard and said, "You're a good man." She got up to go, telling him that she wanted to check on one of the other patients who had gone on a weekend jaunt, but that she'd stop by the following week. Brushing away a tear as she exited the room, she took the elevator to Elizabeth's floor.

Olive noticed the staff huddled near the nursing station and she began to ask if everything was alright when a young aide grabbed her arm and cried, "You'll never believe this! A few minutes ago the business office got a call from a hospital up north. Since the office was closed the call was put through to this floor; apparently last night Elizabeth Billingsley took an overdose of insulin and died! The hospital wanted to know if she had a prepaid funeral plan and it looks like she did."

Olive, too stunned to speak, gently moved the young woman to one side so that she could motion to Elfrieda, who had been shielded from view by the crowd of other nurses. Noticing that she was on the telephone, Olive waited. Elfrieda waved her into the supervisor's room behind the station and sat down after she finished her call.

"What's going on around here?" she sighed. "I wasn't on duty when Irma Weiss died, but two women dying so close together gives me the creeps. I can't say anything, though, because both deaths were from natural causes, but I'm still surprised. I've heard of elderly people accidentally overdosing on insulin, but I've never seen it before. Apparently Elizabeth had some wine with dinner and then took some sleeping medication, which she uses occasionally, so the doctors up there are treating it as a natural death. She never struck me as the suicidal type, that's for sure."

Olive tried to process all of this information, still a little bit in shock. "What's going to happen to her? Will her body be transported back here for burial?"

Elfrieda rubbed her forehead, telling Olive that apparently Elizabeth had a cremation plan, and there was a funeral home in Glens Falls that was going to take care of it. "It's not unusual for people with no immediate family to choose cremations," she explained. "They're cheaper and no one has any decisions about the casket or a funeral service to worry about."

Olive mumbled her thanks and went back to her apartment. She wasn't really tired; she just felt so low. Having talked to Elizabeth only two days before, and having seen her excitement, it was hard to believe Olive wouldn't talk to her again. She felt cheated. Elizabeth was meant to be wheeled back to her room on Monday night, telling Olive every last detail about her trip. She still had her Bible with her from the morning service; but she felt like hurling it across the room. Then she remembered that this had been no act of God. It was Edgar Barnes' doing, and she was going to prove it!

Olive knocked on Jean's door and fell into her arms when she opened it. Jean, again believing that something tragic had befallen Jon, quickly stripped off her rubber gloves and took Olive to sit on the couch.

"Elizabeth is dead too!" Olive told her. "The nursing home just got a call this morning."

Jean was incredulous and told Olive to stay put. She found some brandy and poured them each part of a snifter. Olive looked around, and smelling the pungent odor of cleaning fluid, she apologized to Jean for interrupting her day. Jean told her that she'd almost finished and that it didn't matter anyway.

At that moment, Maggie walked through the door, so Jean mouthed, "Elizabeth died" to her. Maggie took Olive by the shoulders and hugged her, letting her sob a bit before directing her back to the couch.

Olive gathered herself and began to recount the information she'd been given by the floor supervisor, still not quite believing it herself.

"If Elizabeth has been doing her own injections for the past decade, how can she have given herself an overdose?" Maggie wondered aloud. "It doesn't make sense. You'd think the police would have some questions, for God's sake!"

Olive had thought a lot about this on her walk over from the nursing home. "Maybe Barnes gave a very convincing statement, and the fact that she was a diabetic made her insulin overdose plausible. You can bet she didn't do it to herself, though—but I don't know how we can prove it, unless we somehow stop the cremation."

"Same problem as always, I'm afraid," Jean sighed. "We're not next of kin and we have no evidence contrary to what Barnes has given. The hospital knows about the overdose, so holding up the cremation won't stop anything. And I bet if you talk to the sister or Barnes, they'll tell you that Elizabeth was in good spirits about the meeting, so that'll rule out suicide. You said the hospital mentioned that Elizabeth had been drinking at dinner the night she took the overdose? I bet Barnes made sure that the waiter can attest to that, although from what Olive says, Elizabeth was not a drinker."

Maggie nodded. "Actually, that probably helps Barnes, because he can speculate that even a little alcohol may have been enough to cloud her judgment. Who knows? I'll call Agnes at the courthouse to see if anything has been filed for Irma's estate, and I'll ask her to keep a lookout for Elizabeth's. Olive, I'm so sorry, but that's about all I can do for now."

Olive sat back, more despondent than ever. Then she cried out, startling Jean and Maggie. "Why don't we go to the Adirondacks to try to find Beverly, and maybe we can talk to people at the hotel!" She looked up at them hopefully. She couldn't just sit around and do nothing about Elizabeth's death.

"There are a lot of hotels in Lake George, Olive," Jean cautioned her. "It's a real draw for tourists. Although, come to think of it, this isn't summer, so only the big places will be open. Well, first thing tomorrow, why don't you talk to the nursing home staff? That video of Beverly's might have an address with it, or maybe Elizabeth told the nurses where they'd planned to stay. The more we can find out before leaving, the more productive our trip will be."

Maggie looked at Olive and said, "I'm in. I can rent a car, if you like."

Olive grabbed the two of them and started to blubber, but Maggie firmly took Olive's arm and put it around Jean's shoulders. "I don't want you to break my new glasses!" she cried.

Chapter 19

Because Elizabeth's room was paid through the end of the month, there had been no rush to pack up her things when the staff received the sad telephone call. Early on Monday morning, Olive talked to the floor supervisor, explaining her concerns regarding Elizabeth's death.

"I wish I could help you, Olive, but there isn't anything we can do from this distance," the supervisor said. "The hospital in Glens Falls obviously decided her death was accidental, or they would have called the police."

Olive told the supervisor about her plan to travel to Lake George to investigate, requesting a visit to Elizabeth's room to search for clues. The supervisor was reluctant at first, but seeing the torment in Olive's face, she relented, as long as she accompanied her to the room and stayed there while Olive looked around.

"It's for your protection as much as anything, Olive," she told her on the way to Elizabeth's room. "We don't want anyone accusing you of theft after the fact."

Olive appreciated the advice, trying to complete her search as quickly as possible. She found the video in Elizabeth's bed table, but the return address on the envelope was *Kinfolk*, which was not helpful in locating Beverly. Maggie was doing an online search of the property tax records in Warren County to determine whether the house which Elizabeth was supposed to visit was actually titled in Beverly's name, though, so that would help.

Olive knew that Jean also was online, searching the larger chain hotels in Lake George, planning to call each one to locate where Elizabeth had been a guest. Olive asked her to mention Edgar Barnes if her question about Elizabeth brought no result, because Barnes might have booked two rooms in his name. Olive also remembered that when Elizabeth had described her leaf peeping tour, she'd raved about some restaurant that served wonderful crab soup and dinner rolls. Olive couldn't recall the name, but she remembered it had been something historical-sounding.

Jean had also suggested that they call the hospital to get the name of the Glens Falls funeral home, but Maggie doubted whether the hospital could release that kind of information because of privacy rules. But then Olive remembered that the nursing home had given the hospital the name of Elizabeth's funeral home in the Bronx, and that the people there probably had already contacted the Adirondack funeral home to make arrangements for her cremation. Olive asked the floor supervisor to check on it after they were finished searching through Elizabeth's belongings.

Not finding anything else in Elizabeth's room relating to Edgar Barnes, Olive followed the floor supervisor to her desk and waited until she reviewed the file notes. The supervisor found a copy of the cremation plan, giving Olive the telephone number for the Bronx funeral home. Olive asked the supervisor if she would call the funeral home to request the telephone number of the company in Glens Falls, both of them agreeing that the Bronx funeral director would be more likely to cooperate with someone of authority at the nursing home. There was no answer, so the supervisor left a message and told Olive she would contact her when she received a response.

Hurrying back to Jean and Maggie's apartment, Olive rushed through the partly opened door. Jean was seated at the kitchen table, looking at her laptop and making notes on a legal pad. Maggie was on her cell phone, and in response to Olive's look, Jean mouthed "car rental," and returned to her internet research. Olive didn't want to bring over her laptop until she learned whether it would be needed, so she went to the fridge and poured herself some water.

Ending the call with authority, Maggie said, "Well, that's done! We have ourselves an economy rental for tomorrow. They'll even deliver it here! Boy, times have changed. Olive, what did you find in Elizabeth's room?"

"Only the video, I'm afraid," she sighed. "Nothing with Beverly's address on it. The floor supervisor agreed to call the Bronx funeral home and she's left a message. If they tell her the name of the Glens Falls funeral home, we can call it immediately."

Jean looked up from her laptop. "I already Googled the Glens Falls area funeral homes and printed out the list. If we haven't heard from the floor supervisor by two o'clock, Olive can use the list and start calling around. Maggie, you were able to locate Beverly Williams' street address through the Warren County property tax records, right? And I've just gotten some telephone numbers of the bigger chain hotels in and around Lake George."

Olive was amazed. "You two are incredible. You should open a detective agency!"

"Elementary, my dear Olive, elementary," the two responded in unison.

Olive smiled. There was that one brain thing again. "Why don't I take the list of hotel numbers and begin calling while Jean Googles Lake George area restaurants?" Olive suggested. "Jean, I think if you tell me some of the names, I'll eventually recognize the one that Elizabeth raved about."

Olive looked at the alphabetical list of hotels and decided to pick out the most well-known ones to begin calling. Her strategy paid off immediately, because while the Holiday Inn had no record of an Elizabeth Billingsley, the clerk was able to confirm that Edgar Barnes had booked two rooms during the weekend for his party. They'd checked out that morning.

Olive told the clerk that her cousin was one of the Barnes party, and that Olive had hoped to catch her before they left the area. The clerk put down the telephone to check with a colleague who remembered a woman waiting in the restaurant that afternoon with her luggage, but she must have left. Olive told him that her cousin would have been in a wheelchair. There was a very long silence.

"I don't know how to tell you this," the clerk continued, his voice cracking. "The lady in the wheelchair died Saturday night. I was on the day shift when that party checked in, and also yesterday when her roommate called me requesting an ambulance. It was just so sad. Mr. Barnes told me this morning that he'd brought the lady to Lake George specifically to meet her half-sister for the first time, and it had been such a wonderful time for her."

Olive's emotional response was sincere, since she was still trying to accept the fact of Elizabeth's death. She thanked him for his help and closed her cell phone, briefly looking away. Maggie and Jean said nothing, giving Olive some emotional space.

Shaking herself, Olive asked what else she could do. Maggie responded that she could accompany them to lunch, but to bring her cell phone with her in case the floor supervisor called.

There was none of the usual joshing between Maggie and Jean on the way to the dining room, and when they took their seats the three women viewed the menu board without any enthusiasm. But they knew they had to eat something, settling on cups of tomato soup with grilled ham and cheese sandwiches, and fruit cups for dessert. The dining hall did offer wine and beer with lunch and dinner, but they always drank only water or iced tea with lunch.

After they placed their order, Maggie looked around to make sure she couldn't be heard. "What approach should we take with Beverly?" she asked. "She may have been totally innocent in all of this, and Elizabeth might have died before Barnes changed her will, although I highly doubt it. Until the Surrogate's Court receives a file from him for Irma's estate, we can only speculate on his strategy."

"Then maybe we're jumping the gun even driving to the Adirondacks tomorrow?" Jean ventured.

Maggie shook her head. "No, we should try to meet this woman as soon as possible. If we just walk into her home and tell her we're so sorry about Elizabeth's death, we can gauge her first reaction, you know, to find out if her grief is genuine. Besides, we should get Olive away from this gloom-bin for a couple of days. We can make the trip fun, you know."

As they rose to leave, lunch finished, Olive's cell phone ringtone made them stop for a moment. Jon had installed a few bars of the song "Home on the Range" as a little joke, knowing that Olive hated the song, but she hadn't bothered to change it because the phone rang so seldom anyway. Olive acknowledged the caller, nodding a couple of times before motioning to Jean for a pen. She wrote a telephone number down on a paper napkin. Leading Maggie and Jean out of the dining room, Olive didn't speak until they were in the elevator.

"I've got the name of the Glens Falls funeral home and I'll call it as soon we're in your apartment," she announced triumphantly.

The call to the funeral home was frustrating, though. Yes, they'd received Ms. Billingsley's body in the early afternoon, and on instructions from a Mr. Edgar Barnes, who apparently had been named executor of her estate, Ms. Billingsley had been cremated within a couple of hours. It was the funeral home's policy to follow instructions immediately, rather than hold onto bodies unnecessarily. The director had discovered it gave families closure by getting the process out of the way. Families could then plan memorial services at their convenience.

Olive recounted the gist of the call, and Maggie muttered, "I hope tomorrow morning our car rental company is that efficient."

Maggie then called the Holiday Inn to book a room for the three of them, while Jean downloaded a street map of Lake George. She also used Google Earth to show Olive and Maggie the view from above, so to speak, panning over the area. Olive remarked that it must be nice to live beside such a big lake, and Maggie answered that it was probably a very crowded little village during the summer. Jean surfed the weather channel for current temperatures in the Adirondacks; late March could be a particularly cruel time, especially in the North Country. The forecast was pretty favorable, but Olive decided to pack her umbrella anyway, along with some heavier socks for her sneakers.

Jean then began reading out names of area restaurants she'd looked up. "Log Jam, Bucks Tavern, the Montcalm . . ."

"That's it, I think!" Olive shouted. "The Montcalm restaurant was the one Elizabeth liked so much. We can have dinner there and ask if any of the wait staff remember her."

The trio discussed their plan. Maggie felt that if they left at eight o'clock, they'd arrive in Lake George by noon. There was no point in talking further with the funeral home, so they should focus mainly on Beverly. They could eat lunch and then pay her a visit. Maggie wanted to return to Queens in time for the bowling league on Wednesday, and Olive didn't disagree. They decided that when they'd finished with Beverly, they could enjoy being tourists, driving around the area and even traveling into Glens Falls. It would be a nice break from sleuthing. Maggie planned to print out Google driving directions and study them before the morning departure so they wouldn't waste any time getting lost on the road.

Believing that they had all of the relevant information, Olive returned to her apartment, agreeing to meet again later for dinner. Olive took the video of Beverly with her because she remembered she'd brought her little playback video machine from North Dakota. It was a piece of history now that most movie rentals were DVDs, but at least it was useful for this. Sitting alone in her apartment, Olive watched the face of Beverly Williams tell Elizabeth that she was happy to know that she had a sister. Olive couldn't help sobbing a little.

That evening as Maggie, Jean, and Olive approached the dining room entrance, Olive saw Jean gently push

Maggie toward the menu board. Oh, no, not again! She caught up to hear the exchange between them.

"Look, I just forgot them, okay," Maggie hissed. "So quit telling me you don't believe me. See, I'm reading the board, so stop making such a fuss. It's embarrassing."

Olive couldn't help but laugh as she heard a few titters from other diners. They found their seats and Jean chortled. "So, what are you having, Maggie?"

Olive decided to turn in early that night, but watching the video of Beverly that day had had a profound effect on her; she tossed and turned, leaving her somewhat fatigued the next morning. She made her coffee a little stronger, hoping the caffeine would kick start her system. Joining Maggie and Jean in the hallway, they all trooped down to the entrance.

They spied a new small car sitting by the curb. A young man emerged from the car, shouting hello. Maggie approached him and he took her around the vehicle to observe any current dents so that he could compare the vehicle on its return. Maggie then signed some documents, motioning Jean and Olive to join her beside the open trunk. They loaded their suitcases and got into the car, with Jean sitting in the passenger seat as co-pilot.

Watching Maggie look over the various dials on the dashboard, something occurred to Olive. When was the last time Maggie had driven a car? She was almost afraid to ask, so she mumbled a quiet prayer as she clicked on her seat belt. Olive had gotten into the right-hand side of the back seat, which gave her a good view of Maggie and the speedometer—perhaps not a prudent choice either. Should she have called Jon to let him know about the trip? Then she told herself to stop being silly; Maggie hadn't even started the car, for heaven's sake.

Olive could see that the vehicle had an automatic transmission, so that was comforting, and its small size would make it more maneuverable. She remembered the Chevrolet in North Dakota. Bill had always preferred big North American vehicles and he'd normally driven, but when he died, she'd almost traded the Chevy in for a smaller Honda. Then she'd reasoned that the Chevy was still new, so she couldn't have justified the cost of trading it in.

Maggie was her usual confident, noisy self. "Buckle up, it's going to be a bumpy ride," she announced.

Jean laughed, remembering the movie reference. Olive only hoped Maggie would concentrate on her driving and forget about movie trivia.

Maggie started the car and promptly put it in reverse, almost hitting a parked vehicle behind them. Offering up an "oops," she put the car into drive and eased out onto the street. She gave the Google map directions to Jean, so Olive was totally in their care. She said another small prayer.

Maggie's driving style mirrored her approach to all things. Somewhat reckless and voluble, she used only one hand on the steering wheel, leaving the other for gestures at passing landmarks and other drivers. Olive had heard Maggie swear occasionally while viewing televised sports, but driving clearly brought out the best in her. Even Jean had to laugh, listening to Maggie curse at fellow drivers after cutting them off.

They made their way toward the George Washington Bridge. Maggie yelled, "Go back to Joisey!" at another driver while merging into traffic via the on-ramp.

Olive tightened her seat belt, but then forgot her fear as the bridge loomed into sight. Its span over the

Hudson River provided a beautiful view, and Jean offered some travel trivia as they moved along. Olive had not realized that the bridge carried two levels of traffic, chuckling when Jean told her that the levels had been nicknamed "George" and "Martha," with George obviously on top. Incoming traffic was still heavy, but the women were able to move along smoothly going outbound.

With Jean reading directions to Maggie, they turned north after they left the bridge, watching for signs to the New York Thruway.

"Apparently there's a toll booth along here somewhere," Jean mentioned.

Maggie nodded. Eventually they pulled up to a booth and Maggie started to fumble with her left hand, looking for the handle to turn down her window, while keeping her right hand on the wheel and her eyes on the road.

"These foreign cars! How do I get this window open?" Maggie pulled to a stop by the booth, frantically looking around her seat. Jean told her to check the window, and in looking down Maggie punched a button, which only managed to lock them all in. Maggie grew beet red, listening to the sound of blaring horns behind her. Jean told her to try "the other button by the window," to which Maggie only grunted, acknowledging Jean's help when the window finally began to lower. She pulled the ticket out of the machine and handed it to Jean, pushing the button to close her window and offering up a salute of sorts to the driver behind her.

Jean whistled softly as she read out the cost on the ticket, matching it with the exit they had to take. "Hmm, our highways at work, I guess."

Maggie visibly relaxed once they joined the three lanes of traffic going north, reverting to her one-handed style on the wheel. After fifteen minutes or so, Olive was able to relax, too, happy to just sit quietly and look out the window.

She asked Jean whether she'd ever made this trip, and Jean told her that she and Maggie had once taken the train to Saratoga Springs to attend the horse races in August, but she'd never felt the need to drive once she moved from North Dakota. That caused Olive to marvel at Maggie's decision to drive, especially growing up in the city and having precious reason to learn. She murmured yet another quiet prayer.

As they passed the exit to Hyde Park, Olive asked Jean whether it was the Hyde Park connected to Franklin and Eleanor Roosevelt. Jean said yes, and that it was said to house an interesting museum. Apparently, there was also a huge outdoor sculpture garden nearby called Storm King, which was supposed to be awe-inspiring. Olive resolved to search online for tours to the area, given that it wasn't all that far from Queens. Now that she was settled in her new surroundings, she really wanted to explore, and it appeared that Maggie and Jean might enjoy doing so, too.

As they drove down a stretch of fairly boring highway, Olive dozed off. She woke when the car slowed for the exit to Albany, New York. After passing through the toll booth, they saw the capitol building, as well as a huge building shaped like an egg. She must look that up on the internet, too.

Jean directed Maggie to take the exit for Saratoga Springs, which put them on Highway 87 and within a short distance of Glens Falls and Lake George. The roadside was pretty gray with all the melting snow; Olive realized that the Adirondacks welcomed spring a little later than the city. That was understandable, Jean commented, because Lake George was almost as close to Montreal as it was to Manhattan, at least according to the mileage on the highway signs. So certainly a future trip to Montreal was doable. Olive found herself excited by all of these possibilities.

Exit 20 came into view, bringing Olive's thoughts back to the purpose of their trip, and making her speculate on their proposed unannounced visit to Beverly Williams. The three of them could independently make an assessment of her character and then discuss it at the hotel. Olive pointed out the Montcalm as they passed the restaurant, and Jean shouted, "I can't wait to have a steak!" in response.

The Holiday Inn was their first stop, and all of them acknowledged that they were ready to get out of the car. Olive hadn't ridden for this long in ages and her knees were telling her so. After checking in, they decided on soup and sandwiches in the hotel restaurant, not wanting to waste time looking for food in the village. They were all pretty hungry and finished eating in short order.

Jean showed her street map to the desk clerk, who confirmed that Beverly's home was only ten minutes away. Getting into the car, Olive's hands trembled a little. This was more excitement than she'd experienced in a long time, and she wasn't sure if she was ready for it.

Jean looked over and squeezed her shoulder. "Hey, kiddo! She isn't going to hurt us. She's in a wheelchair and there are three of us, remember? If anything, she'll be afraid of us."

Olive knew all of that; she wasn't afraid of any danger. She feared being unable to control her emotions; she didn't want to stand there and blubber in front of a perfect stranger. She asked Jean to do the talking, and Maggie told her to focus on Beverly while Jean was relating Elizabeth's death, because it would be important to get Beverly's immediate reaction. Olive was more than happy with this assignment, having become familiar with Beverly's face through several viewings of her video.

Now all she had to do was wait until they got to Beverly's, and then see what kind of "relative" she really was.

Chapter 20

Maggie eased the car into Beverly's driveway and whistled softly. "What a dump!" she exclaimed. "She mustn't have anyone to help her, and maybe she doesn't have the money to pay for yard work and a paint job. But surely her neighbors don't want to look at this every day."

They all spotted a rustle of drapes in the window as they started toward the front door. Upon knocking, they waited a moment or so. Someone asked who was there.

Olive called back, "My name is Olive Reader and I need to talk to you for a moment."

"Come in, it's unlocked," the voice responded.

There was no real entrance to speak of; the front door opened immediately into a small living room, and sitting in the middle of the room was a wheelchair holding a woman of comparable age. She looked at them quizzically, asking if they were Jehovah's Witnesses, and if so, she wasn't interested.

Jean smiled and walked toward the wheelchair as she spoke. "My name is Jean Corcoran, this is my sister-in-law Maggie Corcoran, and behind her is my sister, Olive Reader. We've heard so much about you, we wanted to meet you," she gushed.

Olive noticed Beverly flinch when she heard the last part of Jean's statement. She watched closely while Jean expressed concern about Elizabeth's recent death. Beverly reacted by blurting out, "But how did you know?"

Jean answered smoothly. "We've become good friends with Elizabeth, particularly my sister here. Elizabeth showed us your video a couple of times because she was so excited about seeing you. We were shocked that she died so suddenly."

Maggie then took over. "I hope you had a chance to meet Elizabeth before she passed away."

Beverly paused before answering, and then said that she'd met Elizabeth during lunch at her home, and that both of them had enjoyed the visit.

Jean took up the questioning again. "So you and Elizabeth were able to learn something about each other? I know she was looking forward to it. I'm trying to remember where she grew up. She told us, but it's slipped my mind. I know she wanted to tell you all about herself, so maybe you can help me out?"

At this, Beverly looked flustered and said she couldn't remember.

Jean went on to tell Beverly that Elizabeth mentioned being in the signal corps in World War II and that she'd become a bookkeeper when she got back to the States—which was obviously false.

Beverly nodded enthusiastically. "Yes. She told me about the war and how boring it was when she returned to civilian life. I can only imagine." Beverly's voice trailed off as she looked from Jean to the other women.

"Did Elizabeth look in good health when you last saw her?" Jean asked. "We're so puzzled that she would take an overdose of insulin. It just isn't like her."

Olive could see that Beverly was becoming quite wary, shifting a little in her wheelchair. Her voice was now somewhat defiant. "Look, I don't know why you're here," she snapped. "She's dead, alright—I'm broken up over it, but I have to accept it. She was fine when I saw her, but accidents happen. I mean, look at me."

Maggie nodded, feigning sympathy and changing the subject, saying that it must be hard for Beverly to cope with her injuries. She asked her how the accident happened.

Beverly appeared to relax a little at this. "Some drunk driver in a big half-ton truck ran a stop sign. I didn't have a chance. But he didn't have any insurance or a pot to pee in, so here I am in this chair, living on next to nothing. Elizabeth immediately understood and told me that when she got back to the city she was going to send me a money order for some cash. That day she also planned to change her will to help me out, but I don't know if she had time to do it before she died. She was such a wonderful person."

Maggie exchanged a glance with Jean. "When is the memorial service? We'd love to attend."

This brought a blank look from Beverly, followed by an expression of panic as she tried to choose her response. "I'm not sure. It's all happened so fast. I have to check with Edgar Barnes, her lawyer. Maybe he's arranging something. I'll let you know, though." Beverly's upper lip was already covered in a slight film of sweat, even though the temperature in the room was fairly cool. "Look, all this talk about Elizabeth is upsetting to me and I need to rest for a while, so I'll have to ask you to leave," she said.

Jean bent down to shake her hand and again offer her condolences, while Maggie and Olive echoed her sentiments on the way to the door.

Backing out of the driveway, Maggie noticed the front room drapes move again. "My butt, she's broken up," she hissed. "What a crock! She doesn't know what we know about her, and if they discussed Elizabeth's life at all, I'll eat my shorts. That was good, Jean, telling her that garbage about Elizabeth in the signal corps and being a bookkeeper. Beverly would've been better off saying she didn't know. Ha!"

Olive suggested a ride around the area, because there was still a lot of daylight left. They drove back to the highway, and she pointed when she spotted Exit 18 for Glens Falls. The exit had the usual businesses—a motel and a McDonald's—and on the street into the city, she saw a couple of small strip malls and a large grocery store. Maggie veered right at the fork in the street which took them by a big hospital, and Olive sighed, realizing that this would have been the hospital which contacted the nursing home.

"I wonder what the death certificate will say?" she mused, speaking to no one in particular.

Maggie answered. "If Barnes does have a new will and starts a file with the Queens County Surrogate's Court, he'll have to include a certified death certificate, so we can look at it then." Maggie then saw the traffic roundabout up ahead and said, "Oh, great. I hate these things—although, truth be told, I've never used one before." There happened to be no travel in any direction at that moment, so Maggie was able to ease the car through the roundabout onto Warren Street without incident.

"Do you know where you're going?" Olive asked. She was enjoying the ride, but she didn't want to get lost either.

"There's no problem," Maggie replied. "We'll just stay on this street until it ends, and then we can drive back the way we came."

Jean pointed out some wonderful old homes along the street. To the right, they all saw a sign for the Hyde Museum and thought about stopping, but Maggie said she wasn't in the mood to wander around looking at paintings. Olive appreciated Maggie's efforts that day, so she agreed that the museum could wait.

Turning around when the street came to another fork, they headed back toward the center of town. When they arrived again at the roundabout, Jean told Maggie to take a right-hand turn, because she wanted to look at the buildings on Glen Street.

"This must be the center of town. I like the facades on these old office buildings. It's nicely kept up, too," Jean said. She motioned for Maggie to go left at the Glens Falls National Bank building onto South Street.

The facades on the buildings along this street weren't as eye-catching, appearing a little run-down, but then Maggie pointed and shouted, "Let's pull in here!" They turned into what looked like a public lot next to a large brick building.

"I'm ready for a drink," she announced, climbing out of the car. "It says Sandy's Clam Bar on the front of the building, so I assume it has clams, and I could use a snack."

Jean and Olive followed her into the building, walking by a pool table on the right.

"Ah, this just gets better and better," Maggie said.

Jean grinned, while Olive looked at the dim interior, wondering what she was getting into. A tall, nice-looking fellow behind the bar introduced himself as Tim, asking what he could get them. They each ordered a pint of beer and Maggie followed him with her eyes as he walked away. Olive whispered to Maggie that she should be less obvious, and that the bartender could be her son, for heaven's sake, to which Maggie responded with a "Huh!" and a request that Olive lighten up.

Tim brought their pints and asked if they were from downstate. "It's that obvious?" asked Maggie, who was convinced it was Olive who had an accent, not her.

"Well, actually, yes," Tim admitted. "But we'll also have a lot of downstate visitors later this week, because the State High School Basketball championships are this coming weekend. The games really bring in a crowd."

Olive had been viewing the menu board during the discussion, and she asked if the clams were fresh. Assured that they were, she ordered a dozen. Maggie suggested that the three of them order two dozen clams and a dozen hot wings, which would hold them until dinner at the Montcalm around seven o'clock.

Jean had been eyeing the pool table and asked Tim the cost. She fished for some quarters and challenged Maggie to a game. Olive had never played, and she hadn't realized that Jimmy had taught the game to Jean.

"Actually, I prefer pool to bowling," Jean explained, "but it's easier to be in a bowling league than a pool league. You know I like to drink, but spending the whole evening sitting around a bar waiting for a turn isn't my idea of a good time. This is good, though."

Maggie racked the balls and Olive pulled out a nearby stool to watch. Jean hit the balls first and Olive flinched a little, surprised that she could do it with such force, watching one of the striped balls disappear from view into a pocket.

"Practice, my dear, practice." Jean was chuckling as she surveyed the table.

"So you get to keep playing after you split up the balls?" Olive asked. She realized that she should have gotten out more in the past.

Jean sank a couple of balls, missing on her third shot, then sat while Maggie prowled around the table.

Jean continued her explanation. "We're playing eight ball. There are solid-colored balls numbered one through eight and striped balls numbered nine through fifteen. Since I knocked in the number two ball, I have to try to put down the rest of the solid balls, and Maggie hopes to knock down all of the striped ones. Whoever puts down all of their balls then shoots at the eight ball, and if I put it in—which I intend to do—it means I win. If I put it in the wrong hole, or pocket, as it's called, or if I accidentally pocket the white cue ball at the same time, it's called a scratch, and I lose."

"But you put in the white ball earlier and you didn't lose?" Olive said, confused.

"Yes, but I wasn't trying to hit the eight ball then, so I only lost my turn."

"It must be hard to make the white ball hit the other ball first."

"First off, call it a cue ball, okay?" Jean said, rolling her eyes. "But yes, it can be hard, particularly if the cue ball is behind the other player's ball on the table. When Maggie and I are done, I'll try to give you a lesson."

Just as Maggie was sinking the eight ball and smirking at a disgruntled Jean, Tim walked over with the food. Thoughts of pool forgotten for the moment, they all reached for their forks and polished off the steamed clams. Olive noticed the "Street of Dreams" T-shirts hung behind the bar, and wondered what that was all about. Maggie shrugged and ventured that since the street was pretty shabby, the moniker was probably meant to be ironic. Maggie never ceased to amaze Olive.

After wiping the hot sauce off their fingers, Maggie and Jean resumed their match; they informed Olive that they were playing the best out of three, so Jean had to win this next game in order to force a third. Fair enough, Olive told them, because she wanted to watch how they held the cues before she tried it herself.

Maggie won, so Jean had to concede defeat. She called Olive to the table and handed her the cue. Olive took it in her right hand and, mimicking Jean, she let the cue rest on the index finger and thumb of her left hand.

Jean was pleased with her form. "That's right. Now push the cue forward in a stroking motion a few times to get used to it. Then you can try to hit the cue ball into one of the other balls."

Olive tried the motion a few times and then lined up the cue ball on the two ball. She was able to hit the cue ball but missed the two ball badly. "What did I do wrong?" she asked.

"Just pick the target and bend down so that you can see the cue ball," Jean told her, "and then look through it to your actual target. In this case, that's the two ball. Then stroke the cue and see what happens."

Olive followed Jean's instructions and made good contact with the two ball. She looked up at Jean in satisfaction.

Maggie started to move toward them and took the cue from Olive. "Let's go," she said. "If I sit here much longer I'm going to want another beer, which I can't have because I'm driving. There's a pool table downstairs at the complex, so we can continue the lessons when we get home. You're showing promise, Miss Olive, and I'd be happy to play some practice games with you."

Olive couldn't help grinning. She loved it when she tried new things and didn't stink. She wished that Jon could see this.

They paid their tab, Tim wishing them well as they left the bar. Back on the street, it had started to snow a little, just enough to be interesting. Maggie's only concern was the following day's drive, so she wanted to check the Weather Channel when they got to the room. They decided to take Route 9 north to the hotel, which took them past the Warren County Municipal Center and courthouse.

"So Barnes probably attended court yesterday as though nothing happened," Maggie muttered as they passed the courthouse. "I hope we can nail his tail to a wall somewhere." Olive and Jean nodded in agreement, but they still had no way to make it happen.

They returned to the hotel around five o'clock, with plenty of time to just lie back and watch a little television before dinner. According to the Weather Channel, the light snow was supposed to taper off that night, giving way to clear skies in the morning. Maggie was relieved. Jean then went to the TV guide and noticed that the Rangers game that night was being televised. She was ecstatic, because the regular season was drawing to a close and the Rangers were in the thick of things.

"This will work out great!" she exclaimed. "I can eat a big steak tonight and then lie back and digest it while I watch the game."

Olive looked over and asked if that's what boa constrictors did. Jean only stuck out her tongue.

Maggie asked them what time they wanted to get on the road the next day so she could ask for a wake-up call, but Jean didn't think it was necessary. "If we get on the road by ten o'clock we'll be back in Queens by two or three, with plenty of time to get to the bowling alley," she said. Olive had no opinion, content to be a passenger.

Around six o'clock, they roused themselves to freshen up for dinner at the Montcalm, which was only a few moments away from the hotel.

Upon entering the restaurant, Olive was immediately struck by the decor. The log walls gave the room a warm, rustic ambiance and the fireplace at the other end was so inviting. They decided to sit near it, and the hostess showed them to a table close by. As the restaurant wasn't busy, Olive took the opportunity to inquire about Elizabeth.

"Oh, I remember them—the lady in the wheelchair on Saturday who was suddenly taken out of the restaurant by the fellow she was with." The hostess told Olive that the man had worn a nice suit, and he'd mentioned that the lady may have had a little too much to drink, although she hadn't noticed that herself. She'd wondered whether the lady had been drinking at some other location, but that was just speculation. When Olive told her that Elizabeth died suddenly that night, the hostess gasped and offered her condolences.

When a server walked up, the hostess told him about the lady dying, and he just shook his head in disbelief. Apparently, he had waited on her table and she'd looked alright to him, but the man with her had insisted that he take her back to the hotel, telling the server that she may have had too much to drink. The waiter agreed with the hostess that he hadn't seen her drink much at all, just a couple of sips of wine. They could provide no other information, so Olive thanked the hostess, who returned to her perch near the door.

Foul play is definitely afoot, Olive thought.

The women dined slowly, enjoying the background music and talking a little about Beverly Williams. They hoped that Agnes at the courthouse would have news later in the week regarding Irma's estate. Olive had already decided that she would warn Howard about Edgar Barnes. She didn't care whether there was hard evidence or not. Based on what the Montcalm staff had told her that night and the outright lies Beverly had told them that afternoon, she had begun to fear that Howard might be in danger. Even Maggie agreed.

Having taken their time over dinner, the first period was over by the time they returned to their room. There had been no goals, though, so Maggie couldn't complain. Jean and Olive both sat on the beds while Maggie pulled up a chair and turned up the volume. Olive hoped that no one was staying in the next room.

The first period intermission ended and the game resumed.

"What do you think you'll tell Howard, Olive?" Jean wondered aloud. "You don't want him confronting Barnes only to find out we still have no proof. You'd be buying yourself a load of trouble."

Olive had considered this, but she told Jean that Howard would hear her out, and if she asked him to hold his tongue until they had proof regarding both Irma and Elizabeth, he would understand.

"What if Barnes tries to involve Howard in some out-of-town scheme like he did with the women?" Jean asked.

"If any invitation is made within the next couple of weeks, I'm going to ask Howard to stall," Olive responded. "Apparently his so-called second cousin wants to meet him in Boston to tour a World War II museum and take in a baseball game."

"Wow, Fenway Park!" Maggie chortled. "That will set his cousin back a few bucks. Remember when we went on that bus tour, Jean? The place was rocking! You can't get any better than a Yankees-Red Sox game. We should do it again someday." She turned to Olive. "You'd like it, Olive."

Olive had to laugh. "The way we've been traveling lately, we'll all be poor old bag ladies within the next ten years." But she thought it was a great idea and hoped they might try it during the summer or fall.

Even though neither team scored, the game was still exciting; there were lots of scoring chances blocked by great saves from both goalies, which drew Olive into the game, too.

Jean and Maggie savored the Rangers' victory while eating ice cream bars. Olive had been tempted, but she was still too full of dinner rolls to add dessert on top.

They readied for bed and tried to fall asleep. The next morning, they set off for Queens. Jean asked to drive, but Maggie told her she couldn't because she'd only rented the car for one driver. It would have cost extra for an additional driver, and she hadn't thought it was worth it.

"Jeez!" Jean muttered. "I hoped to get behind the wheel to see if I can still drive."

Olive said a quiet prayer of thanks. The ride up with Maggie had been interesting enough, but watching Jean relearn her driving skills would be too much for her nerves.

Olive would have so much to tell Jon. She must remember to bring her camera on any future trips, and to ask Jean how to transfer the photos into her computer. She could then email Jon and Karen and attach some photos. It would be a fun project, too.

They pulled alongside their apartment complex a little before four o'clock. Maggie called the rental company and was told that a representative would be there before five. They unloaded their luggage. Deciding to eat dinner earlier than usual, Maggie pointedly suggested that Olive order crow for her meal, because there wasn't one new dent in the vehicle.

Chapter 21

Following their return from the Adirondacks, Maggie hesitated to call the Queens County courthouse, not wanting to be a pest. On Thursday, her patience was rewarded when she heard Agnes' voice on the telephone, asking, "Guess what?"

Maggie quickly retrieved a notebook and pen. "Shoot," she said.

"Late Tuesday, someone from Edgar Barnes' office dropped off the probate petition for Irma Weiss, but I didn't have time until late yesterday to begin reviewing it," Agnes told her. "Barnes is indeed listed as executor, and Irma gives a cash gift to some senior center and the rest to a friend, Matthew Forman. There's an affidavit of heirship with the petition, but it says she has no living relatives, so I don't know whether the judge will order Barnes to publish any legal notice to unknown heirs. Probably not, given that Irma says she has none. I shouldn't be calling you about this, but I agree that it seems a little fishy—too much like the file we got from Barnes eight months ago. Otherwise, the papers seem in order, and you're free to come down and look for yourself, now that we have a court file opened."

Maggie was stunned. She told Agnes that Irma had been introduced to a fellow named Matthew West, who said he was a distant relative whose family had changed its name during the first World War from Weiss to West to avoid persecution. Agnes grunted that it may have been a great story, but the affidavit of heirship made no mention of any name changes.

Maggie asked if Agnes could send her a copy of the affidavit, but Agnes said no. "I can't do that, Maggie. Sorry, but you know the rules. You'll have to come down and do it yourself."

"Okay, I'll be right down." Maggie grabbed her pocketbook and headed out the door, almost bumping into Jean and Olive in the hallway. Olive was carrying her laundry basket. Maggie hurriedly told them about Agnes' call, but said they needn't accompany her to the courthouse.

"Why don't you give us your laundry and we can do it while you're gone?" Olive offered. "I'll keep my cell phone on so you can give us a call when you get back."

"Deal!" Maggie ran back into the apartment and came out with her basket, following Jean and Olive to the elevator. Leaving her basket with them in the basement laundry room, Maggie had just enough time to catch the bus to the courthouse.

During the ride, Maggie tried to work out a plan. The judge who had been her old boss had retired a few years after Maggie had herself, which was unfortunate because she would have felt comfortable requesting a few minutes of his time, off the record. Agnes told her that his successor was an excellent judge, but somewhat younger, and tended to do everything by the book. Maggie acknowledged that because she was not Irma's relative and hadn't been a beneficiary in Irma's previous will, she couldn't oppose Barnes' petition regarding this recent will. And, come to think of it, she hadn't even laid eyes on the previous will; she only had Irma's description of it, and Irma had taken it with her on the trip to Atlantic City. She guessed that the old will was probably in a trash can somewhere.

Arriving at the Surrogate's Court Clerk's office, she waved to Agnes, who pointed at a file set off in the corner. Maggie went into a side room and began reviewing the affidavit of heirship before photocopying it to take home. She also photocopied Irma's affidavit setting out Barnes' entitlement to executor's commission and legal fees, and photocopied the relevant pages from the probate petition. Before leaving, Maggie asked to see the older probate file for the lady who had died about eight months earlier because she wanted to compare the two affidavits, and photocopied that one, as well. Handing the files back to Agnes, she leaned close, telling Agnes that she should expect to receive another file from Barnes within a couple of weeks. When Agnes raised her eyebrows, Maggie told her to call the next day for more details.

Looking at her watch, Maggie made a dash for the bus, catching it just before it pulled away from the curb. The buses traveled fairly frequently, but not as often after morning rush hour, so she was happy to be spared the lengthy wait. Maggie was hungry and hoped that the dining room had something decent for lunch. Within half an hour, she arrived at the complex, and, approaching the elevator, she spied Jean and Olive, weighed down by three laundry baskets and detergent.

Jean looked over. "Timing is all. Here, grab one of these baskets."

They stood silently on the ride to their floor and Maggie suggested Olive drop off her basket and meet at their apartment for a briefing. Olive couldn't wait to learn of Maggie's visit to the courthouse, so she just dropped the basket inside her door and rushed over.

She had just sat down when Jean burst out of her own room. "So, what do you have?" she exclaimed.

Maggie passed around the documents she had photocopied, and Jean whistled when she read Irma's affidavit of heirship. "Why, that lying creep! And this

Matthew guy is just an imposter? I can only imagine the story Barnes cooked up in Elizabeth's affidavit."

Maggie nodded. "I mentioned Elizabeth to Agnes and told her to call me today or tomorrow so I can give her some details. I want to alert her because I'm sure Barnes is already preparing the probate petition for Elizabeth. The problem is still pretty much the same, though. We don't have first-hand proof that Irma didn't know this Michael Forman as a friend, and we have no proof of foul play, given that she was cremated so quickly. Olive saw Forman briefly when Barnes took Irma out for lunch, but it would be Olive's word against Barnes that Forman was introduced to Irma as Matthew West. This just stinks!"

They all fell silent for a few minutes, each one trying to devise a plan to confront Edgar Barnes. Finally Maggie rose, moving toward the door, telling them that she always thought better on a full stomach.

They reached the dining room and Olive laughed as Jean began pushing Maggie toward the menu board. However, Maggie stood her ground, pulling a pair of thin glasses from an equally thin case in her trouser pocket. "Ha! I'll peruse the menu board from our table, if you don't mind," she said triumphantly.

Lunch featured hot turkey sandwiches, which were eerily reminiscent of the turkey dinner the night before, although the sandwiches offered a choice of French fries or mashed potatoes. For some reason Jean did not object to turkey as food, so Olive could only surmise that Jean considered ducks and geese cuter or something. Turkey two days in a row did not speak to Olive, so she opted for a cup of mushroom soup and a side salad. She felt confident that turkey vegetable soup would find its way onto the menu within a day or so anyway. Maggie wanted something more substantial than salad, ordering soup and a tuna sandwich.

The dining room was almost empty, so Olive felt free to speak about the "Edgar Barnes thing." Ever since their talk with Beverly Williams, she'd been anxious regarding Howard's safety. She felt she could no longer remain silent, and asked Maggie whether the Surrogate's Court would listen to her concerns. Maggie didn't think so. She explained that any objection must come from a relative or a beneficiary under the previous will, and they weren't either of those. Maggie's only thought was to contact the law firm which had prepared the previous will, because sometimes firms kept the original in their safe deposit boxes and sent the client a copy for reference.

"Olive, can you remember the law firm's name on the envelope you packed for Irma?" Jean asked.

"I'll go through the Yellow Pages after lunch and see if I can recognize the name," Olive said. "If I find it, I'd prefer that Maggie places the call; she'll know what to ask."

Maggie agreed. If they could locate the original previous will, she would contact the senior center and tell the director about Barnes. The Attorney General might even get involved on behalf of the senior center to prove that the new will was invalid. But it was a long shot.

Olive began her research after lunch and was astonished at the number of law firms in the New York metropolitan area. She kicked herself for not having been more attentive when she'd packed the envelope for Irma. She sighed, opened a beer for herself, and sat down to the long task of reading through all the names of the law firms in New York.

"What to have, what to have," Jean ruminated aloud while sitting down in the dining room. "Olive, I know you'll have the fried sole with Caesar salad, and I'm betting Maggie will go for the lasagna, which I must say is tempting—but I require lots of protein, so I'm ordering the pork chops with mushroom gravy and mashed potatoes. Am I right about you two?"

"Wrong, my dear," Maggie said. "Since we're having pizza tomorrow night, I'm ordering the pork chops tonight."

"Just when you think you know a person!" Jean exclaimed.

Olive had been quiet during the walk to dinner, so Jean now asked if anything was wrong. Olive told them that she'd finished her reading of the Yellow Pages lawyers' ads and no law firm's name had jumped out at her. Jean wondered if the firm might no longer exist, particularly if the older partners had retired.

"I could just kick myself for not noticing the name on the envelope that day," Olive sighed. "I guess I was so focused on Irma that the importance of it didn't register."

Maggie gave her a consoling shrug. "Even if the firm is still around, Irma told you that the will was about twenty years old. The firm may have sent the original to her, or she may have picked it up. It's pretty common practice."

Dinner was served, so the trio fell quiet. Maggie asked Olive whether she wanted to join them in watching the hockey game that night, which brought Howard to mind.

"This would be a good excuse to stop by Howard's room for an hour or so," she thought aloud. "I can take him some licorice since I haven't seen him lately. He'll have heard about Elizabeth's death from one of the aides, I'm sure, because it'll be the gossip of the week, so it'll give me a chance to talk about Edgar Barnes with him."

Maggie finished chewing a bit of pork. "What do you plan to tell him?"

"I'm going to mention that Edgar Barnes took Elizabeth on that trip and then I'll let him know about Irma too. I'm going to say that I'm concerned about his safety."

Jean spoke up. "Here's my suggestion. Ask him if he's heard from Barnes lately. If he hasn't, I think we should use the interval to talk to him alone, outside of the nursing home. He knows Maggie and me from the hockey game last fall. Tell him we're planning a ride out of the city, and you can say that you're curious about his old stomping grounds on Long Island because you've never been there. I'm sure he'd love to get out of the nursing home for a day. Tell him we can have a late lunch at a diner on Long Island, his choice. Maggie can rent a car again for the day."

Maggie nodded enthusiastically. "Sounds like a plan!"

Olive was stunned by both the ingenuity and generosity of the offer. It would be wonderful for Howard to escape the nursing home for a few hours and it would give the three of them his undivided attention in explaining Barnes' scheme. After dinner, Olive almost bounded down the hallway to retrieve the licorice.

She arrived at Howard's room before the game began, striding through the door with ten minutes to spare. Howard looked up in surprise, but his expression quickly turned to pleasure at Olive's company.

"Pull up a chair, partner, the game begins in about five minutes!" he said. "Ooh, licorice. Merci beaucoup."

Olive had learned from Maggie that the Rangers were playing the Flyers that night, a really heated rivalry. Howard turned down the volume for a moment, asking Olive if she'd heard about Elizabeth Billingsley down the hall. Olive nodded and was about to say more when the game came on. She told Howard she could give him more information about Elizabeth during the first intermission, and left it at that.

Olive had begun to realize that she enjoyed watching Howard watch televised hockey. His body contorted at some of the shots on goal, especially when he yelled at the referee's incompetence, which only seemed to trouble him when calls went against the Rangers. Thankfully there were no fights, so the first period passed quickly.

Howard reduced the volume again and asked Olive if she had known Elizabeth Billingsley well.

"I did. When I left your room last Sunday, the nursing station had just received a call from a hospital in the Adirondacks, advising of Elizabeth's death," Olive said quietly. "I was in shock; Elizabeth and I had spoken just a couple of days before."

Howard grimaced. "I'm so sorry, Olive. I didn't know Elizabeth since she was on another floor. So she'd been traveling up north, according to the aide?"

"Yes. Edgar Barnes took her to Lake George to meet someone who said she was Elizabeth's half-sister. Elizabeth was really excited about the idea."

"This is the same Barnes who met with me? That's strange, although it seems like a business to him, hooking up relatives through his website. Hmm."

The game resumed and Elizabeth could see that Howard was torn between continuing the discussion about Edgar Barnes and seeing whether the Rangers could break a scoreless tie. Olive motioned for him to increase the volume, deciding to continue the discussion during the second intermission. Both teams scored during the second period and it featured a lot of end-to-end action. Olive remarked about the players' fitness and Howard agreed.

During the next intermission, Olive asked Howard where he had lived on Long Island. He told her that technically he still lived there, assuming that his rehab allowed him to return home.

Olive blushed a little, as she hadn't meant to appear negative about his prognosis. "Sorry, I was just curious about Long Island, having never been there."

Howard apologized for his abrupt remark, because wanting to return home was a sore point with him.

"You remember Jean and Maggie from the hockey game last fall?" Olive asked.

"Those two would be pretty hard to forget!" Howard laughed.

"I've always wanted to visit Long Island, so they suggested renting a car for the day. I told them that you'd be a good tour guide since it's your old stomping grounds, and they think it's a great idea. We haven't set a date yet, but Saturday might make sense because there won't be as much commuter traffic. That's according to Maggie, anyway."

"I'd love to do that," Howard said. "I can buy you all lunch at this great little diner near my home. After Winnie died, I went there every morning for coffee, so the owners will be relieved to see I'm not dead yet. Can I chip in on the cost of the rental?"

"No. We've already got it covered," Olive said. "If you buy us lunch, that's a fair trade. So let's say we meet you by the front door at ten o'clock on Saturday? It's supposed to be sunny and mild."

"I'll be there. This is wonderful!"

At that moment, the game resumed, and Olive took the opportunity to bid Howard goodnight. She walked down the street for a while before returning to the apartment complex, not wanting to interrupt Jean and Maggie during the third period, but not really caring about the game either.

She thought about Howard and realized how much she liked him. He'd already told her so much about his beloved Winnie that she looked forward to traveling through the neighborhood in which Howard and Winnie spent the better part of their lives. She supposed that Howard might feel the same if she ever took him on a tour of her old farm in North Dakota. She flushed a little at the thought and headed back inside.

The game had three minutes left and the Flyers led 2-1, so Maggie and Jean were on the edge of their seats, hardly noticing when Olive walked through the door. Olive helped herself to a beer, knowing that she'd be in the apartment for at least a half hour following the game, telling them about Howard and planning the outing to Long Island. Despite the seriousness of what they planned to discuss with him on Long Island, she was excited at the prospect of another trip—especially with Howard.

Chapter 22

In the car, Maggie looked over at Howard, asking if he needed help buckling up. He told her that he wanted to try it himself, although it might take a few minutes. Usually impatient with any kind of delay, Maggie surprised both Jean and Olive by telling Howard to take his time; there was no hurry. As he slowly worked on his seat belt, Howard asked Maggie if she was familiar with the route to his home on Willow Street in Wantagh, about thirty miles away.

"Olive told me your home address, so I printed out directions from the internet, but if you'd point out major route changes, I'd really appreciate it," she told him.

Maggie's driving skills had improved with the ride to the Adirondacks, which pleased Olive because she didn't want Howard to be anxious. Maggie had a tendency to tailgate—probably because she refused to wear her glasses—and she drove too fast for Olive's comfort. But today, Maggie was a changed woman, with her glasses on and acceleration moderate. Olive sat back, relieved.

The ride began in silence until Jean asked Howard what he had done for a living, and Olive listened while he repeated some of the information she already knew. He described his work as a foreman in the meat packing plant, interrupting his monologue occasionally to point out a landmark along the route. He told them that, after returning from the war, he'd considered the GI bill, because he'd done well in high school and could have attended college. Being married, though, and wanting to start a family, he'd decided against college, reasoning that immediate employment and a chance to buy a home in the new Levitt developments springing up around Long Island would be best for Winnie and him.

"Besides, I felt restless after months of danger and the stress of combat, so I couldn't imagine sitting in a college classroom for three or four years," Howard explained. "Over time I've tried to make up for my lack of formal education by reading as much as possible. Winnie was a great reader, too, so we'd share our impressions of the same books. We always enjoyed sports together, but we liked going to museums and that sort of thing, too. She was such a wonderful woman." Howard started to tear up and then gruffly told them that the damn medication he was taking sometimes made him so emotional. "It's pretty embarrassing."

Olive leaned over and patted his shoulder while Jean jumped in with another quick question. "So, how come you like the Rangers instead of the Islanders? I mean, isn't the Coliseum right in your back yard?" she asked.

"Winnie and I used to watch the Islanders, especially during their glory years in the 1980s," he responded. "More recently, I began following the Rangers, and since it's easy to see them on cable, I've gotten to know the players better and just enjoy the games."

By this time they had merged onto the Grand Central Parkway East, heading toward eastern Long Island. Howard advised Maggie that the name would soon change to Northern Parkway East, and a few miles after that, she should look for Exit 33 to merge onto Wantagh State Parkway. Not long after that, Howard pointed to the Seaford exit, and within a few minutes, they were turning from Merrick Road onto Willow Street.

Olive told Howard that she was amazed at the similarity of the homes in the neighborhood. She was used to farmhouses back west, where no two were alike. Howard explained about the Levitt developments after World War II, which had allowed young veterans a chance to own small homes in the New York metropolitan area, a dream come true for so many veterans from the northeast who had grown up in apartments during the Great Depression.

They stopped in front of Howard's home while he continued his explanation. "Our original home looked like the home two doors down," he said, pointing out a small Cape-Cod-styled house. "When Winnie received a small inheritance three years into our marriage, we used it to add two dormers on the front of the home and one dormer spanning the back, turning the attic into space for three rooms and a bath. When we realized there would be no children, the extra space proved unnecessary, but we made the best of it by using one of the upstairs rooms as a sewing room for Winnie, where she could enjoy the elevated view from that room's windows, and we christened the extra bath the 'tub' room, because I used it to soak after a long day at work."

After helping Howard out of the vehicle, they walked toward his home. It was brick with white trim, and Olive remarked on the rose bushes in the tidy front yard. Howard's voice cracked a little when he described Winnie's skill at gardening.

As they walked up the sidewalk, a younger man opened the front door, calling out to Howard. He had already told the women that his tenant's name was Jake Smith, and that he was a college professor with a six-month contract at Hofstra University. Howard had telephoned him about the visit, hoping that he would be home that day to show the ladies around. Howard made the introductions and they all followed Smith into the house. The professor asked if they wanted coffee, but they all declined, not wanting to take up too much of his weekend.

Howard pointed out features in the home and the women were impressed with the color schemes, furniture, and wall decorations, all very tasteful; each of the women silently wondered whether the choices had been Winnie's, Howard's, or both. Howard pointed out the backyard and Olive could see a small garden space at the back next to a tool shed. Howard described how Winnie had set up the space each year, enlisting his help in planting and weeding. He told them how he couldn't wait for tomato season, because he took a whole tomato with his lunch each day.

"Along the shed Winnie used to grow sunflowers, which were pretty colorful," he said, gesturing to the area. "Then she'd harvest them and get the neighbor kids involved in picking out the seeds and roasting them in the oven, so each one could take a bag home. But I'm guessing the kids ate them before they ever got there." He chuckled and turned to the professor. "Jake, would you mind if the ladies took a brief look upstairs? I'm feeling stronger every day, but I don't want to attempt the climb just yet."

"No problem. I'll take them on a quick tour," the young professor said with a smile.

Olive enjoyed the view from the second floor, but felt a twinge of sadness when she peeked into Winnie's old sewing room. Howard must have left it unchanged as a memorial to her, or perhaps only from inertia. With the warmer weather, the backyard was green, and Olive could almost smell the earth, making her wish she still had a garden—albeit one much smaller than the one she grew on the farm. The garden size here was perfect.

Sighing, she joined the others as they walked downstairs.

Back in the car, Howard directed Maggie to the end of the street to show them the Jones Beach Hotel. According to Howard, the hotel was used as a military barracks during World War II and afterward fell into disuse, but was reopened as a European-style accommodation—spare, but pleasant and well-reviewed.

They proceeded downtown past several businesses, with Maggie following Howard's directions to Long Island Cheeseburger. "Howard, you definitely know the way to my heart!" she exclaimed as they pulled into the parking lot.

Inside, Howard was greeted warmly by the wait staff while the women found a place by a window. After they all ordered cheeseburgers and coffee, Jean and Howard began comparing the food offered in the dining room with the cuisine at the nursing home. Like Olive, Jean had begun to notice the repetition on the menu board, while Howard only scoffed, telling them that the poor nursing home patients were being served leftovers from the dining room. Olive thought this was highly unlikely, but she had to laugh.

Howard went on. "I miss eating fried onions and garlic in my food, and something I can sink my teeth into. And a little salt, please, for God's sake!" he exclaimed. "I know there are patients who don't have their own teeth and I know that my diet is restricted because of blood pressure, but my medication works fine, so some salt in my food won't kill me. Even though Winnie wasn't Italian, she made the best marinara sauce, ever! Lots of garlic, onion, basil, and other herbs, and she'd let it simmer and then freeze some of it for later. Fresh tomatoes from the garden— oh boy, I can still taste it!"

Howard had obviously piqued Maggie's Italian pride, because she gently grabbed his shoulder, sputtering, "Well, how about this, mister? In Winnie's memory, I'm going to cook you up some sauce next week and the four of us will have a spaghetti and meatball dinner at our apartment. Do you think your taste buds are up to the shock?"

"This cheeseburger will remind me what real food is all about, so I'll be ready," Howard laughed, sitting back so their plates could be put on the table.

They ate in relative silence, but when they finished, Jean told Howard they had something serious to discuss. Howard looked quizzically in Olive's direction, so she began her explanation. As Olive discussed the similarities in the deaths of Irma and Elizabeth, she could see Howard straighten in his chair. With a clenched jaw, he just nodded until she finished her narrative.

"So no one has caught this guy?" he demanded. "He's pretty clever, though, from what you've described. I'd like to nail him, too, so maybe I can help?"

All three women looked startled.

"No!" Maggie exclaimed. "We're only telling you about this to warn you, Howard. We don't want to put you in any danger. We're asking you to refuse any invitation from Barnes for travel of any kind. It's just not safe."

"I'll think about it. How about this? You feed me spaghetti and meatballs this Tuesday and I'll give you my answer then," Howard said. "I feel well enough to act as a guinea pig to trap this creep, but we have to come up with a plan. We can discuss it on Tuesday, but I don't want to talk about it anymore today. I'm enjoying this outing too much to worry about Edgar Barnes."

Olive was a bit taken aback by Howard's courage. She hadn't known he was going to react this way. She almost wondered if she shouldn't have told him, knowing that he was so enthusiastic about catching Barnes.

Following lunch, Howard directed Maggie toward Jones Beach State Park, which was about ten minutes away. The parking area near the beach was almost empty at that time of year, so Howard didn't have a particularly long walk to view the surf. The waves were a little wild that day. Howard explained that there was also a bay side of the park, but Olive, coming from North Dakota, stood mesmerized by the sight and sounds of the waves. Conscious that Howard might require some rest, Jean nudged Olive and they returned to the car.

Howard told Maggie to drive to the bay side so that he could show them the Nikon Amphitheater. Maggie remarked that she felt guilty for never having been to Jones Beach, even having lived in the city so long. They stopped to look at the amphitheater in the distance.

"The theater was really great in the old days." Howard grinned. "I took Winnie to see *South Pacific* once." He launched into a version of "Some Enchanted Evening," startling the women with the strength and quality of his voice.

He cleared his throat. "In recent years, it seems they don't have musicals anymore. There's music, or what they call music, anyway. A lot of retreads like you see in Atlantic City, but some decent shows too—you know, Jimmy Buffett, for instance. I'd like to go again sometime, just for old times' sake. Sitting in the amphitheater and looking at the stage with the water in the background is quite a view."

The women all made a mental note to search the Jones Beach website for acceptable offerings that summer so Howard could choose a performance. Looking at him, Maggie nodded to the others and suggested that they head home so Howard wouldn't miss his dinner. He laughed and agreed. Maggie began retracing their route, and luckily had her written directions, because Howard had begun to doze and she didn't want to disturb him.

He woke up with a start when they arrived in front of the nursing home entrance, complimenting Maggie on her smooth driving. She asked him to repeat his praise for the benefit of the naysayers in the back.

Passing through the front door, Howard was offered a wheelchair by one of the aides, but he refused, saying he could make it to his room. Olive accompanied him to ensure he returned to it safely.

"Are you going to do the Sunday crossword puzzle tomorrow?" she asked as they reached his room.

"Of course. And I don't want to try it without you, if you're free."

"Alright. I'll stop by after church. See you then."

As Olive turned to go, Howard took her hand and thanked her for the great day. Olive blushed and bade him a good evening.

Walking back to her apartment, she thought about Howard's desire to trap Barnes, and about the possible danger. At dinner she'd raise the issue with Jean and Maggie and get their thoughts, hoping that they'd agree to try and dissuade Howard from any plan he might devise.

Maggie called the rental company while Jean and Olive looked at the Jones Beach Theater website, curious about whether the summer entertainment had been booked yet. There was a partial line-up available, and as Howard predicted, it contained a lot of "nostalgia" acts featuring aged rock stars and crooners. They decided to check back a month or so later, hoping that additional performers were booked in the meantime.

After Maggie returned the car keys to the rental people, she joined the others for a drink before dinner. They decided on cocktails rather than wine, giving Jean a chance to dip into her well-stocked bar. She and Maggie usually preferred wine and beer to hard liquor, but she also said there was a time for cocktails, and when that time came, she wanted to be ready. Maggie was always ready for scotch, while Jean opted for rum and Coke. Olive, having first tried whiskey and ginger ale during her honeymoon in Winnipeg, had been partial to that Canadian favorite ever since. They toasted the nice afternoon with Howard, feeling good about giving him a break from the nursing home.

Olive shuddered, though. "I don't want Howard playing the hero and getting himself hurt, and I know him well enough to believe that he'll come up with some cockamamie plan which will put him in danger."

Jean shrugged. "He strikes me as pretty sensible, and he's a big boy, so at least let's hear him out," she said. "When he mentioned wanting to be a guinea pig, it got me thinking. I'm tempted to call Gerry Biggs, one of the fellows I remember from the force. He's a detective now, although he should be pretty close to retirement. Maybe he can tell me the name of someone on the Boston force we can contact when we get there, assuming that Howard goes through with his plan."

"What do you mean we, Jean, or am I missing something?" Olive gurgled.

Jean just shrugged again. "I'll bet you each twenty bucks that Howard suggests he accept the Boston invitation, knowing that they'll somehow try to kill him. If he wants to do that, there's no way I'm going to let him unless we tag along, or at least follow them. Assuming he has a cell phone, we can stay in contact. I mean, they'll have to let him go the bathroom by himself, won't they? Anyway, if I explain the problem to Gerry and he can set us up with a contact in Boston, we can call in the cavalry if things get hairy."

Even Maggie was skeptical. "So the NYPD and the Boston police are going to believe a story from three dotty broads about another old codger, and drop everything to ride to the rescue?" She snorted. "What actual proof do we have about any wrongdoing that's already occurred, let alone something that might happen? If you can set this up, then you have connections even the governor would envy."

Jean bristled. "Okay, okay. I'm not going to say anything to Gerry unless Barnes actually sets a date for Howard to travel. And if Howard accepts, we'll make sure he has Barnes confirm the hotel they're using, and that Howard tells Barnes he intends to call his doctor during the trip, something like that."

Olive just shook her head. "I think I'll have another drink."

Chapter 23

Howard refused Olive's request to discuss the Barnes matter during their Sunday crossword puzzling. He told her that he'd been thinking about it; he also winked, and told her he was a one-channel processor and could only concentrate on the crossword puzzle, so they should focus on that if they wanted to complete it before they both got old. Olive sighed, realizing that he would not be moved, resigning herself to wait for Tuesday's dinner. She decided not to mention Jean's plan either, not wanting to encourage him.

On Tuesday, Olive stopped by Maggie's before lunch and asked if she could help with the dinner preparations. The unmistakable aroma of garlic, onions, and herbs wafted through the apartment, making her mouth water.

Maggie grinned and told her to take a taste, although the sauce wouldn't reach its full goodness for a little while. Apparently Jean was making a salad, so Olive offered to buy bread and a bottle of wine. Maggie told her that she already had wine, but the bakery down the street made great cannoli, which would be a real treat for Howard. Olive promised to make those purchases after lunch.

"Ah, spaghetti, meatballs, salad, bread, and wine. That makes life worth living," Jean said, stepping into the kitchen.

Maggie added, "Don't forget the cannoli. Olive's picking some up when she buys the bread."

Jean sighed and gave Olive a little hug.

After a quick lunch, Olive walked down the street to buy the bread and dessert, knowing that her hair appointment on the second floor was scheduled for three o'clock.

Olive enjoyed having her hair washed. Not only was it relaxing, but being a widow, it was pleasant to experience any human touch, even something that mundane. As usual, the stylist extolled the virtues of hair coloring, but Olive was unmoved.

She had begun to gray around the age of fifty and had been tempted to correct it, but Bill had told her that he loved her natural look and convinced her to forget about coloring. He'd argued that he'd been almost bald for a few years and wasn't trying to hide it, so Olive had agreed to not color her hair. By the time Bill died, Olive's hair was fully gray, going on white, but it had developed into a look that she liked, so she always resisted anyone's attempt to change her mind, and just brushed it daily to maintain its luster. That day, she also wanted it trimmed, because it was getting a little ragged around the edges.

Olive decided to swing by Jean and Maggie's to drop off the bread and cannoli after her hair appointment. She would still have time to change into something more presentable before walking to the nursing home to pick up Howard. She knocked and Maggie yelled to come in, but when she entered, she realized that Maggie must be in the bathroom, so she simply set her parcels on the counter and left, assuming that Maggie would figure things out.

Going through her closet, Olive chose a sleeveless tailored grey-blue dress which looked nice with her hair, and decided to put on grey pumps rather than sandals. Bill had given her pearl earrings for their thirtieth wedding anniversary, and looking in the mirror, she saw that they complimented the dress. She knew that Maggie and Jean would tease her, but she felt like dressing up a little for Howard.

Olive arrived at Howard's room a few minutes to five. He was sitting in the wheelchair already, dressed in black trousers, a starched white shirt, and a striped tie. He was holding a bottle of wine and some daffodils.

"I hope Maggie likes flowers. Something for the cook, you know," he chuckled.

Olive laughed, telling Howard that Maggie would be shocked and pleased by his thoughtfulness. As she went to take hold of the wheelchair, Howard looked at her appreciatively, remarking on her dress and earrings. Olive quickly moved past him to disguise the blush which had risen up her neck, and, taking hold of the chair handles at the rear, thanked him for the compliment.

As they were leaving the room, some young aide called out, asking if they were going on a date, and this time there were blushes all round.

Olive guided the chair to the tunnel connecting the two buildings and then caught the elevator to her floor. Knocking on the apartment door, Olive stationed the chair for easy entrance and Jean appeared, holding the door open for both of them.

"Why, you shouldn't have!" Maggie grinned as she gave Howard a peck on the cheek, graciously accepting his gift bottle of wine. She told Howard that she intended to offer everyone a cocktail.

He enthusiastically ordered a scotch, while the women reprised their choices of the other night.

They settled themselves around the living room, with Howard's chair to one side, creating a comfortable circle. Not surprisingly, Maggie opened with a comment on the Rangers, with Jean and Howard joining in. While Olive had little to offer, she enjoyed being part of the group, although with the playoffs approaching, she hoped that the four of them could still find some interests in common other than hockey. But then again, she thought ruefully, by the time the hockey playoffs ended, baseball season would be in full swing. Oh, well.

They finished their cocktails and Olive moved Howard toward the dinner table while Maggie and Jean set out the salad and wine. The bread had been cut and put in a basket next to the place reserved for Howard.

"If you all don't mind, I'm just going to serve individual plates," Maggie said, "but there's lots of food for seconds if you're hungry."

Serving Howard first, Maggie stood back and watched with the others while he bent over to enjoy the aroma before actually tasting the meal. It then occurred to Olive that she'd never seen Howard eat food which required cutting, wondering whether she should offer to help him. He obviously caught her look of concern, because he just smiled and told them that he'd gotten much better with utensils, but if he had a problem he'd holler, because he wasn't going to let any infirmity get in the way of a great meal.

His comment lightened the moment and Jean was relieved to propose a toast to great Italian food. Maggie told Howard that even if Winnie's sauce bettered hers, he had a duty as her guest to lie and pronounce hers the best, ever.

With that, they all dug in, murmuring their appreciation to the chef, and slurping a little as they almost inhaled the sauce-laden noodles.

The women glanced at each other as the dinner was ending, wondering when Howard would share his thoughts on Edgar Barnes. Perhaps he'd decided against pursuing the matter, which would have pleased Olive in particular. However, as Maggie set out coffee cups and cannoli, Howard cleared his throat, asking whether they were ready to discuss the issue at hand. They all nodded somewhat glumly.

"Cheer up! I've got a plan," he said, a twinkle in his eye. "Firstly, I should let you know that Barnes called me yesterday. He told me that John Case, my long lost relative, plans to visit Boston in about two weeks and wants to meet me. Barnes rather coincidentally plans to attend a legal seminar on the same weekend, and as luck would have it, the Red Sox also play at home. I asked him whether it might be too early in the season to sit through a ball game, but he assures me that everything will be fine. Oh, to have his optimism, I guess."

"How is he proposing to get you there?" Olive asked, clearly concerned.

"He told me that he intends to drive, since it's less than four hours. Apparently he has a big car and a driver, so that allows him to work during travel. He asked me to bring along my financial documents and my current will, because he's offered to review them for free. He's even going to bring a wheelchair in case I get tired during all the excitement."

To the women, this scenario sounded all too familiar.

Jean just shook her head. "Have you seen a photo of this relative yet?" she asked. "We're concerned that this Matthew Forman person will pose as John Case, or whatever name he gave you, and then they'll try to poison you or something during the trip."

"Does Barnes know whether you take any medications?" Maggie demanded. "He managed to give Irma a barbiturate overdose somehow, and he did the same thing to poor Elizabeth with insulin."

"Well, given that I have a heart condition, he's probably guessed that I take Digitalis, and since my stroke, I also take Coumadin as a blood thinner," Howard said. "I suspect he'll want to feed me Digoxin. It's really toxic in larger quantities, and he might also try to withhold my blood thinner. That sounds like his M.O."

Olive shuddered. "This is giving me the creeps.! Howard, you can't be serious about taking the trip, knowing what Barnes probably has in store for you."

"Actually, knowing about Irma and Elizabeth gives me the confidence to catch Barnes in the act," Howard said. "I'll insist on my own room, and if he tries to offer me orange juice—like you said he was giving Irma—I'll just decline it, and I'll make sure that any water I drink comes from unopened bottles. He doesn't seem the type to try brute force, especially since bruises will raise suspicion. I can take my cell phone with me to report to one of you periodically, and if I feel like I'm in danger, I'll call the police."

Maggie, Jean, and Olive shook their heads in unison. This was a ridiculous plan.

Jean spoke first. "No way, buster! We're going to follow you to Boston, but before you leave, I'm calling a detective I know with the NYPD to ask if he has a contact in Boston we can speak to beforehand. I still don't like this idea, but it may be our only opportunity to close down Barnes' operation."

They all pulled out their cell phones so that Howard could exchange his number with each of them, and although he could call any one of them, they agreed that he should first try Jean's number in the event of an emergency. Howard had Barnes' cell phone number already, so he passed that on to the women. He agreed to insist that Barnes give him the name and telephone number of the Boston hotel, using Howard's physician as the excuse. He also promised to get more details about the itinerary, again to supposedly convince his physician about the trip.

It was approaching nine o'clock when Howard mentioned the witching hour, as he called it, so Olive began pushing his chair toward the door. He thanked them all, and then asked if they liked Chinese food. They laughed and nodded in response.

"How about next Monday we meet here again and I'll buy some Chinese take-out," he suggested. "They're probably only having mystery meat at the nursing home that night, so take-out will be a welcome change for me. By then I should have more information and it'll give Jean a chance to talk to the detective."

The women nodded. Once Barnes told Howard the name of the hotel, Maggie could confirm it and then book a room for the three of them. They'd also scope out directions in Boston, first to the World War II museum and then to Fenway Park, assuming that Barnes actually planned to take Howard to the game.

Olive took Howard back to his room, enduring the titter of the young aide who'd seen them earlier. Leaving Howard to the aide's tender mercies, Olive walked back to her apartment.

She had trouble falling asleep, imagining the final hours for both Irma and Elizabeth, and speculating on Barnes' plans for Howard. She agreed that Barnes probably would avoid outright violence, fearing detection, but he was clearly a cold, unscrupulous creep, and Howard shouldn't be blasé in dealing with him. Rather than getting out of bed, Olive turned her mind to more pleasant thoughts, remembering Howard's home on Long Island and the vacant garden in the backyard. She fell asleep soon after.

On Wednesday morning, Jean called Gerry Biggs' precinct, but was told that he was out of town at a conference until the end of the week. She didn't want to discuss the Barnes' matter with anyone else, so she left a message.

She sat back for a while, trying to think of various contingencies for the plan. Assuming that Barnes did threaten Howard during the trip, would Howard be able to call her? Assuming that Howard was able to call her, would the Boston police react, and if so, what evidence could Howard provide of any threatened or actual attempt to kill him? Should she ask Gerry whether Howard could be fitted with a wire? That idea made Jean laugh. She'd obviously been watching too many movies.

Nevertheless, she'd discuss the issue with Biggs to ensure that Howard faced only minimal danger. She liked the old coot and could see that Olive really liked him and that he liked her back, so Jean wanted this to go as smoothly as possible.

The women met again for lunch that day in the dining room. Turkey vegetable soup had indeed found its way onto the lunch menu, but all of them were in the mood for it, and were also pleasantly surprised at the hot corned beef on rye to accompany it. The chef had thoughtfully placed two or three types of mustard on each table, so Maggie immediately reached for the hottest one possible.

Jean told them about her call to the precinct and they discussed the car rental. Olive wished that Barnes would travel by train, because it would be easier to keep track of him, but Jean said they had to assume that once they were on the Interstate, they could pick up his trail. Jean offered to drive, but both Maggie and Olive were adamant that Maggie do it.

Olive glared at her sister. "I don't want you taking driving lessons on the way to Boston, and besides, Howard plans to call your cell phone in an emergency, so you have to be free to take the call," she said. "If we take a trip this summer, you'll have plenty of time to play Mario Andretti."

Maggie turned to Olive. "I want you to tell Howard that Jean wasn't able to speak to Biggs yet," she said. "Could you go to the nursing home and ask Howard to call Jean as soon as he finds out the name and location of the hotel? She should have this information when Biggs calls her at the end of the week."

Olive nodded; Maggie's idea made sense. She felt a bit better now that she had something to do regarding the whole Barnes plan, but she still felt uneasy about the whole thing. Surely it was better for Howard to not be involved with such a dangerous man.

After lunch, Olive took a walk to clear her head. She needed to take stock. Her harmonica efforts had fallen by the wayside and she'd been reluctant to meet any new patients at the nursing home. She knew that Irma and Elizabeth had appreciated her visits and she was aware of three new admissions who might gain something by meeting someone new, but she still felt raw about their deaths, and worried that she might be too emotional to bring any cheer to new patients.

Then it occurred to her that she could do at least one thing. She walked back to the nursing home, waving at Bea Jones as she went into the business office.

Greeting Olive with a smile, Bea called her over. "We've missed you in the past couple of weeks," she said. "There are three new patients who could probably use a visit. Their files are in the front of the cabinet if you want to take a look."

Olive thanked her and began reviewing the files. The new patients were all women, two of them not much older than she, for heaven's sake. Health was such a curious thing. However, she was pleased to see that all three women had family living locally, so they would be spared the attentions of Edgar Barnes. She made a note of their names and rooms, vowing to drop in on at least one of them following her visit with Howard.

When Olive peeked into his room, she found it empty, although the television was on. She didn't want to enter in case he was using the bathroom. Instead, she dropped by the nursing station and told Elfrieda that she'd brought him some licorice.

"Howard's physiotherapy was changed from ten o'clock this morning to one o'clock, but he should be along shortly," Elfrieda explained after consulting a chart on the wall.

She had no sooner finished saying so when Olive spotted Howard being wheeled toward his room, looking worn out and grumpy. He brightened considerably when he noticed Olive, motioning her toward his room.

"I can come another time if you want to rest," Olive offered.

"No. I'm glad you came. The folks in physio are a mean bunch." Smiling ruefully, Howard said loudly, "The better I get the more awful they get. It's cruel and unusual punishment, I tell you."

The aide pushing him just laughed, telling Olive that Howard went through this routine daily after physio, but that he wouldn't miss it for the world. Waiting in the hall until Howard was settled in bed, Olive crept into the room somewhat cautiously. Howard grinned, telling her that his outburst was really for effect; he very well acknowledged that the exercises had made him noticeably stronger than when he'd begun them a few months before. Olive had to agree, because he appeared much better on the trip to Long Island compared with their evening at the hockey game the previous October.

Howard told Olive that he had some news. "I called Barnes this morning and told him that my doctor will allow me to take the trip if I can give him an itinerary to evaluate the amount of activity I'm facing, and also to confirm the hotel and its location," he told her. "Barnes hemmed and hawed, saying he hadn't been able to work all that out yet, but I told him there is no use talking about the trip until I have the specifics for my doctor, so he told me he'd call back. Could you hand me my cell phone?"

Olive found the phone in the bedside table and Howard checked it for messages.

"Ha! Looks like he wants this to happen, alright," Howard crowed. "He left a message while I was in rehab, so I'll call him while you're here, if that's okay."

Olive nodded and waited for Howard to make the call. He began speaking with Barnes, motioning for Olive to get him a pen and paper from the table. There was a small notebook, and she signaled to him that she would write the information he got from Barnes as he received it. It took a few minutes to jot down the text of the call, and when Howard clicked off the phone, they both laughed.

"Wow, Barnes has been a busy fellow. So we're staying near Fenway Park by the look of things," Howard remarked.

Olive read her notes back to Howard to confirm the details. Barnes planned to pick Howard up at ten o'clock a week from that Friday for the drive to Boston. Howard's relative was supposed to fly into Boston early that morning. They all would meet later that afternoon for cocktails and dinner, allowing Howard and Case to get acquainted before the weekend's activities began.

Barnes' driver would take Howard and Case to the museum on Saturday while Barnes attended his seminar, and they would dine again later in the day. On Sunday they would enjoy the Red Sox afternoon game before driving back to Queens.

Howard chuckled when Olive read the part about Barnes bringing a nurse along for his safety.

"Oh, I'm sure she'll do everything she can to make me feel safe," he scoffed. "Let's see, orange juice whether I need it or not?"

"This isn't funny, Howard. I'm still really worried about you," Olive protested.

"Don't be. I promise I'll have my wits about me at all times. I plan to only nurse whatever cocktail I'm offered and I'll watch what I eat. I'll have the Digitalis and Coumadin in my pocket so they can't tamper with that."

Olive could see that Howard should have a little nap before dinner, so she presented him with his licorice and told him she'd pass his information on to Jean. She figured she had enough time to visit a new patient, but finding the room empty, Olive promised herself to return the following day.

Arriving at her floor back at the complex, Olive spotted Jean, caught up with her, and suggested that they all meet to discuss Howard's Boston itinerary. Jean grimaced when she heard about nurse Betty's inclusion in the trip, but said little other than that.

After dinner, Olive decided to walk back to the nursing home, thinking she should visit at least one of the new patients. She was heartened to see that all three appeared to have visitors, so she popped in to check on Howard again. He quickly set down his newspaper when he realized it was Olive at the door.

"Come in, come in, my dear!" he hollered. Olive laughed and pulled up a chair.

"Jean and Maggie are headed for their bowling league so I planned to introduce myself to the new patients, but was glad to find them all occupied," Olive explained.

"I never got into bowling," Howard said. "Too loud. Pool was more my game, and Winnie was good at it too. The VFW lounge had a great table and sometimes they sponsored tournaments. Do you play pool, Olive?"

"No. Jean tried to show me but I haven't been able to practice. There's a table in the rec room in our complex, if you'd like to give me a lesson sometime," she said.

Howard said he would love to, so they agreed to a game the next day. Olive asked him if he was steady enough on his feet for pool, and Howard thought he could do it. He pointed to the tripod cane in the corner. He'd used a regular cane on their trip to Long Island, so Olive looked at him quizzically.

"I just used the regular cane on the Long Island trip because there were three of you to help, but when I go to Boston I want more stability, so I also have this one," he explained. "Actually, playing pool with you will be a good test for using it. I'll have you walk with the wheelchair beside me, so if I get tired I can always get back into the chair. Before lunch I wandered up and down the hallway with the cane. The nurses were so dang proud of me."

When Olive returned to her apartment, she tried some stretching exercises and then drifted into a nap on the couch. She was awakened by a knock on the door and sprang up, a little disoriented, only then realizing that she'd fallen asleep.

She let Jean and Maggie into the apartment, scampering to the bathroom to freshen up, hearing hoots of "sleeping beauty" behind her.

Olive told Maggie and Jean about the pool match she'd scheduled with Howard the following day, which pleased them both.

"The more Howard exercises and walks around, the less I'll worry about him in Boston," Maggie said. "And that cane you mentioned sure is a good idea. The steadier he is on his pins, the less monkey business for Barnes to try. Jean, I hope Biggs calls you soon as he returns to the precinct on Friday."

"Oh, that reminds me," Olive interjected. "Howard told me that he called the Boston hotel and confirmed the reservation. There are three rooms under Barnes' name, so it looks like he'll have his privacy anyway. He'll want to call us without locking himself in the bathroom, so at least that part's okay. I still don't have a very good feeling about this, though."

Maggie patted her arm. "Once Jean gets the name of a Boston cop from Biggs, things should fall into place, so don't lose any sleep over this," she said. "I'm sure once we've got the whole thing planned out, it'll go off without a hitch."

Olive could only hope she was right.

The following day found Olive and Howard looking at the pool table in Flushing Village's basement. The walk from Howard's room had been slow, but he'd appeared confident with his cane and they chatted while Olive wheeled the chair beside him, asking occasionally if he preferred to ride. He leaned on it a couple of times when they stopped, but otherwise arrived at the recreation room in good condition.

Olive started to put the balls in the triangle, but Howard stopped her. He showed her the pattern of alternating striped and solid colored balls within the frame, leaving the black eight ball in the center of it. Before beginning play, Howard asked Olive to describe the game so that he could correct any misinformation she may have received. Satisfied with her answers, he suggested she take a couple of shots on the white cue ball to ensure she could make consistent contact.

"Not bad for a first timer," he remarked as she practiced. "I don't know whether I'm strong enough to break out the balls, so why don't you give it a try? Just focus on making contact with the cue ball initially, and the rest will take care of itself."

Olive clapped when her cue ball sent some of the other balls around the table, spreading them out as she had seen Jean do in the Adirondacks. Since no ball had gone in a pocket, it was Howard's turn, and he aimed for the solid blue two ball. Olive immediately recognized his skill, and admired it.

Howard braced himself carefully before each shot and was able to use surprising force when the shot demanded it, and Olive could see his confidence grow with each turn. They chatted a little, but like her days with Bill, she just enjoyed the moment and didn't clutter it with unnecessary blather.

After six games, with Howard leading four to two, Olive put her cue in the wall rack, signaling to Howard that it was time to go. "I don't want your nurses angry with me for tiring you, or at least that's my story, given that you beat me handily," she exclaimed.

"Yes, I suppose I shouldn't overdo it," Howard sighed. "But thanks, Olive, that was fun. If you're free on Saturday, I'd love to do this again; I don't have any physio that day."

Olive agreed, telling him Jean hoped to talk to Biggs on Friday, so maybe she'd have some news to report by then.

After accompanying Howard to his room, Olive remembered she had precious little cash, so she ran to the bank before it closed. She recalled enjoying the whiskey and ginger ale at Jean's, so she bought some diet ginger ale and licorice at the market before stopping at the liquor store on the way back to her apartment.

Olive knocked on Jean's door, asking if she wanted to try the whiskey. Jean declined, but told Olive to come in anyway.

While Olive constructed her cocktail, Jean poured herself a scotch. It gave both of them the chance to reminisce a little, and they found themselves giggling at childhood foibles and high school lore. They had just rinsed out their glasses when Maggie returned from the hair stylist's, so they headed to the dining room.

"Well, I think the chef shot the bolt with last night's creativity," Maggie sighed. "This must be cholesterol night or something."

They stared glumly at the menu board, trying to decide between chicken tenders with fries, salmon croquettes with fries, or hamburgers with fries.

"Maybe it's kids' night," Olive ventured, not sure what to do. "I've never seen it like this before. I guess I'll try the salmon croquettes, although it's probably made from last night's poached salmon. No, you know, on second thought, it's Thursday, so the grocery store is open late. I'm going to buy us three little steaks and I can bake potatoes in the microwave. Jean, if you have any salad fixings, you can make one up while I'm gone, and Maggie, I think there's bread left over from Tuesday. You can just heat the bread in my oven for a couple of minutes while I cook the steak. I'll buy some mushrooms to go with it, too."

Jean jumped up, grabbing Olive and giving her a little push. "You are a temptress, my dear. We'll be waiting for you."

Olive couldn't help laughing as she made her way to the store. By necessity, life on the farm didn't allow much spontaneity in the kitchen. She'd cooked a lot of meals, and during harvest season they had to be done exactly on time so that she could send the men out to finish their work. To be able to run across the street for ingredients for a meal that could be cooked in under twenty minutes was exhilarating, so Olive was almost a little breathless when she came back and unlocked the door to her apartment.

She gave Jean a call and they arrived at her apartment a couple of moments later. She told them to look through the movies she'd recorded to see if any suited their fancy. Olive had been careful to go through the guide every morning, recording some films which she thought they could all enjoy. Maggie spotted *Casablanca* and convinced Jean that it was worth seeing again. When Olive heard Maggie begin mimicking some of the characters, repeating their lines verbatim, she rolled her eyes at Jean, who mouthed, "Careful what you wish for."

Olive knew she could fry up a great steak and watched Jean attack it. Between bites, Jean told Olive that she was a great chef.

Maggie grimaced when Olive told them about her six-game pool match with Howard. "I just hope he doesn't overdo it. He has to be rested and strong for the Boston trip," she said.

Olive shrugged. "He looked fine. We walked slowly and he carried on a conversation, so I don't think he was winded by the activity."

She still didn't want him to go to Boston, but she kept that thought to herself.

Chapter 24

Jean was jumpy all day Friday. She wanted to talk to Gerry Biggs as soon as possible, but she understood that he probably had to catch up on department matters before returning her call. Her message had been brief so maybe he thought it was a social call, not giving it much priority.

By four o'clock Jean couldn't stand the suspense, so she placed a second call. On the third ring, the detective picked up. After the usual greetings, Jean gave Biggs a summary of the Barnes matter.

He listened quietly during her narrative, continuing his silence well after she'd finished. At first Jean thought that the line had gone dead, but when she spoke his name, he responded.

"Yeah, I'm here," he grunted. "I'm just trying to get my head around what you're telling me. Let's see. A local attorney killed two old ladies but neither the nursing home here in Queens nor the hospital in the Adirondacks suspected foul play, and now you think this Barnes guy is going after an old gent friend of yours. I dunno, Jean. I'm not sure what we have to go on if we're trying to tail him. I don't want to call someone on the Boston force and look like a fool if nothing comes of it."

"I know it sounds crazy, Gerry, but could you just call someone up there and give me a name and number to call if something does come up?" Jean pleaded. "We're booking ourselves into the same hotel and hopefully we can stay in contact with Howard by cell phone. We'll only call your Boston contact if there's an emergency."

Biggs paused again. "I'm not sure I like that either, Jean," he said. "Let's say this Barnes guy is desperate. You say he has a driver who's a big guy. That might not be the safest place for you to be. Why don't I call my contact in Boston and give him Howard's phone number? You won't have to go to Boston and put yourself in the middle of it that way."

"We promised Howard we'd be there for him!" she protested.

"Jean, mind if I ask you a personal question? How old are you and how old are your two friends? I'm guessing around seventy? Tell you what I'll do. Before I leave on vacation after work today, I'll call Boston and then I'll call you back. Hopefully within the next half hour or so." With that, Biggs hung up.

Jean clicked off and sat down, a little dejected. Hearing some noise at the door, she looked up to see Olive and Maggie, with four raised eyebrows between them. She'd just begun to explain what had happened when her phone rang again.

She answered and heard the sound of Biggs' voice once more.

"Jean, do you have a pen and paper handy?" he asked. "The fellow I tried to reach is named Lorne Spector. His phone went to voicemail, so I tried to give him a decent message, and I also left him my phone number. Problem is that my wife and I leave for fishing in the wilds of New Hampshire soon, and I won't have my phone on. No phone contact is a promise I make to her each trip. Here's Lorne's number, and I've also given him yours, so maybe he'll call you before your friend leaves for Boston. All I can do, Jean, is plead that you and your posse stay home. You can't do any good up there and you may get hurt. Do you read me?"

Jean told Biggs that she read him loud and clear, thanking him for his help. She told him she'd give Lorne's number to Howard and would give Howard's number to Lorne, provided she was able to speak to him before Howard's departure. Wishing Biggs a wonderful vacation, she clicked off.

"Jeez!" she exclaimed after she hung up.

Maggie and Olive glanced at each other, realizing that the call had not gone well. After Jean recounted Biggs' advice, they all just shook their heads. It was only a week until Barnes would set his plan in motion, whatever it was, and they felt totally unprepared.

They knew they required an actual contact in Boston. If Barnes began making threats, a general 911 call wouldn't work. Jean knew that a dispatcher wouldn't understand Howard's situation, and she understood Biggs' concern regarding their ability to intervene. She wondered whether they should just call the whole thing off. It was Howard's decision, but hopefully he would understand.

Olive resolved to convince Howard to call off the plan on Monday when they met for Chinese food. In the meantime, she would just enjoy playing pool and doing the crossword with him. She didn't want the Barnes thing to take over their whole lives—just as much as she didn't want it to be the end of Howard's. She couldn't imagine how she would live with herself if something happened to him at this point, given how she felt about him.

By noon on Monday, Jean was beside herself. Knowing that she couldn't reach Biggs and not wanting to bother Spector, she could only pace and mutter. When she stopped in the laundry room that morning it was already full, so she couldn't even use that as a diversion.

Maggie was at a dental appointment and Olive had resumed her volunteering at the nursing home. Jean doubted whether either of them would be free to meet in the dining room, so she began making a sandwich for lunch. She was sorely tempted to pour herself a glass of wine, but told herself that would be silly. Luckily, ESPN was running highlights from the previous night, so Jean took her plate into the living room and ate on the couch.

Her phone rang a little after one o'clock and she lunged for it, letting out a huge breath when Detective Spector identified himself. Jean gave him the same narrative she had given Biggs, and not surprisingly, Spector was similarly wary.

"Ma'am, are you Mr. Kenner's daughter?" he asked.

"No. He lives in the nursing home next to our apartment complex. The two ladies who died also lived there." Jean was becoming annoyed; she thought she'd already explained that, loud and clear. She kept her voice calm, though, realizing that Spector probably had her pegged as an elderly busybody who would just be a nuisance to his department.

"So Mr. Kenner will travel to Boston this Friday with this Mr. Barnes, who is an attorney?" Spector asked.

Jean was beginning to grit her teeth. Spector kept asking her questions which she'd already answered, and she got the definite feeling that he was trying to downplay any possible danger for Howard.

He finally told her that, yes, he was willing to take down Howard's number, and, yes, it was alright if Howard had his, but he still wasn't sure if he could assist, given that nothing had been done to Mr. Kenner and that even Jean agreed no threats had yet been made. He ended the call by telling Jean that he was very busy with other investigations, giving her a number to pass along to Mr. Kenner.

Jean clicked off her phone and sat back, deflated. She had hoped that Spector would take their concerns more seriously, but his reluctance only made her more fearful of Howard's plan. Jean had promised Biggs that she and the others wouldn't go to Boston, but she realized they had no choice. Someone had to watch out for Howard, if only to call the police in the event the trip took a dangerous turn.

Howard was expected that night for Chinese food, but Jean wanted to discuss Spector's call with Olive and Maggie before then. She called Olive's cell phone, not sure whether Olive intended to remain at the nursing home prior to wheeling Howard over for the meal.

"Hi, it's me," Jean said when her sister picked up. "Sorry to call if you're in the middle of visiting a patient, but I have to talk to you and Maggie before we meet with Howard."

She listened while Olive confirmed that she was meeting with a patient, but would be free in half an hour. This worked well, as Maggie should have returned by then.

Fifteen minutes later, Jean heard Maggie whistling as she came down the hall.

"Have you had lunch?" Jean asked her. "We have some salami in the fridge for a sandwich, and I think you might enjoy a beer as well."

By the time Olive arrived, Maggie had finished her sandwich and both she and Jean were sipping beer together. Olive looked at them as she entered and went directly to the fridge, retrieving a cold one for herself.

"So, what's up?" Olive asked, popping open her beer.

Jean recounted her call from Spector, and wondered what they should do.

Olive knew that Howard was determined to go to Boston, but perhaps they could work on him that night and dissuade him. "So we're agreed that if refuses to call off the trip, we'll follow him to Boston?" she asked.

Jean and Maggie both nodded.

"Okay. That's fine with me," Olive said. "Howard will probably bring his cell phone tonight, so let's give him that other police number. Let's also try to sort out a plan in case we can't convince him to give it up, and make notes to review with Howard. He may also have some suggestions on how to proceed."

Olive had brought along the itinerary which Barnes had given Howard, so Jean called the hotel in Boston to make reservations. During the call, she mentioned that their friends, Howard Kenner and Edgar Barnes, also had reservations, and they wanted to stay as close to them as possible. Both Olive and Maggie gave a thumbs up to Jean's ingenuity, hoping that there was a room available on the same floor. As luck would have it, the reservations clerk was able to book them into a room only two doors away from Howard's.

Jean took down the information from the clerk. "Oh, good!" she cried. "We're all planning on going to the Red Sox game on Sunday, so we want to be near each other in the hotel. So we're in room 703? And you said Howard Kenner is in 707? I think he and Edgar, Mr. Barnes, planned to book adjacent rooms? Oh, yes. Edgar's in room 709? And it's an adjoining room too? Hmm. Howard hadn't mentioned that. Well, thank you for your help, and we'll see you on Friday. Have a nice day."

The three women just looked at each other. This was not good. Barnes had cleverly arranged for adjoining rooms, while telling Howard that he would have his own accommodation. Hopefully there was a lock on Howard's side, but interior doors in adjoining rooms probably weren't that secure. They could discuss this with him that night.

Maggie brought out a Boston street guide that she had bought on the way to her dentist. Their hotel was listed in it, allowing the women to trace its proximity to Fenway Park and the World War II museum, which was a little out of town.

Maggie whistled. "I can probably drive to the museum, which appears to have some parking according to the website," she said, "but there's no way we can drive to Fenway."

"Is there any point in going to Fenway anyway?" Olive asked. "We don't have tickets, and even if we did, how will we find Howard in such a crowd?"

Jean started to chuckle. "My dear, you can always get tickets. There are these helpful people called scalpers who wait near the stadium, and for their mere five hundred percent profit, depending on the popularity of the visiting team, you give these people all your money and they give you tickets. It works out rather well—for them."

Making a face, Olive continued her questioning. "Okay. So we get into the game. Then what?"

Maggie looked at Jean. "I'll take this one," she said, rolling her eyes. "Olive, you know the cell phone you carry around? It works in a stadium too. Howard can ask Edgar's driver to wheel him to the entrance of the men's room so that Howard can walk inside to use the facilities. He can call us from there and give us the location of their seats. It should work."

Olive nodded slowly. "We're counting on a lot of things going according to plan, aren't we?" she murmured.

Maggie and Jean shrugged in agreement and they all fell silent, trying to think through the various ramifications.

Jean began pecking away at the computer. She discovered that the Red Sox were hosting Cleveland, and told Olive that tickets would be more easily purchased; the Indians were much less of a rival than the New York Yankees. She also searched the hotel's website, and then printed out the emailed reservation. "Anything else I should look up?" she asked.

Maggie, who was studying the street guide, looked up and gave Jean the address of the museum so that she could input it along with the hotel address. Jean then printed out driving directions, giving them to Maggie to keep in her pocketbook.

"Can you check the weather forecast for the weekend?" Olive asked Jean. "We should let Howard know whether he has to bundle up for the game. That's one good thing about the rental car, we can throw in extra clothing in case we need it."

Jean showed Olive the weather forecast; it turned out to be surprisingly favorable.

The women then discussed whether Olive should acknowledge Howard if they happened to pass by each other in the hotel lobby. Would that be enough for Barnes to call off whatever plan he might have? Would Howard want Barnes to call off the plan? They agreed they should discuss the issue with Howard that night. They weren't sure whether either Olive or Howard were good enough actors to pretend they didn't know each other. Since no other wrinkles came to mind, they parted for a couple of hours prior to dinner.

When Olive entered Howard's room at five o'clock, he again was ready in his wheelchair. This time he'd forgone a tie, wine, and flowers. Olive was not surprised; he was paying for dinner, after all, and having gotten to know Maggie and Jean much better, he probably felt he needn't be so formal. Olive was wearing blue jeans herself.

Arriving at the women's apartment, Howard smiled when he accepted a scotch, and sighed a little after his first sip. "This is good stuff. Single malt is the only way to go," he said appreciatively. "Do you all want to talk about the Boston trip now, or wait until after dinner?"

Maggie spoke up. "I had a sandwich earlier, but I'm still pretty hungry. Besides, delivery will be quicker if we order before six o'clock, so unless anyone is violently opposed, I say let's eat first." With that, she took out the menu and passed it over to Howard. He noted pencil marks beside three of the dishes and asked if these were their favorites.

"They are," Maggie responded. "But it's your treat, so we're willing to try something new."

"Well, why don't we try hot and sour soup first?" he suggested. "Winnie and I always enjoyed it, and I just crave pungent, spicy food after so many months on the nursing home diet. You've marked pork lo mein, which I like. Garlic prawns also sound good. Since there are four of us, let's add in chicken fried rice and egg foo young. They make good leftovers, too, if you ladies are watching a movie later."

Maggie grinned ear to ear, knowing that Howard had found his way to her heart. She took the menu and made a quick call, figuring that they could finish their cocktails by the time the food arrived. Jean had already put out plates, bowls, spoons, and chopsticks, along with glasses for beer or water.

Rather than mention Boston outright, Maggie asked Howard if he had caught the Rangers' game.

In answer he threw up his hands. "These referees have been reached!" he cried.

Olive smiled a little as Jean launched into an even more vitriolic description of the officials. Olive looked over to see Maggie watching her, and they both shrugged at Howard's passion for the game.

The cartons of food soon arrived and Jean started to transfer the contents into bowls, but Howard stopped her, saying they should just use the cartons and not bother dirtying any more dishes. He walked over to the table to sit down, foregoing the wheelchair, and Olive could see why. Even though Howard was a tall man, the chair put him somewhat lower at the table, which couldn't be all that comfortable for eating.

He now sat tall, and took hold of his soup spoon, murmuring at the taste of the spicy broth. The soup was a first for Olive, so she was a little tentative in taking a sip. She declared it delicious, while the spicy heat started tears all around the table.

They enjoyed a leisurely dinner, discussing dim sum and other Asian foods, and noting the increase in the number of Thai restaurants in the past decade. As he'd done with Olive in their early meetings, Howard recounted some funny food stories from overseas trips he and Winnie had taken, and had Maggie and Jean collapsing in laughter.

After dinner, they returned to the living room and let Jean bring Howard up-to-date. He nodded when she told him about the call from Detective Spector, taking out his cell phone to input the numbers which Spector had given Jean. He began shaking his head when he heard about the adjoining hotel rooms, his eyes narrowing at the thought of Barnes' manipulations.

"Actually, Winnie and I were put in one accidentally once and you can lock them on each side, so that's what I'll do," he told Jean. "I might even try to drag a chair over and just put it in front of the door. We'll see. I can always call housekeeping pretending I need some more toilet paper, and when the person arrives I can ask her to move a chair for me."

"Howard, are you sure you want to go through with this?" Olive asked. "I can't help but feel that this is far too dangerous."

"I know," Howard replied, taking her hand, "but we have to do this to keep Barnes from hurting anyone else. If I can accomplish that, I'll be happy."

Olive nodded and brushed a tear from her eye. Howard's bravery touched her, and she knew in her heart that they were doing the right thing.

Maggie then told Howard about the ball game and her suggestion about calling Jean from the bathroom. It reminded her that they should all charge their cell phones before leaving Queens, and Howard said that he planned to take his charger with him. It would be important to call Jean whenever he could, hopefully even on the highway to Boston if Barnes happened to pull off at a rest stop.

"One thing about being an old man, I can always ask him to stop, because he won't want the nice leather in his car damaged, if you know what I mean," Howard chuckled.

They also broached whether Olive should acknowledge him or pretend to be a stranger, but he just shrugged, not sure which would be the better option.

Olive offered her opinion. "If I see you in the lobby and come over to say hello, it would allow me to pop into your room without raising suspicion, but then

Barnes might decide to call the whole thing off." She paused. "Howard, I don't know how you feel about that. You still don't have to go through with it, you know."

Howard clenched his fists. "Someone has to take a stand with this creep. If they start threatening me, I'm going to press Jean's number and leave the phone on. They won't do anything to me in the hotel, and so as long as you know I'm in my room, you can call hotel security and that detective fellow. If need be, Maggie can call him with her phone and hold Jean's next to it so he can hear what's being said. Believe me, I've been thinking a lot about this."

Maggie broke in. "But let's say we call the police. It'll save you from harm, but unless there's something physical, how can we prove that Barnes is the bad guy?"

Howard nodded. "I've been thinking about that, too. You said that Irma signed a will the day before she died, so Barnes must have made her do it in Atlantic City. My guess is he'll do the same thing to me. If the cops bust in, I can tell them to search his briefcase. That will back up my story."

Olive sat staring into space. Howard and the others seemed so sure that the plan would work, but they were forgetting that he wasn't forty years old and he was in a wheelchair, for heaven's sake. Howard obviously noticed her concern, because he rose from his chair and sat beside her on the couch.

"Cheer up, Olive," he said. "The sooner we get this done, the sooner we can get back to regular life, although I have to say, I'm truly enjoying all of this cloak and dagger stuff."

Maggie and Jean were looking at Howard with true admiration. Maggie said she knew why he'd won a medal during World War II, but he just waved off her comment.

He looked at his watch and told them that he was scheduled for physio the following morning, so he should get some extra rest. Olive deposited him in his room and came back to help Jean and Maggie clean up, then returned home and poured herself a glass of wine. She knew that sleep would not come easily that night.

The rest of the week flew by. Howard had insisted on a pool match on Thursday, but didn't make any mention of Friday's trip during the entire game. Thursday night, the women met to finalize the travel plans, as the rental car was being delivered the following morning. Howard told them he'd asked the front desk to buzz him when Barnes signed in, giving him time for a quick call to Jean. They could then be waiting in the rental car when Barnes brought Howard out of the building.

Olive was a pile of nerves that night, so Jean suggested a glass of red wine—cold from the fridge, of course—to help her fall asleep. Olive gladly accepted, and soon she was snoozing, despite her concerns about the trip.

Chapter 25

Barnes arrived promptly at ten o'clock Friday morning. Howard had been able to speak briefly to Jean beforehand, and since they'd already packed their luggage in the rental car, the women were able to walk down to the vehicle while Barnes was helping Howard out of his room.

Jean sat up front with Maggie, the driving directions and cell phone on her lap. They shrunk down in their seats when Barnes emerged from the building. He was followed by his driver, who was pushing Howard in his chair. Barnes appeared intent on his vehicle, so he didn't even glance their way, and the driver had his eyes on the sidewalk, so the women felt sure that neither had seen them.

Maggie waited until Barnes' car turned onto the cross street before easing the rental from the curb. She assumed that Barnes' driver would take the same route as she out of the city, so she felt no need to get particularly close and risk detection.

Traffic was relatively light, and Maggie was able to merge onto the I-95 North within about twenty minutes. Then, after another twenty minutes or so, Maggie fell in one car behind Barnes' vehicle, heading northeast. She wondered if Howard planned to ask for a bathroom break early in the trip or wait until they were closer to Boston, or maybe both. Time would tell.

In Barnes' car, the lawyer introduced his driver and the nurse to Howard; they rode up front while Barnes and Howard shared the plush back seat, complete with a small bar and a tray for "legal work on the go," as he described it. Barnes told Howard that they would be on the road a while and offered him a cocktail, but Howard declined, telling him that his old kidneys probably couldn't take the shock. Barnes appeared to accept this and changed the subject to Howard's finances. Barnes had already removed the envelope of documents from Howard's suitcase.

"We might as well put this time to good use, Howard, because you'll be pretty busy with John when we arrive in Boston and I want to stay out of your way," Barnes said. Howard watched Barnes read through his investment and bank statements, complimenting Howard on the size of his estate. "Did you sell your home to increase the value to this amount?" he asked.

"No, I still own it," Howard answered. "Winnie and I both believed in Christmas Club deductions each week, and we also bought a lot of savings bonds. We bought stocks, too, and got lucky with some of the newer tech stocks, but we basically stuck with the blue chip variety, which have appreciated over time."

"You worked in a plant, you told me? This is fairly sophisticated investing you're describing," Barnes exclaimed.

Howard didn't know whether to be complimented or insulted. "You can learn a lot by studying as you go. You don't have to attend school to be smart, you know."

"Oh, sorry, I didn't mean that. I'm just impressed, that's all."

Howard pretended to be mollified, all the while wanting to call Barnes an asshole and give him a poke in the nose. But he also remembered his mission, and the fact that there was a rather large man driving the vehicle.

Barnes then turned his attention to Howard's last will and testament. "This is pretty old, almost thirty years old, in fact. It hasn't been updated since then?" he asked.

"No need to. Winnie and I left everything to each other, and then to our church if we both croaked. Why should I change it?"

"It isn't strictly necessary, but if a will is updated, it's clear that you've looked at your current circumstances and either confirmed or changed your estate plan. It's pretty commonly done," Barnes informed him.

Howard had been looking out the window and turned to tell Barnes that he'd think about it, watching James' jaw clench. In Howard's mind, this was all going according to plan.

He decided to wait another half hour to request a bathroom break; then he could contact Jean and confirm that they were on the highway, too. Barnes appeared to have nothing more to say, which was fine with Howard, leaving him free to watch the scenery—such as it was—go by.

You could travel faster on interstate highways, but the only points of interest appeared to be the monstrosities built every forty miles or so, featuring fast food outlets and fuel pumps. Necessary, but not pretty by any stretch of the imagination. Howard thought about a book he'd read a number of years before. He remembered it was called *Blue Highways*, or something like that—a more modern version of *Travels with Charley*, the Steinbeck narrative written about a cross country road trip with his dog. This more recent book involved a trip taken only on non-interstate roads, shown in blue on maps, and the interesting sights and people that the author had found off the beaten path, so to speak. Howard wanted to recommend it to Olive.

He began thinking about Olive. After Winnie died, Howard never thought he could meet a woman even close to her in temperament and interest. He found Olive a little shyer than Winnie, but maybe that was a good thing; he'd mellowed a lot with age himself, not having the piss and vinegar of a younger man. He couldn't imagine himself keeping up with either Jean or Maggie, for instance, although they were fun to visit once in a while. Olive had a quiet confidence which attracted him, and so far, they appeared to enjoy a lot of the same things. He wondered whether Olive would consider an old coot like him worth her time once he was able to leave the nursing home. He hoped so.

He was brought out of his reverie by the sound of Barnes' voice pointing out a sign signaling a rest stop in fifteen miles. Howard agreed that they should stop, if that was alright with Barnes, so a few minutes later, James began pulling into the right lane.

He let them out at the entrance to the rest stop and Howard stepped carefully out of the car, using his cane for support. Betty offered to help, but he declined, telling them that he would meet them back at the entrance. He wanted to get to a bathroom stall before Barnes or James came in, hoping to complete his call undetected. In any event, he planned to be as non-committal as possible, just in case they could hear his conversation.

Jean picked up the cell phone on the first ring. "Jean Corcoran speaking."

Howard was brief. "We're stopping for a few minutes at the rest stop near Hartford. I feel fine, Doctor. The car is huge and comfortable, and it looks like we're making good time. We're just using the time to look at some documents and enjoy the scenery. Yes, you have a good day ,too. Thanks. Bye."

Jean looked over at Maggie in their car. "Sounds like everything's fine," she reported. "They're about ten minutes ahead of us. I wouldn't mind a break, too. By the time we get there and park, they'll probably be on their way and we can catch up with them again after a potty stop. Howard's pretending that I'm his physician. Smart move in case Barnes is in the next stall. Apparently they've already looked at his will."

When Howard exited the stall, he found Barnes and James standing next to the sink. He nodded to them, washed up, and then followed them back to the car. Barnes asked casually if he needed more time to make any phone calls, so Howard realized that he must have heard part of his conversation.

"No, that's fine," Howard replied. "My physician in Queens is going off shift, and as you know, he wasn't that keen about the trip, so he called me. Not the greatest timing because I was in the bathroom, but I let him know that everything is fine and that we're making good time. He asked me to call once we reach the hotel."

Barnes appeared satisfied, because he nodded to James to start the car. Howard assumed that Barnes had something else on his mind, and he didn't disappoint.

"I'm curious about the church in your will, Howard," Barnes said. "When you and your wife made your wills almost thirty years ago, you probably didn't have the assets you do now?"

Howard nodded, asking Barnes if that concerned him.

"No, not really, but as an attorney, I can tell you that it's nice to spread your money around. There are a lot of good charities out there. I'm also wondering about the attorney named as executor in your will. He must be pretty old by now. Do you know whether he's still in active practice?"

Howard was beginning to enjoy this. "Actually, he was the son of the founding member of the law firm, so I'm guessing he's about ten years younger than me," he said. "He can't be my executor if he's retired from legal practice?"

Barnes started to color somewhat. "He can serve as executor, of course, but it's often better to have someone currently in practice, because they know the modern law, that sort of thing."

"Well, can't he just hire a law firm?"

Howard could see that Barnes was trying to appear nonchalant yet concerned about his welfare. "That's true," Barnes said slowly. "But often, if the executor is also a lawyer, he can save the estate some legal fees. I know that I always reduce my usual fee when I'm also the executor."

Howard couldn't help but smirk. "Yes, but if I'm dead, what will I care? And the church will be so happy to get the money, I don't think its people will care either. But maybe I'm missing something?"

Barnes just grunted a little and sat back. Howard continued to gaze out the window, feeling smug that he was pulling one over on this horrible man.

Meanwhile, Maggie pulled out of the rest stop. Jean had bought a small cup of coffee and Olive had brought along some water, but none of them wanted to drink too much liquid in case Barnes made no other stops before Boston. They were also totally immune from temptation in the food court.

The builders were clever, making motorists walk through food vendors on the way to the bathrooms, but frankly, putting all of the vendors so close together only made the women want to gag. The strong smell of pizza mingled with the cinnamon sweetness of hot rolls, and the McGrease permeating the whole building left Olive wanting to wash her hair. Maggie estimated that they were still about ten miles behind Barnes, but she wanted to be a little closer once they drew near Boston.

They soon crossed over the Massachusetts border and finally got onto the Mass Pike toward Boston. Earlier, Jean had put on the radio, but with Maggie concentrating on the road and Olive apparently lost in her own thoughts, she just turned it off, sighing. The drive to the Adirondacks had been a lot of fun, and the view was definitely better than this, but she reminded herself that they were on a mission, not a vacation. There would be plenty of time later for that kind of thing.

After an hour or so of traveling on the Mass Pike, they could see the dim outline of a metropolitan area. Soon after, Maggie negotiated a number of turns, and they finally arrived in front of the hotel. They spotted a bellhop removing luggage from Barnes' trunk.

"We'd better give them time to check in so we don't run into them in the lobby," Maggie said. "Poor Howard must have to use the bathroom. That was a long haul from the rest stop to here."

Barnes and Howard had already gone inside. There was a spot by the curb across the street, so Maggie parked there and looked at her watch.

"We'll wait fifteen minutes before we go in," she decided. "Parking is just an extra ten dollars a night, but I can't get the rate until we check in."

The women were all on edge, hoping that Howard would call them soon. Fifteen minutes passed and Maggie began to ease the car into the hotel's driveway. A valet appeared immediately and took the keys from Maggie.

"This is great," she said, smiling at the valet. "We can just grab our luggage and go inside."

Another young man appeared and began removing their bags, so Olive and Maggie stood to the side while Jean went ahead to register. Just as she walked up to the desk, her cell phone rang, and after looking around to ensure that neither Barnes nor his driver was lurking, she stepped back outside to take the call.

"Hi, it's Howard," he said on the other end. "So far, so good. I'm in room 707 and I've told them I need to lie down for an hour or so. The nurse offered to stay with me, and she's twice offered me juice. But I told them I'm fine, just a little tired, so hopefully she won't come back. When you get your room number, please call me back to confirm. I've called housekeeping and asked for assistance, so once someone comes I'll have a chair put in front of the adjoining door. James left the wheelchair in my room, but I placed it right next to the hallway door so they don't have to come into the room to get me."

Jean was satisfied with Howard's arrangements, but before clicking off, she asked whether Barnes had given him his baseball ticket. Howard said he hadn't, but it had occurred to him that if he was in a wheelchair, he'd have to go in a special area in the park. Jean had brought her laptop along, so she promised to look at the seating chart to confirm that. They said goodbye and ended the call.

Heading back into the foyer, Jean met Maggie and Olive at the front desk. She winked to allay their concerns, and checked all of them into room 703.

Following the bellhop, they arrived at their room, and after sending him off with a tip, fell onto the beds. Jean then called Howard to confirm their room number. She cautioned him to actually get some rest, because the next forty-eight hours would certainly be tiring.

Maggie looked out the window. "What is it with me?" she grumbled. "I always manage to look out onto parking lots. Jeez!"

Olive and Jean were content to let Maggie vent, knowing that she'd been at the wheel for a long time. They realized they were hungry, and because they didn't expect to hear from Howard for a while, they took the elevator to the first floor restaurant.

Then Olive had a thought. "The bar probably has some kind of lunch menu," she mused. "I could use a drink, and if they bring Howard down for some food, they'll probably go to the dining room because it has more room for wheelchairs. We'd better not be in there when they are."

Within ten minutes, they were enjoying cold beers and hot cheeseburgers at the bar. Olive said that she wished Howard could have joined them, and Maggie nodded, but they all knew that wasn't part of the plan.

As they were finishing, Jean looked up and croaked, "Oh my God. There's Barnes!"

The women quietly watched Barnes, his driver, and the nurse walk into the far end of the lounge and take a seat in the corner. Jean motioned Maggie to take care of the bill so that she and Olive could walk out without drawing any attention. She knew that Barnes had seen Olive briefly when he'd picked up Irma, and it was Jean who would take Howard's calls, so the further they got from him, the better. Barnes and his cohorts were deeply involved in conversation, so their departure went unnoticed and Maggie could pay the bill in relative peace.

The nurse ordered some calamari to share with the driver, and they all spoke in hushed tones over cocktails. Barnes looked a little stressed, in Maggie's opinion. It probably had something to do with Howard refusing to drink any of their "special" juice.

Jean was normally fairly calm under pressure, both by nature and from watching Jimmy do police work while he was alive, but even she was a little breathless when they all finally returned to their room. "Man, that creep was only about fifty feet away. I'd love to hit him over the head with something," she said.

Olive had an idea. "Call Howard and see if he's awake," she suggested. "If they're still in the lounge having drinks, that should give us a few minutes alone with him. And Maggie, go down to the end of hall and buy a couple of snacks. He must be starved. Jean, I'll keep an eye on the door while you talk to him."

Jean started to protest, thinking that Olive might want time alone with Howard. Then she realized this whole situation was probably too emotional for Olive, so she agreed to make a quick trip to see him.

Howard answered his phone immediately, telling Jean he'd be at the door to let her in. When she brought in a candy bar and a bag of pretzels for him, he grinned in gratitude.

"Have they given you any idea about things, other than the itinerary Barnes mentioned over the phone?" Jean asked.

"If they're changing it at all, he hasn't said," Howard responded. "I'm supposed to meet Case later today and then we're to talk lovingly into the night about his grandfather and my father, and I guess I'm supposed to conclude that he's so special that I'll change my will to give him a chunk of my estate. But that's just a guess."

Jean couldn't help but laugh at Howard's attitude. No wonder Olive was falling for him. He had a lot of spunk for an old guy. She lightly punched his arm, telling him to take it easy.

She wished that he would have dinner at the hotel so Maggie could spy on them, but Howard wasn't sure of Barnes' plans. He told her it would be easier on Barnes if they just ate in the restaurant because they wouldn't have to cart him around, but Howard would call her just before they left his room to update her. Hopefully he could call her from whatever restaurant they went to, too. The pick-up time was scheduled for five o'clock, apparently for cocktails.

Jean left quickly, and she and Olive went back to their room. They had about an hour or so until Howard's departure for dinner. Maggie set the alarm and closed the drapes, telling them to try to steal a few moments of sleep.

Not surprisingly, they all drifted off for a deep nap, only to be awakened by the buzz from the alarm. They splashed water on their faces, brushed their hair, and sat waiting for Howard's call.

Promptly at five o'clock, Jean's cell phone rang, with Howard telling her that Barnes was at the door. He would tell Barnes that he'd been in the bathroom when he heard his knock, accounting for the delay caused by his call.

In the other room, Howard answered the door, expecting to be introduced to his long lost relative. Instead it was only Barnes, asking if he was ready. He told Howard that the restaurant in the hotel appeared to have a good menu, and it would be easier for him to eat closer to home, so that's what they would do for dinner.

"Great idea, Edgar! I can just walk to dinner using my cane instead of bothering with the wheelchair." Howard had been standing in the doorway holding his cane, so there was no reason for Barnes to go in the room. Howard had also planted a couple of items around the room, knowing that if they were moved, it would confirm his suspicion that Barnes had a second key. Barnes didn't seem the type to leave these things to chance.

Maggie peeked out the door following Howard's call and spied Barnes standing in his doorway. She left her door ajar in an attempt to pick up any of their conversation. When she saw Howard walk with Barnes toward the elevator, she knew from Howard's lack of wheelchair that they weren't leaving the building, so she closed the door and reported back to Jean and Olive.

"Neither James nor Betty were with Barnes, so maybe they're done for the evening. How should we handle this?" she asked.

Jean spoke up. "We ate a big lunch late enough that I don't care to eat anything for the next couple of hours. Maggie, you should wait until they get settled in the dining room and then have a drink in the lounge. I looked into the dining room earlier, and if you sit at the bar, you have a pretty good view of things. When you find a spot, give me a call and we can take it from there."

Olive still thought she should do the surveillance. "I'm the only one who's actually seen Forman, or Case, if that's what they're calling him now," she cried.

Jean and Maggie immediately vetoed this.

Jean tapped Olive on the arm. "We worry that you'll be too emotional worrying about Howard, and besides, what if Forman recognizes you? Then everything goes out the window," she cried.

Olive reluctantly agreed. She described Forman to Maggie as athletically built, around six feet tall with sandy, somewhat longer hair—quite handsome, actually.

Maggie used the bathroom and grabbed the complimentary newspaper from the desk so that she would have some kind of camouflage if Barnes happened to look over into the bar. By this time, she felt that Howard would be settled in the dining room, so she took the elevator to the first floor.

Being careful not to look for Howard on her way to the bar, Maggie found the seat Jean had recommended and ordered a glass of merlot. She opened the newspaper while looking beyond the bartender and was able to just see Howard's table. Perfect! Barnes' back was toward her, but she had a clear view of "Case" and Howard.

Looking closer, she could see that Case was indeed Matthew Forman—he looked just like Olive had described him.

Forman had been waiting at the table when Barnes and Howard entered. He rose quickly, and with a big smile, strode over to them, extending his hand to shake Howard's.

"Howard, I'm so excited to meet you! I've been trying to imagine what you look like!" he exclaimed.

Retrieving his hand from Forman's grip, Howard nodded and grunted, "Old! I look old, I'm afraid."

He noticed that Forman laughed a little too heartily and appeared to glance over at Barnes as if to check that he was doing alright. They sat down at the table and Barnes called to the waiter. After checking with the others, he ordered scotch for all of them.

Just as the waiter began to leave the table, Howard changed his order to gin and tonic, telling Barnes that he hadn't enjoyed one of them in a long while. It occurred to him to keep his drink different from theirs, so there could be no switch made without his knowledge. Barnes looked a little puzzled, telling Howard that gin and tonic was normally a summer drink, but Howard chose not to respond.

"So, John, tell me about yourself," Howard said, turning to his supposed relative. "I'm curious about how you found me."

Forman launched into a well-prepared monologue: his grandmother had told his father about Howard's Uncle Johnny and how she'd met him toward the end of World War I. She'd given Johnny a photo as a keepsake, and only found out about her pregnancy a couple of weeks after he was killed. She then married a local boy—John's grandfather—who knew about the pregnancy, but agreed to take her son as his own when she gave birth the following spring. She'd kept the secret from her son for many years, only disclosing it on her deathbed. "John" went on to say that his father also kept the secret for many years, only sharing the information with his son a few months before his death.

"It's probably hard for you to understand, Howard, but this has bothered me for a while," Forman said. "I wanted to find my roots, so to speak—to honor my father, if nothing else—and I can't tell you how happy I am that Mr. Barnes was able to make it happen. When he took your blood sample and had it matched with mine, it was the end of a long journey for me."

Howard smiled and told "John" that he was happy, too. "By the way, Edgar, I've been waiting to read the report," he said, clearing his throat. "Do you have it?"

Barnes smoothly told him that he had only received verbal confirmation, but hoped to have the written report on Monday; he would send a copy to both Howard and John. Then he smiled and took a sip of his scotch.

The waiter reappeared and took their orders. Barnes ordered a bottle of wine for the table in celebration of a happy reunion.

Forman began asking Howard all about World War II, saying that his father fought for Britain and thought perhaps they'd actually fought together in Europe. Howard said he doubted it, given that the troops he fought with were all American.

Forman continued. "The museum I found online seems pretty interesting. I had to write to request a tour, so we'll do that tomorrow morning. Mr. Barnes' driver will take us there."

"John, please. It's Edgar. My father is called Mr. Barnes," Barnes said. Forman responded with more hearty laughter.

Howard's meal was good. He hadn't eaten a thick steak in a long time and found himself only half-listening to the conversation. He thought to ask Forman if he'd ever seen a picture of his Uncle Johnny.

"No," Forman answered. "Apparently there wasn't time to take a photo before he shipped out."

"When did your grandmother die?" Howard asked. "Did your father have a photo of her when she was young? I imagine that you must have a photo of your father when he was young. He might have had his portrait taken in uniform before he shipped out during World War II. I'm curious to see if there's any family resemblance between him and me, since we would have been cousins."

Up to that point, Forman had been fairly glib in his explanations, but these questions appeared to unsettle him and he glanced at Barnes a couple of times until the latter mentioned that while the DNA test had been conclusive, he agreed that it would be nice for Howard to see a photo of John's father. Taking his cue, Forman told Howard that he should have thought to bring a photo with him, but when he returned to England he would have a copy made and mail it promptly.

Howard reached for the dessert menu. "I want to thank you for getting tickets to Sunday's ballgame," he said. "Do you know what section we're in? I've been to Fenway a few times over the years, so I'm pretty familiar with it."

Forman again appeared to stumble, and Barnes broke in, telling Howard that he had taken the liberty of getting the tickets, rather than having John try to do it from England. Barnes told Howard he had the tickets in his room and would check on the location, as he'd never been to Fenway.

Forman again took the cue and began talking about seeing live baseball for the first time; he was especially excited since the owner of the Red Sox also owned the Liverpool football club. It was all so grand.

Howard smiled and told them that he was a little tired and wanted to turn in early. Barnes agreed, bidding "John" goodnight, because his room was on another floor.

Howard and Barnes walked toward the elevator.

"So, what do you think of John?" Barnes asked. "He's had a tough life, Howard. He was in a bad accident a few years ago that he doesn't want to discuss with you, but apparently it's been a hard go for him ever since. He has trouble concentrating, so it's difficult for him to keep a job. You and I discussed your will and I know you want to benefit your church, but I'm asking that you give John some thought, and maybe leave him part of your estate. We can talk about it tomorrow sometime, of course."

They got off the elevator and walked to Howard's room. Howard said goodnight out in the hall, not wanting Barnes to come into his room. He shut the door behind him, used the bathroom, and then called Jean.

Meanwhile, Maggie paid her tab at the bar and waited a few minutes before following Howard to their floor. She had watched their table during dinner, with Forman waving his arms about in excitement while

Howard sat back calmly. She also noticed the glances between Forman and Barnes when Howard bent his head to eat his meal. She'd wanted to walk over and hit Forman as hard as she could.

She was careful to read the newspaper a little, though, so she couldn't be observed staring at Barnes' table, and she'd actually found the paper interesting. It was local, so the sports section was a hoot. Maggie was so used to partisan New York papers that it was fun to read the same stuff about the Bruins, Celtics, and Red Sox somewhere else. She was already looking forward to the ballgame on Sunday; she and Jean planned to root loudly for the Indians. Olive would be mortified.

Maggie got back to her room to find Jean already on the phone with Howard. When Jean clicked off, she reported that everything had gone according to plan.

She quoted Howard's final comment: "If that lad is my relative, I'll eat my shorts, waistband and all!"

Maggie and Olive laughed, happy that Howard still had a lot of energy.

Jean confirmed that the trip to the museum was scheduled for ten o'clock, but there was a new wrinkle. "Apparently it's a private museum, so we can't go in without an invitation or something," she said. "But I still think we should follow them and wait in the car, just in case they try any side trips on the way back. We all don't have to go, Olive, if you want to stay here."

Olive shook her head vigorously, finishing up the soup she'd ordered from room service. She would see this through to the end.

Maggie turned on the television and whistled softly, having forgotten that Boston was hosting the Rangers that night. She leaned back against her pillow, engrossed in the game. Olive joined Jean as a spectator, but began to lose interest, picking up Maggie's newspaper and finishing it before falling asleep. A whole day of staking out the enemy had wiped her out, and she needed the rest for the harder days to come.

Chapter 26

On the way to the museum the next day, Howard looked out the window as the car wound through the city. Barnes had apparently gone to a seminar, leaving Forman, James, and Howard to enjoy the morning. He hadn't seen Betty since the previous day, so maybe she'd been smart enough to forgo the excursion, particularly since her efforts at giving him orange juice had failed. He'd been careful to decline the wine with last night's meal, too, so he felt comfortable he hadn't ingested any drugs other than those on his person. He felt fine, anyway, albeit bored to death.

This young supposed relative kept trying to interest him, but Howard had to force himself to listen to him; he didn't want to draw any suspicion at this point, after all. Forman's English accent was also a little strange, like he'd just learned it or something. Howard should have asked Olive if she'd actually heard the man speak when he'd talked to Irma.

James was supposed to drive them back to the hotel around two o'clock for a late lunch, after which Howard assumed that Barnes would try to work on him again with hard luck stories about young Johnny.

They pulled in front of a building and were met by a fellow who introduced himself as a volunteer. Once inside, Howard steadied himself with his cane and let the volunteer lead the way, while Forman made the recommended donation to the facility. They wandered through the exhibits, which Howard found interesting in a ghoulish sort of way, and left the building a little while later. James noted they had some time before lunch, so he offered to drive them around the city. Forman enthusiastically agreed.

The women were waiting outside the parking lot during the museum tour. Seeing Howard and the others emerge, they shrunk down in their seats to avoid detection, although as Jean pointed out, anyone with a brain might notice the New York license plates on the rental. Luckily they'd parked at a curb across from the building, and a couple of cars had pulled in behind them.

They began following Barnes' town car, thinking it was headed to the hotel.

"Oh, boy! The driver's taking some weird route and I don't know beans about Boston streets!" Maggie yelled.

Olive got out her street finder, which she'd read to kill time while they'd waited for the tour to end. "What street are we on?" she asked.

Jean looked up and called out the street and an upcoming cross street, giving Olive time to get her bearings. Olive told Maggie to try to keep the town car in sight, and told Jean to call out major intersections as they came up. It was their only option.

Fortunately, it became clear that the driver was taking Howard and Forman on a general tour of the city and seemed to be in no hurry. With Jean still calling out intersections, Olive was able to determine his planned route, more or less, allowing Maggie to relax a little.

After almost an hour, they followed him back to the hotel entrance, and as before, waited until Howard was in the lobby before driving up to the valet.

Back in their room, Jean took the opportunity to call Howard, hoping that he was alone. He sounded troubled when he answered, telling Jean that he'd arranged a couple of items in his room to alert him of any entry by Barnes, but housekeeping was so efficient that everything was back in proper order. He'd have to try again that day.

He told Jean that Barnes was taking him to lunch at two o'clock, and then he and "John" were supposed to enjoy dinner that evening. Howard told her that he didn't feel afraid; he just felt bored and ready to go home. Jean almost told him that the trip had been no picnic for them either, but kept it to herself, asking him to take care.

"Howard's getting ready to explode and I don't blame him," she reported to the other ladies after hanging up. "He wants to get this over with. I don't know how detectives do it, sitting there watching someone, just waiting for something to happen. I remember Jimmy was involved in a couple of stakeouts, and he hated them. Now I know what he was talking about."

Olive stood by their partially-opened door, waiting for some activity. She noticed a young Thai woman passing with her housekeeping cart, so she closed the door quietly. She opened it again after the woman passed.

She heard men's voices, somewhat hushed, in the hall, and had an idea. She put on her hat and walked down the hall following the cleaner, and when she reached her, Olive turned a little to get a look at the younger man with Barnes. Seeing his profile, she almost gasped—Matthew Forman was John Case!

The cleaner looked at Olive quizzically, so regaining her composure, she asked for extra toilet paper, telling her that a friend in room 703 wasn't feeling well. Olive kept her back to the men during this exchange, but could hear Howard's voice telling them that he was ready for lunch. After she heard the elevator doors shut, she thanked the cleaning woman and went back to her room with the toilet paper rolls.

Olive told Jean and Maggie about Howard's lunch plans. This time Jean volunteered for the eavesdropping mission. She grabbed the same paper Maggie had been reading the other day and headed down to the lounge.

Jean seated herself at the bar and ordered a Bloody Mary, opening the paper to the sports section. Her beloved Yankees had started out strong. Between glances at the paper, Jean watched Howard and company in the dining room.

Forman appeared to do a lot of talking, smiling and laughing, while Barnes and Howard just seemed to watch, responding only occasionally. If body language told her anything, Howard was already fed up with their company. It made her anxious because Howard was a stubborn old cuss, and if he didn't want to go along with Barnes' estate plan, he could be in a lot of trouble. She wondered whether she should call Detective Spector again and ask him to at least stop by the hotel. She'd talk it over with the girls first.

Back in the room, Olive told Maggie that she was a little hungry. Maggie called Jean, who quickly answered to keep the phone from ringing out in the lounge, and told her that she and Olive were going to the burger place down the street and that Jean should order some lunch for herself at the bar.

"Already ahead of you on that one, my dear," was Jean's response. "Keep your phone on in case I need to reach you. And buy a couple of beers if there's a package store nearby. I'll probably want one later after this stakeout."

Howard was finding Forman even more tiresome than he had been in the museum that morning. "John" was supposed to have suffered some lasting brain damage, so Howard asked him about it, and Forman immediately fell into a kind a patter, a well-rehearsed story about his accident and its residual effects. Howard even noticed Barnes nodding at certain parts of the narrative. He had to give them credit; they were creative.

Howard was trying to anticipate their actions. *Let's say I do agree to put "John" in my will,* he thought as "John" went on. I still have to die for their plan to work. So let's say I force the issue and tell them I want to go home. What will they do? I'll just have to be patient and see if Barnes brings me a brand-new will.

With lunch over, Howard mentioned that he had to call his physician, and he wanted to lie down for a while. Forman looked concerned. "Are you alright?" he asked.

"I'm supposed to check in with my doctor sometime today, but I feel fine, just a little tired," Howard answered. In answer to Forman's next question, he said he took Digoxin and Coumadin for his heart and post-stroke issues.

Forman's lips began to quiver. "Gee, Howard, don't go dying on me now that I just found you!"

Howard thought he would puke. But he just smiled and waved off Forman's offer of assistance in rising from the table, steadying himself with his cane.

Barnes called out that he had a meeting later, but would visit Howard that evening. Howard gave him a thumbs up, wanting to return to his room as quickly as possible so that he could call Jean.

Jean watched Howard make his way to the elevator, thinking that he looked very tired. Perhaps the itinerary was proving too difficult for him. She knew that Howard would call her soon, so she paid her check, used the ladies room in the hallway, and then took the elevator herself. She planned to ask Howard to think very carefully about continuing this charade. She hoped that Olive and Maggie were still out of the hotel, because she wanted to have a very frank discussion with Howard.

So much for that idea—both Olive and Maggie were lounging in the room and wanted a report as soon as Jean entered. Her cell phone began ringing immediately, so they quieted to let her answer it.

Howard told Jean that, yes, he was tired, but, yes, he intended to carry on. He suspected that Barnes would make his move that night, because he probably had no intention of taking Howard to a ballgame. He couldn't tell Jean why, necessarily; it was just a gut feeling from watching Barnes and Case. He told her that Barnes planned to "stop by" his room early in the evening, which hadn't been on the original itinerary.

Howard signed off, wanting some rest before what promised to be the big showdown. Maggie and Olive watched Jean blanch during the conversation and began peppering her with questions the minute she ended the call.

"Just let me think this through for a minute, okay?" Jean said. "I'm going to call Detective Spector and tell him we're here and we're concerned about Howard. Maybe he'll get off the couch and lend us a hand."

Jean called his number, but only got his voicemail. She tried to leave Spector a short, coherent message, but found herself getting emotional, so she left her phone number requesting that he return her call as soon as possible. There was nothing more they could do.

Then Jean thought of Detective Biggs from Queens. He'd told her that his cell phone would be off during his New Hampshire fishing trip, but everyone said that. She'd at least try to call and ask him to contact Spector again on Howard's behalf. She wrote down Spector's number on a piece of paper so she'd have it handy.

She called, and Biggs answered: "This better be good."

Apparently, he thought that it was someone from his office because of the Queens area code, and now Jean didn't know what to say. But, recovering her composure, she launched into her story, asking his forgiveness in advance for interrupting his vacation.

"Well, luckily for you, I'm in town enjoying a beer with my wife, who happens to be in the ladies room at the moment, so let's make it quick," Biggs told her. "Okay. Spector wasn't convinced, which doesn't surprise me. And, by the way, I thought you promised to stay home—and now you're in the thick of it. So you want me to call Spector again, and tell him what? That Barnes is putting your friend up at a nice hotel, buying him dinners, and having his driver take him places, and so far with no harm at all to the old guy? Come on, Jean, should we call out the SWAT team?"

Jean began to wonder how many beers Biggs had enjoyed at that point. "Could you just call him and confirm you spoke to me and that we're all at the hotel?" she pleaded. "Howard's worried that Barnes will make his move tonight."

Biggs sighed. "Alright. I see my wife coming back. It's my turn to take a leak so I'll call Spector, but if he doesn't answer, all I can do is leave a message. You understand?"

It was Jean's turn to sigh, but she thanked Biggs and hoped he could get through to Spector.

Now there was truly nothing more that they could do. She wanted to cry, but she knew that Olive was hanging on by a thread, so she had to be strong. Walking across the room, she reached for the remote and surfed until she found a baseball game on one of the networks.

All they could do was wait.

Howard heard a knock at the door and roused himself as quickly as he could.

"Who is it?" he called. "I'm just on my way to the bathroom."

His question was met with silence, so he looked through the peephole to see Barnes and James waiting patiently out in the hall. He hobbled to the bathroom and punched in Jean's number while looking at his watch. Seven o'clock! He'd slept longer than he planned.

"Jean. It's me!" he said into the phone. "Barnes and James are at my door. Bye."

When he came out of the bathroom, though, he was startled to find the two men waiting for him in his room. "Just a minute," he muttered to them. While pretending to get a tissue from the bathroom counter, Howard reached into his pocket and hit redial, leaving his cell phone open. When he emerged, he walked slowly to the chair by his bed.

"How did you get in here?" he demanded.

Barnes smiled. "The desk clerk gave me a second key in case you have any difficulties in the night," he said smoothly.

James just stood there, staring at Howard until Barnes caught his eye and directed him to call Betty.

Barnes opened his briefcase and pulled out a sheaf of documents. "I promised to talk to you tonight about your will, Howard," he said. "I've made a new one for you—which you're going to sign."

"I don't want a new will! I already told you that!" Howard shouted in response.

At that moment, Olive and Maggie were watching Jean frantically try to call Detective Spector. She had obviously only gotten his voicemail, because she shouted a message pleading for help.

The three women looked at each other, wondering what to do next.

"Maggie, you and I'll go to Howard's room and pretend that we're old friends who just happened to be in town and thought we spotted him in the lobby earlier today," Jean decided. "If we can get inside the room, I don't think Barnes will try anything funny. Olive, you stand guard outside and call security if you hear anything. The number's on the back of the door, so write it down."

Inside Howard's room, Barnes was reading the terms of the new will aloud, which he said gave a three hundred thousand dollar cash gift to Howard's church, and the rest to John Case.

Betty arrived. She pulled out a syringe and sat on the bed next to Howard's chair.

"See, here's the thing, Howard," Barnes said. "If you don't sign, Betty is going to inject you with enough Digoxin to send you to Neverland. If you do sign, then Betty will put the syringe away. How about it? You're still giving a lot of cash to your church, and I promise to do a fine job as executor. And there will be no need for you to sign any other will when you get back to Queens, if you understand my drift. Right, Howard?"

Acknowledging his situation, Howard nodded, holding out his hand for the pen.

Barnes smiled, telling him that he'd made a good decision. He led Howard through the will execution formalities and Howard initialed and signed the will.

While James and Betty were signing as witnesses, Barnes had Howard sign the affidavit of heirship and the acknowledgment of Barnes' entitlement to commissions and legal fees.

Howard's shoulders slumped when he was done. He was feeling angry and helpless.

The three women ran past a cleaning lady in the hallway. Olive briefly thought she recognized her from earlier—she'd gotten toilet paper from her at one point—but was too focused on Howard's situation to greet her properly.

Maggie knocked on the door, and it opened.

"Howard, we thought it was you in the lobby today!" Jean exclaimed, and they pushed their way inside, letting the door slam shut behind them.

Olive remained outside in the hall, trying to listen through the door. She couldn't help but feel that everything was going horribly wrong.

Jean was startled when she saw Howard's face; he looked so weary and defeated. She attempted to maintain her ruse, telling him that she and Maggie hadn't seen him in years, and that they were wondering how Winnie was doing.

Howard just shook his head, telling them that Winnie had died some years before. Maggie went over to him and took his hand, expressing her condolences. It gave her the opportunity to see the signed will and to sit between Betty and Howard.

Betty had put her hand behind her back and kept glancing at Barnes. Jean noticed Barnes raise his eyebrows, and then he nodded at Betty.

Betty began to pull Maggie away from Howard. "Hello, ladies. I've seen the two of you in the bar every time Howard was in the dining room, so you didn't just find out about him today, did you?" she asked with a smirk.

Jean colored, wondering how Betty could have known about their surveillance—but then again the bar was large, and both she and Maggie had been focusing on Howard when they'd eaten there.

Just then, there was a knock on the door. Barnes motioned James to get it.

A cleaning woman held a roll of toilet paper and announced "Housekeeping!" as she slipped inside. She delivered the roll to the bathroom.

Howard tried to stand, but Betty gently sat him back down, and the cleaning woman gave them a strange look as she left the bathroom. She opened the room door to leave, and just as she was stepping out, Olive came in.

Jean blurted out, "Olive, what are you doing here?"

"I wanted to see Howard, too. It's been so long." Olive fidgeted in the doorway. She'd panicked just standing there outside.

Barnes and Betty exchanged knowing glances.

Barnes then smirked and addressed all three women. "Ladies, ladies," he admonished. "Have you been spying on poor old Howard? And what's your name? Ah, Olive. I remember you from the nursing home. You're quite a busybody, aren't you? And now all of you are causing me a problem. What brand of car are you driving?"

Betty waved the syringe, and Maggie told him the information about their rental car. What could she do? Otherwise, Betty would kill Howard!

Barnes nodded to James, who went to the telephone and called the valet station for both vehicles. The women all exchanged puzzled glances, while Howard just closed his eyes.

He shook his head sadly, thinking that just now when he had something to live for, it might be taken away.

There was a loud knock on the door then.

Barnes motioned Betty to take Howard into the bathroom while James looked through the keyhole. He opened the door to let a security guard step in.

The guard greeted the guests. "Our housekeeper was concerned about an elderly gentleman here," he said. "But I don't see him."

Olive exchanged a glance with Jean. The housekeeper had come to their rescue!

But Barnes explained that his father-in-law was in the bathroom with his nurse, because sometimes he needed assistance. They were planning on taking him out for some fresh air shortly, along with his old friends, who just happened to be staying at the same hotel.

Maggie, Jean, and Olive stood silently, not wanting to endanger Howard any further, but also stunned by Barnes' glib explanation to the guard. Apparently satisfied, the guard bade them goodnight and left.

Olive began to sob softly, realizing she'd blundered in joining the other women in the room. The telephone rang and James answered, telling the valet that they would be down shortly.

"Come on, all of you," Barnes said, a hard edge to his voice. "Let's go for a ride."

Barnes and James directed everyone out of the room and down to the lobby. Betty stood very close to Howard the entire time, hypodermic syringe poised to enter his arm should any funny business arise. James and Barnes took up the rear, and Jean felt the unmistakable press of a gun against her back.

"Move along," James said gruffly, poking her with the gun.

Olive grasped Jean's hand, praying that somehow they would get out of this. She knew they should never have gone to Boston!

They passed the same cleaning lady in the lobby; Olive didn't know how she'd gotten downstairs so fast, but the woman clearly looked concerned. "Help us!" Olive mouthed to her as they left through the front doors. The housekeeper just looked shocked.

Betty shoved Howard into the backseat of Barnes' town car and sat next to him. James motioned with the gun for Olive to climb into the front seat, and then passed the gun to Barnes before entering the driver's seat himself. In the rearview mirror, Olive could see Maggie and Jean getting into the front seat of their rental car, and Barnes get into the back.

They slowly pulled out of the hotel's driveway.

"Now, ladies, we're going to follow my town car, and I don't want any funny stuff. This gun in my hand might go off accidentally and kill someone," Barnes threatened in the rental car.

Maggie could have kicked herself for gassing up on the way into Boston; she had no real excuse to pull over now.

Barnes called Betty. Maggie and Jean exchanged worried glances. They couldn't hear Barnes' conversation, but they assumed it didn't involve restaurant choices.

In the town car, Howard and Olive got the picture, because Betty and James were exchanging ideas on how best to get rid of them. Olive started to cry again. Howard told her it would be alright, but Betty snapped at him to shut up.

Maggie had an idea then. She put on her turn signal. Because Barnes was directly behind her seat, he wouldn't be able to notice it. She left the signal on, hoping it would attract attention. She drove as she was directed, trying to keep the town car in sight.

They proceeded without incident, but Maggie was becoming concerned that the turn signal would start to beep. She pointed to it, looking quickly at Jean, who then began talking to Barnes to keep him occupied, giving Maggie time to disengage and then reengage the signal.

One car behind her, she could see the glow of a patrol car's lights, which then used its siren to pull her over.

"What!" Barnes yelled. "Were you speeding or something?"

"No. I was just following your driver like you told me," Maggie said.

"Okay. I'm calling James to tell him we're being pulled over. You just answer the nice policeman's questions, and don't get cute or Betty will make Howard a very dead man. You got that?" Barnes ordered.

The patrolman walked up to Maggie's window and she opened it, shutting off the turn signal. "What seems to be the problem, officer?" she asked.

"Can I see your driver's license, ma'am?" he asked. "You had your turn signal on for a lot of blocks."

"What do you mean?" Maggie burst out. "Are you telling me I don't know how to drive, you little piss head? Why I could be your grandmother, you little punk!"

Jean heard Maggie drop the F-bomb and the patrolman stepped back, startled. Then he ordered Maggie to get out of the car.

Maggie shoved the door open, stumbling into him as she stood up. "The man in the back has a gun and they're holding our friend in another car," she whispered to the officer. "Help us, please!"

Barnes was trying to look out, but he only saw Maggie stumble and didn't realize she was talking to the cop. He'd put the phone in his lap and had returned the gun to his jacket pocket.

Jean watched him through the rear view mirror and quietly released her seat belt. She lunged over the seat and grabbed the phone, calling "Maggie!" to get her attention. She didn't want to close the phone connection, though, because it would alert Betty that something was wrong.

Up ahead, James pulled the town car to the curb, not wanting to get too far ahead of Barnes. Betty had set down the syringe to pick up the call from Barnes, feeling pretty secure that Howard wouldn't give her any trouble. He'd been sitting with his eyes closed, so she thought the old codger had drifted off.

She was wrong. James hadn't thought to lock the vehicle's doors in leaving the hotel, so Howard yelled, "Olive, jump!" before bringing his cane down on Betty's hand and reaching across her for the syringe. Betty was startled, allowing Howard to plunge the syringe into the seat before she could retrieve it. She began to punch him, but he was partially able to fend off her blows with his cane.

James jumped out of the car to get into the back seat, but then realized that Olive had run into the street, flagging down a passing motorist. He reached for his gun, but then remembered he'd given it to Barnes.

"Betty, let's get outta here!" he yelled. "I'm not taking the fall for that suit. I'm not going back to prison. Run!" He motioned frantically and turned to flee.

Unfortunately for Betty, Howard began pushing the tripod end of his cane into her face. She wasn't going anywhere.

Olive heard the wail of a couple of sirens, and two patrol cars screeched to a halt behind them, followed by a dark sedan.

A man in a suit jumped out and ran ahead of the uniformed officers, asking Olive if she was "Jean."

"No. I'm Olive," she answered shakily. "Jean is my sister and she's in a car behind us. It's a rental with New York plates."

The patrolmen pulled Betty out of the car, and Olive heard Howard cussing, still waving his cane about. Olive asked the man how he knew about Jean.

"I'm Detective Spector, and I owe her and you an apology," he replied. "Originally, Jean's story sounded pretty farfetched, but when I got her message tonight, it seemed legit, so I stopped by the hotel. Some little Asian cleaning woman is your guardian angel, I'll tell you. She saw you leave and told me all she knew—she'd even written down your license plate number. We sent out an APB, but apparently a patrolman had already pulled over the rental because the driver had the turn signal on for way too long. We pull those people over because most times they're drunk."

Olive could only laugh. Good old Maggie! She certainly deserved a drink after that maneuver. And Olive would have to find that housekeeper and thank her—she might very well have saved their lives.

The patrolman helped Howard out of the car and steadied him on the curb. Olive ran over and hugged him. "You were so brave!" she exclaimed, squeezing him tight.

Howard shrugged and grinned. "I haven't had this much excitement in years!"

A patrolman climbed into the town car, pointing to the syringe stuck in the seat. "Detective, I think you should see this," he said, and Spector came over to inspect the scene.

Howard explained to Spector about Betty, telling them that James had taken off a few moments before. Betty was already in handcuffs, but wasn't saying anything at that point. She just looked angry and sullen.

Spector laughed at her. "So your husband ran off on you? Brave man! I bet you're real proud."

Soon, two more vehicles pulled up behind. Olive saw a patrol car in the lead, followed by the rental, with Maggie at the wheel.

Maggie and Jean got out and ran to Olive, and Jean gave Olive the biggest hug of her life. Olive recounted Howard's bravery, to which he just shrugged once again. Maggie and Jean both shook their heads in awe. Olive looked around Maggie, spotting Barnes in the back seat of the cruiser.

Olive turned to the Detective and asked whether he'd looked in Barnes' briefcase. He told her they were going to look at it when they got back to the station.

"You might want to open it now while Howard is still here," she said. "They forced him to sign a new will, so he'll want to tear it up."

"It's evidence now, ma'am, so he can't destroy it, but he can identify it and give us a statement before you all return to New York," Spector informed her.

Olive had another thought. "Could you also check it for baseball tickets? Barnes was supposed to take Howard to the game tomorrow, so we can use the tickets instead."

Spector couldn't find any baseball tickets. He asked Barnes whether he'd bought any in the first place; Barnes just grunted and looked away.

Olive gave Spector a quick description of Matthew Forman, telling him that Forman was posing as John Case. When Howard looked at the will he began to laugh, telling the Detective that it was just like the will

Barnes had prepared for Irma Weiss, naming Matthew Forman as Howard's friend, stating in the affidavit of heirship that Howard had no living relatives. Spector apologized again, saying that Detective Biggs of the NYPD also owed them one, and he'd make sure they got it.

Olive started to pull Howard toward the rental. "Come on, Howard, it's been a long day," she said. "Detective, can we just give our statements tomorrow morning? We'd like to get on the road around noon."

Spector agreed, and after confirming that Howard required no medical attention, helped him into the front seat of the rental car. He ordered the patrolman to lead them back to the hotel.

Maggie thanked him. "Detective," she added, "can you offer my apologies to the young man who pulled me over? I used some strong language because I wanted him to order me out of the vehicle. I don't usually talk that way."

Jean and Olive had to stifle smirks at that little lie, but remained quiet.

Back in the car, Maggie said, "Well, this should put that crook out of business permanently! I bet Betty sings like a diva, and if they find James, he'll probably join the chorus." Always the most excitable, she was almost bouncing off the seat, making her passengers more than a little wary of her driving.

After arriving at the hotel, they all agreed to a drink in the lounge. On the way past the front desk, Olive asked the name of the cleaner on the seventh floor. Telling Jean to order her a whisky and ginger ale, Olive detoured to the elevator and caught up with the housekeeper just as she was leaving for the evening. Olive brought her down to the lounge and asked her to sit for a few moments so they could buy her a glass of wine.

Her name was Sa, and she had only recently come to America, mainly to cook and clean for her brother's family. She shyly recounted her part in the adventure—calling the security guard, writing down the license plate numbers, talking to Spector when he arrived at the hotel—fighting for the correct words in a few places. She had been worried when she saw everyone sneaking about on the seventh floor, and had spotted James motioning them to leave with his gun, so she'd rushed downstairs to the lobby to see if she could prevent them from leaving.

"You really were our guardian angel!" Olive exclaimed, taking her hands in hers.

Sa blushed.

Jean took down her full name, address, and telephone number, saying that she wanted to seek a commendation from her employer for her role in their rescue. Sa protested, but was pleased with the recognition at the same time.

The following morning, Detective Spector arrived promptly at ten o'clock and, after two hours of taking statements, told Howard and the women they could go. Spector also relayed what he'd learned from a brief interrogation of Barnes; he indeed had scams running in all five boroughs, and had hired Matthew Forman to pose as his victims' relatives. James, his driver, had already been convicted of aggravated assault, so when the police finally caught up to him, he would be going to jail for a long time.

"I'm glad to hear it!" Jean remarked, remembering the press of his gun on her lower back.

As they got into the rental car, Olive heaved a sigh of relief, muttering that there was no place like home, and then realized that for the first time she'd just called

New York "home." She grinned in satisfaction, patting Howard on the shoulder.

Chapter 27

Howard turned and took one last look at his room. Following his return from Boston, he felt strangely invigorated, realizing, as he told Olive, that he still had some gas in the tank. He resumed his physio sessions with even more vigor, and his social life continued to break the monotony of the nursing home.

At least twice a week he accompanied Olive to the apartment complex, either for home cooking or Chinese take-out with Maggie and Jean, but sometimes just for a quiet meal alone with Olive. He thoroughly enjoyed the evenings with Jean and Maggie—they were a real panic—but he treasured Olive's quiet presence and their discussions on everything from art to politics. He realized how much he'd missed by living alone so many years after he lost Winnie.

He had to admit that he'd fallen in love with Olive and was like a school boy when he thought of her. She seemed to like him and cared a lot about his well-being, too, but for a few weeks, Howard had lacked the courage to share his deeper feelings with her. He wanted her to reciprocate, knowing he'd be crushed if she told him otherwise—gently, he was sure.

He wanted Olive to move to Long Island with him. His tenant had finished his college contract, but Howard decided to leave the house vacant for the time being, at least until the doctor cleared his return. But his outstanding progress convinced the physician that he could return home as long as the public health nurse stopped by twice a week to take his vitals, and more importantly, that Howard agree to continue physiotherapy at a nearby clinic. Howard also agreed to wear a Lifeline bracelet in case he fell while alone.

Howard knew that he could survive at home with all of these safeguards in place, so he wasn't looking at Olive as a helpmate. He wanted her to be his friend and lover, as silly as he knew that sounded for an old coot like him. He couldn't help it. He felt twenty years younger around her, and he wanted Olive to share the rest of his life.

Following their return from Boston, he began joining Olive in church. The weather was much better, so he wasn't worried about ice. It was good to get out, wear a suit, and hear what the preacher had to say. They went outside to the courtyard to do the crossword puzzle, because it was much more comfortable than his room.

The Sunday before his return home, Howard set the puzzle down and took Olive's hand, haltingly sharing his feelings for her. As he spoke, tears welled up in Olive's eyes, and after a couple of minutes, he found himself unable to speak.

Olive said nothing, but she nodded and squeezed his hand, so he took it as a "yes." He asked her if they could tell Jean and Maggie right that minute. She just nodded and squeezed his hand again, so he grabbed his cell phone, telling Jean to bring Maggie to the courtyard right away.

They burst into the courtyard soon after.

"What's up?" Jean exclaimed, looking around wildly. "Olive, are you okay?"

Howard just grinned, saying they both were fine, but that he wanted them to be the first to know that he planned to put an extra ring on Olive's finger.

Jean squealed and grabbed her sister in a bear hug, while Maggie pumped Howard's hand.

The following week passed quickly as he and Olive visited his home to walk through it again. Howard was even able to climb the stairs. Their bedroom would be on the first floor, a convenience for both of them, but he specifically told Olive to do whatever she wanted with Winnie's old sewing room. She replied that it was too early to make big changes, but that they could plan them together.

And now it was time to go. Olive was trying to pack and had asked Jean and Maggie for help.

"Christ on a bicycle!" Jean exclaimed, looking at the big mess Olive had made in packing up. "Are you taking half of Queens with you?"

Olive just grinned.

THE END

ABOUT THE AUTHOR

 Prior to retiring with her husband to Vancouver Island, Canada, L.V. Nield practised law for many years in New York State. Working primarily in Elder Law, Laura was always aware of the vulnerability of seniors.

Kinfolk Killers, while a work of pure fiction, incorporates information regarding potential abuses of the old and frail.

Please visit L.V. Nield's Facebook page at: https://www.facebook.com/LV-Nield-1879141138769244/ .

www.ingramcontent.com/pod-product-compliance
Lightning Source LLC
Chambersburg PA
CBHW050401260626
47156CB00003B/827